W
Cox

HELLGATE

HELLGATE

P. GRADY COX

FIVE STAR

A part of Gale, a Cengage Company

Farmington Hills, Mich • San Francisco • New York • Waterville, Maine
Meriden, Conn • Mason, Ohio • Chicago

LIBRARY OF CONGRESS CATALOGING-IN-PUBLICATION DATA

Names: Cox, P. Grady, author.
Title: Hellgate / P. Grady Cox.
Description: First edition. | Waterville, Maine : Five Star Publishing, 2018.
Identifiers: LCCN 2017047956 (print) | LCCN 2017060632 (ebook) | ISBN
    9781432838089 (EBook) | ISBN 9781432838072 (EBook) | ISBN
    9781432838195 (hardcover)
Subjects: LCSH: Outlaws—Fiction. | BISAC: FICTION / Historical. | FICTION /
    Westerns. | GSAFD: Western stories.
Classification: LCC PS3603.O924 (ebook) | LCC PS3603.O924 H45 2018 (print) |
    DDC 813/.6—dc23
LC record available at https://lccn.loc.gov/2017047956

First Edition. First Printing: April 2018
Find us on Facebook–https://www.facebook.com/FiveStarCengage
Visit our website–http://www.gale.cengage.com/fivestar/
Contact Five Star™ Publishing at FiveStar@cengage.com

Printed in Mexico
1 2 3 4 5 6 7 22 21 20 19 18

Dedicated to the many women who unconditionally love, encourage, nurture, and support children not their own, including my aunts: Ida Yeaw Coppage, Jeanne Grady Ottavianno, and especially Mary Alice Grady Brierley.

ACKNOWLEDGMENTS

At the risk of leaving someone out, I must thank my classmates from the Phoenix College creative writing program: Ray Carns, Jonathan Bond, Jonathan Levy, Hirsch Handmaker, Amy Nichols, Amy McLane, Nanor Tabrizi, Dean Burmeister, Lynn Galvin, Martha Blue, Marty Murphy, Deb Whitford, Sheila Grinell, Kate Cross, and Karen Reed.

To my friends Eric Pflum, David Waid, Liz Marshall, Janice Russell, Diana Douglas, and LaDonna Ockinga, who supply continuous support for all things writing and beyond, thank you!

Thanks to Vakula Law Firm and Maureen Vakula for the gracious tour of the historic Marks Home in Prescott, Arizona, which served as the blueprint for Mary Alice's home; Cale Morris of the Arizona Herpetological Society; the archivists at Sharlot Hall Museum in Prescott; and Janet Cooper and Jock MacIver for the back roads exploration that led fortuitously to the inspirational town of Stanton.

Special thanks to Susan Tone, who has read innumerable versions of this manuscript throughout the entire process without complaint, for her invaluable comments, suggestions, and encouragement, for accompanying me on many research field trips, and for being my friend.

To James Sallis, without whom no novel of mine would be published, thank you for years of patient help and guidance. I am grateful to Thomas Cobb for taking me under his wing and pointing the completed manuscript in the right direction with unrelenting confidence in my ability to tell a story. Anything good found in my writing is due to these two dedicated and kind-hearted teachers and friends. Anything not good is due to my not listening when I should have.

CHAPTER ONE

"In this land of precarious fortunes, every girl should
know how to be *useful* . . ."
Mrs. Lydia Maria Child, author of *The Girl's Own Book*

*Somewhere between Phoenix and Wickenburg, Arizona Territory,
November, 1879*
Rose LaBelle lay where they had shoved her, sharp pebbles
pressing into her cheek. The boot poked her ribs again.

"You know how to cook?"

She closed her eyes against the image the deep southern
drawl evoked—the recent memory of him hauling her from the
stagecoach, a big man with big hands that had held fast against
her struggles—but now her eyes shot open as bloody bandaged
fingers hooked into her blouse's collar. He pulled her up a ways
from the ground, then let her drop.

"Ah said, kin you cook."

"No!" She threw a handful of dirt at him; he swore and
slapped her. Blood dripped from her lip, and her full bladder
released warm wetness down her inner thigh.

There were four of them. The other three busied themselves
setting up camp for the night. The tall one, called Caleb, knelt
over a pile of sticks, held a match to them, and blew gently. His
hair hung down on either side of his face, and she hoped it
would burst into flame, but the flickering fire erupted without
incident.

"Jesus, Sam!" A high-pitched voice came from behind her. "You oughta know a fine lady like her woulda *had* a cook."

"Shut up, Eddie. She bit my finger half off. Since when does fine ladies do that?" His heavy boots scraped the sandy dirt, and a shadow fell across Rose as Sam passed between her and the campfire, on his way to join the others.

They'd tied the horses nearby. Steam rose from a pile of fresh manure, and scurrying beetles crawled over the droppings while the outlaws finished setting up. She guessed the one called Dodger was the leader, since he was always yelling orders. She sat up, pulled her clothing together as best she could with her bound wrists, and huddled into her cape. Images stabbed her mind, fresh and vivid and brutal. She couldn't stop the memories that carried her back to what had happened only hours ago, when she was on that road with her arms pinned behind her and Sam's hot breath huffing against her neck.

The driver and the guard, sprawled across the top of the stagecoach, stared with dead eyes. Dangling arms waved each time the nervous horses pulled against their harnesses. Caleb spoke soothing words and settled the team. On the road behind the stage, the bodies of the extra guards lay beneath the film of dust their fleeing horses had left behind.

A bolt of fabric unraveled in the dirt where Eddie threw it as he searched the stage's boot for valuables. White silk for her wedding gown fluttered in the breeze like a flag of surrender.

Sam's hold on her arms tightened when Dodger sank dirty fingers into her cheeks, and turned her head so she had to look into his jaundiced eyes framed by stringy black hair.

"You married? Ever been with a man?"

The wind shifted; she could smell them, a rotten smell. The sour stench of dried sweat and the same stinking clothes worn for a long, long time. She pulled up her legs and put her arms around them. Buried her face in her knees. It was all her fault. Her father had warned against the trip but she had insisted, and her father would not let her go without him.

She raised her head. A horse tied nearby pissed a pungent stream that splashed on the dirt and seemed to go on forever. The puddle spread toward her feet, and she scrambled backwards. Tucking her skirts close around her legs, she sat with her back to the men and twisted her wrists, but the rope Caleb had bound her with held tight.

When she and her father didn't arrive in Prescott, Auntie would notify the authorities. Surely she would send a telegram to Arthur in Tucson. He'd raise a posse and come after her. But that could take days. Where would she be by then? She wondered if she would still be alive.

Caleb tied her wrists to the saddle horn with a length of rough hemp and spotted the silver chain hanging from her neck. He hefted the locket suspended by it. "What do we have here?" With a sudden, hard yank he broke the chain and opened the locket. Inside were pictures of her parents, the only picture she'd ever had of her mother.

"You son of a—" She swung her leg to kick him, but he caught her shoe.

"Son of a what, huh?" He laughed. "You'd best behave or you'll get yourself hurt." He pushed her foot to the horse's flank and kept his hand on it.

"Caleb, don't you put no bruises on her," Eddie said. "I like my women pink—not black and blue." He laughed at his own wit as he buckled the last of the saddlebags filled with payroll money meant for her father's businesses in Wickenburg. He flung them over the back of his horse.

"Yes, suh," Sam chimed in. "Pink. Rosie pink." He and Eddie laughed again. "That's what we'll call her: Rosie Pink."

Caleb released her foot. Yellow hair fell across his face as he looked down at the treasure he held. Bile stung Rose's throat at the sight of her precious keepsake lying upon the dirt-filled creases of his long fingers. He tossed the locket to Dodger, who shoved it in a pocket without even looking at it. Caleb swung up onto his horse, pulling her reins taut as he passed, and she grabbed for her horse's mane as it lurched to follow him.

They crossed the road and headed into the desert. Each giant saguaro cactus cast a long, black shadow beneath the pounding hooves, shadows that turned to blurs as they rode ever faster and the sky darkened to gray.

She clung to the horse with numb hands, her wrists already chafed an angry red. She pressed her knees tight against the saddle and matched the rocking of her hips to the horse's gait. They galloped toward the sunset's long scarlet gash on a horizon edged by the black teeth of distant mountains.

She drew her knees closer and rocked herself as if she were still on that ride. It had lasted far into the night.

A hand touched her shoulder, bringing her awareness back to the present, which was just as bad as the memories.

Caleb stood over her. "You must be hungry." He bent down, offering a plate of beans.

She shrugged back her cape, took the plate, then flung it at him, spraying beans across the front of his shirt. The plate rattled across the graveled ground.

"She's more fucking trouble than she's worth," Dodger yelled from his place by the fire. "We oughta just shoot her now. I don't give a shit if McCabe wants us to bring him the women."

Caleb crouched down beside her. "That wasn't very polite." A slight smile played across his mouth, the creases around his eyes deepened, and he spoke to her in the same gentling voice he had used earlier with the horses. "You married? Pretty enough. You *oughta* be married." Then he laughed. "You're old enough." His tone turned cruel. "Hell, past old enough."

She looked away.

"You didn't say nothin' when Dodger asked if you ever been with a man. You know how to . . . you know?"

She felt heat rising from her neck, burning her cheeks.

Caleb raised his voice, ensuring Dodger and the others by the fire heard him. "I don't think we should shoot her. I think Mason will be pleased with this one. A real lady." He gave another soft laugh and got to his feet. Before he walked away, he said to her, "Can't cook. Can't fuck. Probly can't clean these beans off my shirt neither. You ain't very useful."

CHAPTER TWO

Dark shapes against a black sky, the horses ripped desert grass, and bits jingled as they chewed. A faint scent of sweet hay clung to them, vestige of the livery in Phoenix. Rose's legs ached, and the discomfort in her inner thighs grew more intense. She longed for her own mare, not as wide as the horse they forced her to ride hard for hours. Stretching her legs to ease them only caused her thigh muscles to cramp. She gasped from the sudden, hard pain.

Dodger raised his head and looked at her. "You want a drink?"

She nodded. He brought his canteen to her, and she took a long swallow. "Thank you."

He pushed his battered hat back on his head. Hair fell from beneath it, greasy strands that straggled across his forehead. He was the thinnest man she had ever seen—creases lined sunken cheeks and the hollows around his eyes. He took the canteen and returned to his place by the fire.

"Yeah, give her lotsa water," Eddie said. "I hear it keeps their skin soft."

"Shut up." Dodger rubbed his temples.

Rose wanted to stay as far away from them as she could, but the warmth of the fire called to her and she stood. Her legs had stopped aching and cramping, but now they shook, threatening to give out. The smell of warmed beans wafted toward her. Her stomach rolled, and she wished she hadn't refused the plate Caleb offered earlier. Before she could reach the campfire, another hard cramp in her thigh made her cry out and she limped, bent over, back to the rock she'd been sitting on.

Sam picked up a plate and started ladling more beans onto it.

"Hey! You had yours. Get outta there." Eddie tried to grab the ladle.

Sam jerked it away. Caleb and Dodger ducked as beans flew across the campsite. "They ain't for me! They's for Rosie Pink."

"You want beans all over *your* shirt?" Eddie laughed. "What do you care if she eats anyway? Better to leave her hungry. We'll fill her up." He pulled Sam's arm but the big man shook free and cuffed Eddie on the side of the head. A glancing blow, but it sent Eddie flying backwards. He scrambled to his feet. A knife flashed in the firelight.

Dodger drew his pistol. "That's enough, God damn it."

Eddie and Sam backed away from each other, grumbling.

"We're just gonna have to kill her." Dodger stood up, pistol in hand. "This is too damn much trouble. And I ain't puttin' up with you two"—he waved the gun toward Sam and Eddie— "fightin' over her all the way to—" He looked at her. "Well, I don't s'pose a fine lady like yourself would've heard of Hellgate?"

"She's heard of it all right! Look at her face!" Eddie burst into laughter, pointing at her with the knife before sliding it into its sheath.

"Mad Mason? That's the McCabe you're—?" Lawmen often paused at their ranch to visit with her father. She wished she had paid more attention to their conversations. What little she'd heard was enough now to fill her with terror.

"Heard of Mr. McCabe, have you?" Dodger asked. "So, you see? Ain't it better if we just kilt you now?" He walked over, grinning.

Rose dared not look up. She clenched her jaw and fists to

15

keep from trembling. The hammer of Dodger's pistol—metal sliding against metal—pulled back and cocked, and the scent of cold, oily steel stung her nostrils. He pushed the barrel of the gun through her dark hair, loosened by the long ride to fall across her shoulders, tangled with hat and ribbons.

"Mr. McCabe don't like being called Mad Mason. Says it's disrespectful."

"Aw, come on, Dodger. If you're gonna kill her anyways, why can't we do her first?" Eddie shifted his weight from one leg to the other until Sam shoved him.

"Me first. Ah'm the one she bit."

"That's enough!" Dodger said. "Do what you want with her. I'm sick of it." He lowered the hammer and shoved his pistol into its holster. Returning to his spot by the fire, he took out his tobacco pouch and started to roll a smoke. "Just quit all the Goddamn whining."

Eddie and Sam wrestled, fell to the ground, rolled, and grunted, inching ever closer to her. Then Caleb stepped around them and grabbed her bound hands. He pulled her up beside him.

"We're not gonna kill her, and we're not gonna take turns with her. I want her. For myself."

Dodger choked out smoke. The fight stopped. Everyone, Rose included, stared at Caleb.

"Who do ya think—"

"You ain't got no right—"

"Now what makes you believe you got a claim on the woman, Caleb?" Dodger asked.

"Mason will be mad if he hears we had a perfectly good woman and then killed her. And if these two get at her, they *will* kill her. With their—" He hesitated, then found the right word. "Enthusiasm."

"Take her, then."

Eddie and Sam yowled. A lone coyote answered them from a distant hillside.

"We don't even gotta tell Mr. McCabe we found us a woman," Eddie said. "We kept women for ourselves before."

"That's true." Dodger dragged on his cigarette and took his time exhaling. "But Caleb did shoot the marshal in Phoenix. You'd be hangin' from a gallows if not for our friend here. Don't we owe him something?"

Rose tried to twist free, but Caleb's grip tightened.

"Let's go." He dragged her to the blackness beyond the campfire and shoved her down in a clearing encircled by creosote bushes. He tossed a few strips of jerky onto her skirt. "Thought you might still be hungry."

While she chewed, faint voices came from the camp, and fire flickered through the far side of scrub and cactus. There was a familiar rushing sound behind her. She thought at first it was wind, yet the bushes were still. Not wind but fast-moving water, a river surging over rocks.

Caleb scraped the drying beans from the front of his shirt with his knife. She slid her hands under her skirt, reaching for her own knife, always carried at her father's insistence and hidden in her high shoe. Her fingers touched the hilt but Caleb spoke and she jerked her hand away.

"This is gonna stink in a day or two, Miss Rosie Pink." He removed his coat, laying it on the ground, and slipped out of his braces, leaving them to dangle from his trousers. Then he unbuttoned his shirt and pulled it off, crouched down and rubbed scoops of sand into the damp stain. His slender fingers worked the sand into the fabric.

"You already stink," she said.

He laughed.

Behind him, branches of cholla cactus, covered with a thick fur of silvery needles, shimmered in the light of the stars, bright next to the thin sliver of moon.

"You sure took me by surprise," he said. He sprang to his feet, pulled on his shirt and buttoned it, then held out a hand to her. *Never show fear,* she thought. She put her hands in his and let him help her up.

"You've had a very bad day, haven't you?" He pulled her closer.

"Don't touch me!"

Laughter came from the camp.

She tried to push him away, but his arm tightened around her.

"When I was very young," he said, "my sister had a doll. Wore a frilly dress—all lace and ruffles, you know. Its face, tiny hands, they was made of porcelain."

Crazy madness, but that voice lulled her. His horse-soothing voice. He stroked her hair, pressing her cheek to his chest. She felt the thump of his heartbeat.

"That doll," he said. "It had long silky brown hair. White skin with pink cheeks painted on, a little red mouth. Great big blue eyes rigged so that when you laid her down they closed." He gave a little laugh. "I thought that doll was beautiful. I guess I thought it was alive. My sister and I would play husband and wife, and it was our child. She named it Mrs. Coppage. She took it with her when she got married." He moved back a little, and with a hand under her chin, raised her face. "I used to wonder if she still had it or what happened to it. Then I saw you standing in the road. Looked just like that doll, come to life."

She pushed him. "Saw me standing by my father's dead body!"

He took hold of her wrists. "Whoa. I'm not gonna hurt you."

"The hell you aren't."

He pulled her sideways, then edged away until he could see beyond the bushes that surrounded them, see the men around the fire. "I guess you better scream."

"What?"

"They'll be expectin' it."

He snaked his fingers into her hair and pulled her close. "I said scream." He raised his arm as if to hit her and yanked her head back.

She screamed.

Muffled laughter followed by Eddie's hooting voice floated from the camp.

"Now sit. There." He crouched a few feet away, drew his pistol, and cracked open the cylinder. He removed each spent shell and replaced it with a bullet from his cartridge belt.

"What are you going to do to me?" she asked.

He snapped the cylinder shut and holstered the pistol. Then he was beside her, his hand on her arm. He pushed her down and picked up handfuls of dirt, threw it on her skirt, and rubbed it into the dark blue velvet of her cape.

She screeched, bringing more laughs and hoots, and struggled to reach her shoe.

"Quit fighting me." He pinned her wrists above her head with one hand and hooked fingers into the lace collar of her blouse. A hard yank and the lace ripped open, exposing her chemise. Cold air pricked her neck and the upper curves of her breasts.

"Dear God," he whispered, and closed his eyes.

"You're hurting me."

He released her and rolled onto his back. He lay beside her and grabbed her when she tried to roll away. His heavy breathing turned into a loud grunt when she raked her fingernails across his cheek, drawing blood.

The laughter from the camp increased. Sam's southern drawl called out, "Was it that good, Caleb?"

He jumped up and wrenched her to her feet, dragged her to

the camp, and threw her down near the fire.

Dodger glanced up. "Hard to tell who got the worst of it."

Caleb walked into the darkness and returned with his bedroll. He threw a blanket at her. She spread it out and lay down, pulling her cape close. He dropped another blanket and sat beside her, holding a length of rope, which he attached to the one binding her wrists, then he turned away from her and lay down, holding on like she was a dog on a leash.

She moved as far away from him as she could, then lay on her back and stared up at the stars. Each of them was an angel, her papa had said, after her mother died. Whenever she looked up at night, her mother would be there, in heaven, watching over her. She believed that. When she was six years old.

She started to slip into sleep but the images came again.

Gunfire all around them. The stage slammed to a stop, throwing her and Papa from their seats. The door flew open. Blinded by sudden sunlight. Rough hands hauled her into the road. Her father, roaring, followed, pistol in hand. A dark stain blossomed on his vest and surprise on his face as he lurched and then collapsed, thudded to the ground. Dust danced around his body. He lay still. Deathly still. She screamed, screamed until Sam's big hand pressed over her mouth—

Under cover of darkness, she moved her lips in silent prayer, *Hail Mary, full of grace* . . . She hoped her parents were reunited and happy in heaven. One last look at the stars before she rolled onto her side and closed her eyes, shivering.

CHAPTER THREE

"Suppression of undue emotion, whether of laughter, or anger, or mortification, or disappointment, or of selfishness in any form, is a sure mark of good training." *Sensible Etiquette of the Best Society,* Mrs. H. O. Ward

Prescott, Capital of the Arizona Territory

Down the hill, toward the center of town, one flicker of light in a window followed another one by one, as lamps flared. The breeze carried faint piano music and laughter from Whiskey Row, then shifted direction and filled the air with fragrant woodsmoke from fireplaces and stoves. Mary Alice settled herself more comfortably into the rocking chair and pulled her shawl up over her shoulders. Soon winter weather would put a stop to the routine, but for now she clung to this ritual she used to share with Joseph of an evening, enjoying the covered porch that wrapped around half the house. From here she looked down upon the brick courthouse, the businesses locked up for the night, the revelers going in and out of the saloons on Montezuma Street.

She lifted the china teacup to her lips. Already cold.

Kam Le appeared in the doorway.

"Missus, please come in now. It is warm by the fire."

Kam Le picked up the tea tray as Mary Alice leaned on her walking stick to rise from the rocker. She limped into the house and stopped for just a moment, as she sometimes did on nights when nostalgia threatened to overwhelm. All the little touches Joseph included during construction: parquet floors, dark mahogany woodwork, and brass doorknobs with plates stamped with a flowery design. In the hallway, a carved floral design embellished the stairway's baluster post.

Mary Alice turned right off the entry hallway. The parlor's three curved turret windows were dark and reflected the flames in the hearth. Hand-painted tiles, inlaid with geometric designs, framed the fireplace beneath a carved wooden mantel. Joseph had overseen its construction with much care. With much love. Yes, a lovely home. An empty home.

She sank into Joseph's favorite chair, leather softened by the years he'd relaxed there, and let her shawl fall from her shoulders as the crackling fire's warmth enveloped her. Kam Le had closed the heavy wooden pocket doors separating the parlor from the music room in order to hold the heat in. Now she held a match to the lamp, then sat on the footstool and lifted Mary Alice's feet to her lap.

Kam Le removed Mary Alice's shoes and began a gentle massage, which eased her pain. "Kam Le, what would I do without you?" The young woman seemed to know just the place to apply pressure, just the place to caress or stretch. Mary Alice thanked God every night, in her evening prayers, that Joseph had insisted they hire help during the last months of his illness. In the five months since he'd passed away, Kam Le and her brother, Kimo, an excellent cook, had become like family. Her only family. Except, of course, for her beloved niece, Rose.

The fire hissed and popped. A carriage passed outside. The horses' hooves clopped on the hard-packed road, and her thoughts turned to Rose and Walter. Travel by stage was so harsh, dusty, and, more recently, dangerous. They'd be arriving within the week, their first visit to Prescott since Joseph's funeral, a visit lost in a haze of sadness and details and obligations.

"You need time to mourn," Walter had said, when she questioned why Rose would not spend the summer as usual. Now she suspected the real reason was that this man, Arthur, whom Rose now planned to marry, supplied the distraction. Well, this time the visit would be a happy one. An exciting time, making plans for a wedding. And she was to sew the gown. She could hardly wait to get her hands on the bolt of silk Rose had picked out.

"Kam Le, did you remember to air the mattress in Rose's room? Did you beat the rugs?"

"Yes, Missus." Kam Le smiled.

"You enjoy her visits almost as much as I, don't you, dear?"

Kam Le's smile widened and she nodded. "She promised to teach me to play, to play . . ." Kam Le searched for the word.

"The piano?" How heavenly it would be to hear music fill the house again. The music room, on the other side of the pocket doors, sat silent when Rose was not visiting. The Story & Clark upright served no purpose, except to be admired after Kam Le polished its oak wood until the exquisite grain gleamed.

"Oh, I wish I could teach you." Mary Alice looked with disdain at her crippled fingers. "But Rose will be a fine teacher. Then you can accompany her when she sings. She has such a lovely voice."

"No, Missus. Not the piano. Five something . . . five card studs!"

"A card game? That girl has spent way too much time with her father! And all those ranch hands. It's been all I could do to civilize her, with only summer visits! It's a wonder she found a respectable man willing to marry her, though God knows it took her long enough. Kam Le, stop smiling!"

Kam Le eased house slippers onto Mary Alice's feet. "Time

for your brandy." She hurried off to the kitchen.

Mary Alice turned up the flame in the lamp and put on her spectacles. She opened her Bible just as Kam Le returned and, before touching the crystal snifter to her lips, she raised it and said, "Here's to Rose and Arthur, the happy couple." She sipped, staring into the flames. "I'm so looking forward to seeing my Rose. I do hope she's having a pleasant trip."

"I also hope that is so, Missus." Kam Le used the poker to push the remaining logs toward the back of the fireplace for the night.

Mary Alice tipped the decanter to fill her glass again. "She has a wonderful future ahead of her." She dismissed Kam Le, waving the girl away.

Mary Alice raised her glass to the wedding portrait over the fireplace, to the young couple whose faces glowed with the promise of their own future. Joseph had whispered in her ear, said things that made her laugh and caused the photographer to start the exposure all over again. This went on until the photographer claimed he was about to run out of plates and threatened to bring out the stands with braces to hold their necks still. The stays of her wedding dress pressed so tightly she feared fainting, but they managed to stand still long enough for the plate to capture their image. Mary Alice smiled, looking at the ornately framed photograph. How the wedding styles had changed. All those hoops probably would have held her up, even unconscious. She imagined Rose's dress. It would have a tasteful bustle and overskirt and . . . she looked up at her own wedding portrait again.

Joseph stood behind her, his hand at her elbow. All the decades of their marriage his hand had been at her elbow. She poured another glass of brandy.

★ ★ ★ ★ ★

Mary Alice blinked awake, aware only of a stiff neck, a headache, and a tingling hand wedged between her hip and the chair's arm. Sunlight streamed through the sheer lace panels at the parlor windows. A quilt covered her. Kam Le must have placed it over her, and she pushed it aside. She grasped her cane with aching fingers and struggled to her feet.

"I see you are up," Kam Le said from the doorway. "Kimo is fixing breakfast."

Kam Le's expression was a mix of concern and obvious judgment, her lips a thin line, although Mary Alice couldn't imagine why. Anybody could get tired and fall asleep in a chair. Joseph used to do so regularly. Maybe the Chinese had some particular aversion to sleeping in chairs. "Thank you, dear," she said, and shuffled on stiff legs while Kam Le slipped past her and picked up the tray holding the empty brandy decanter and glass.

Mary Alice crossed the hall to her bedroom, took care of her morning ablutions, and fixed her hair. By then the smell of coffee and bacon filled the house. Her morning stiffness had passed, and her stomach rumbled in anticipation. She carried her cane, occasionally touching the hallway wall for support, and hesitated when she reached the door to the dining room. She needed to stop and collect herself, as she did every morning since Joseph had taken ill. The carved walnut table, covered with lace cloth and set with fine china, used to bring her a fulfilling sense of satisfaction. Joseph always made it to the table before her. His booming "Good day!" and beaming face always made her smile. Now a single place setting and Joseph's empty chair greeted her.

But this morning a light tapping at the front door brought a welcome delay. "I'll get it," she said. She pulled the door open. Alvenia Pumfrey stood on the porch, a hired cabriolet tied to the hitching post by the road.

"Alvenia! Come in out of the cold. What are you doing here so early in the morning? It's not Friday, is it?"

Alvenia came in, laughing. "Of course it's not Friday!" The women of the town and the officers' wives from Fort Whipple met regularly on Friday afternoons. The tradition began with the governor's wife giving talks on her travels and continued, even though Mrs. Fremont had moved back east. "Nor is it so early in the morning. You're such a card, Mary Alice."

Mary Alice glanced into the parlor where the rumpled quilt still draped the wingback chair. The mantel clock read fifteen minutes past twelve. "Why, I had no idea. I must have overslept."

Alvenia removed her cloak, hat, gloves, and walking stick and hung them all on the hallway coatrack. "Shouldn't have worn the heavy wool. It's unseasonably warm. We had talked of speaking with the new dressmaker today. Did you forget? I guess we can go another day."

"Oh, no, we can go this afternoon. Just a little later than we planned." Mary Alice took her friend's arm and led her toward the dining room. "Kam Le, please set another place for Mrs. Pumfrey. Yes, of course, now I remember. To speak with her about a dress for me to wear to Rose's wedding. God knows it will take all I have to make the wedding gown."

Alvenia smiled. "We understand our priorities, don't we? It's not as if the guests will be looking at anybody except the stunning bride."

"Good thing. I'll be a depressing sight all dressed in black."

"It will be over a year by then. Perhaps a touch of lace or buttons in a summer color? Cream? Or pink, to match your roses?"

"Perhaps. I'll need to think about it."

Alvenia reached across the table to take Mary Alice's hand in a gentle grasp. "You are feeling up to it? The meeting with the dressmaker?"

"Oh, Alvenia! Yes, yes. I'm fine. Actually, I've been feeling quite a bit better lately."

"I'm so glad to hear that."

While they ate, Alvenia gossiped about the new family at her church, just moved to the city from a farm in Skull Valley. "Too much talk of robberies and kidnappings. They have young children—didn't like the isolation out there."

Another knock at the door, this one loud and forceful.

"My goodness, who could that be?" Mary Alice felt almost giddy. This was like before Joseph fell ill, when the house was busy all the time with callers, both social and business. Then Kimo appeared in the doorway.

"Missus, the city marshal wishes to speak with you. He's waiting in the parlor."

"What on earth? Excuse me, Alvenia."

Marshal Duval stood by the fireplace. He was, as usual, overloaded with guns and cartridge belts. Large spurs jutted from his heels, and he always tucked his trousers inside his boots like the cavalrymen from the fort. "Good morning, Mrs. Bradford." He dragged a hand across his long, drooping mustache and waved toward Joseph's chair. "Ma'am, you'd best take a seat."

She sat down, pushing the quilt to one side. Alvenia and Kam Le hovered in the hallway near the door.

"Ma'am, there's been an unfortunate incident on the Wickenburg Road—"

Her napkin was still in her hand and she raised it to her mouth. "Has something happened to my niece?"

"Ma'am. It was a robbery." He puffed up straighter, pushing back his coat so he could hook his thumbs in his braces. "Outlaws. Killed all the guards and the driver and—"

Alvenia gasped.

Mary Alice dug her fingers into the quilt, bunching it into

her fist. "Not Walter. Not my Rose!"

"No, ma'am. No. Your family members are alive." The marshal stood back as Kam Le brought a tray with glasses of brandy. Mary Alice held hers to her lips with a shaking hand. She wanted to throw it at the man, to get him to say what he had come to say quickly. Yet she dreaded the words that might be coming.

Duval downed his brandy in one gulp and put the glass on the tray. "Mr. LaBelle got took to Wickenburg and is being doctored there. He's the one said to send a telegram up here and let you know of the delay."

"Doctored?"

"The outlaws shot him, ma'am, but he'll be all right. A posse from Phoenix come across the stage and carried him on to Wickenburg."

"Then my niece stayed there to look after him?" Of course, her brother-in-law would never let anything happen to Rose. She placed her glass on a table and willed herself to be calm. Alvenia was sobbing. Mary Alice disapproved of such displays, and her disapproval gave her the strength to resist joining in.

"This here will explain the situation." Duval stuck his fingers into a trouser pocket. "Ma'am, your niece, Rose, is mentioned in this note." He dug a folded paper out and handed it to Mary Alice. "Mr. LaBelle had one of his men ride up here with this. Got to my office afore the telegraph clerk brought the message about the robbery."

Walter's handwriting scrawled across the smudged paper. She couldn't decipher every word but one line was clear enough until tears caused it to shimmer. She blinked to hold them back.

"As soon as I can travel I will arrive to conduct the search for Rose from your house."

CHAPTER FOUR

Exhausted despite having slept a few hours, Rose opened her eyes and lay still, legs and back aching. The first rays of sunlight broke over the hills and illuminated the rope tied to a creosote bush.

She knelt, then stood, testing each leg to be sure it would hold her.

"Well, look who's back from the dead," Sam said.

Eddie looked up from rolling his bedding. "God, she's sure a mess, ain't she?"

"I need to . . . I have to . . ." Heat rose in her face. Caleb and Dodger stopped in the middle of saddling their horses to stare at her.

Dodger nodded at Sam. "Take her to find a bush."

"Ah ain't takin' her. She can piss where she stands." Question settled, he went back to saddling his horse.

Dodger glanced at Eddie, but Caleb said, "Don't let him take her. He won't keep his hands off her."

Eddie laughed. "Who'd want her now? Look at her!"

Caleb brushed past her and untied the rope from the bush. "Let her go by herself. She ain't going nowheres with no water and her hands tied."

Remembering the sheltering bushes, she headed for the clearing where Caleb had dragged her the night before. To the south the distinctive domed mountain that held the Vulture Mine rose above the horizon. They couldn't be more than five or six miles from Wickenburg.

Crouched behind a creosote bush, she fumbled with her skirt and petticoats, pulled the knife from her shoe, and began to saw through the ropes that held her wrists. Her hands shook. She dropped the knife. She cut her finger when she picked it up but ignored the blood, held the knife tighter, and sawed faster. She looked to see if anyone was coming and, even though she nicked her wrist several times, she felt no pain. She sawed away, each strand breaking apart with excruciating slowness. The frantic rasping of blade against rope matched her breath. Finally she was free. She squatted, pulling apart her drawers. As soon as her bladder emptied she broke into a run, pulling clothing into place, and almost toppled over the edge of a deep ravine. She realized the drop-off just in time to skid to a stop at the edge and stumble backwards. Far below, the muddy waters of the Hassayampa River flowed around boulders and tree branches piled high by late summer storms.

She ran for the long piece of rope, tied it to a stunted mesquite tree, and let it dangle over the edge. It fell short of the river.

Digging at the knot of ribbons tangled in her hair until she worked them loose, she pulled the ties and sash off, hoping to use the wide ribbon to extend the rope. But she dropped the hat, and it toppled over the edge.

It sailed across the chasm, hovered—suspended in midair for a second—then began a slow downward spiral. Impaled on an uprooted tree, the wide brim flapped in the breeze.

She pulled the rope up. Hands shaking uncontrollably, she fumbled at tying the pieces together.

"Where the hell are you?" Caleb yelled. "Come on, Rosie Pink, you must be finished by now." Heavy footsteps approached.

Flinging the rope over the edge, she backed into a mesquite

thicket and pushed herself deep inside, ignoring thorns that tore at her clothes and scratched her hands and face. When she could go no farther, she clutched the blue satin sash and pressed it against her lips, willing herself to be motionless. She could see him through the leaves. A dry leaf near her mouth moved and she held her breath.

He looked over the edge of the cliff.

More footsteps nearby. "Where the fuck is she? Dodger's ready to go." Eddie followed Caleb's gaze, shuffled closer to the edge, and peered over. He looked up at Caleb with round eyes and open mouth.

"Hey, Dodger!" he yelled. "The woman done kilt herself! Jumped in the damn river! And you said me and Sam was gonna kill her—with our enthoo . . . enthoo . . . Ha! Just look what you done!"

Caleb grabbed Eddie around the throat, then twisted him and bent him over the edge. Dodger came running and pulled the two men backwards. "No point in fighting over her now. She was just gonna slow us down anyway."

Eddie rubbed his throat and slinked back to the camp.

Dodger put a hand on Caleb's shoulder.

"She didn't jump," Caleb said. "Look. She climbed down the rope—"

"And fell the last fifteen feet? If she ain't dead, she will be soon enough. Let's go."

"I'm gonna look for her."

"Do what you gotta do. We'll meet up with you in Stanton."

Loud voices came from the camp and then the sounds of them riding away while Caleb stared down into the river, hat in hand, head hanging. Rose feared she could not stay still much longer, waiting for him to go with the others.

But instead of leaving, he threw his hat down and took off his coat, his boots, and stockings. He walked barefoot to the edge of the cliff, lowering himself over, and his head disappeared below the rim.

CHAPTER FIVE

An expanse of tawny grass stretched for miles. Swaths of colored fronds, cream and wine, rippled and released spore into the breeze. It all created the illusion of a soft blanket cushioning the earth. Illusion it was, for after two miles Rose pined for the heavy work boots she wore around the ranch. Reality poked at her with each sharp rock that penetrated the soft leather soles of her traveling shoes. Blisters blossomed on her feet.

The sun's warmth, welcomed earlier in the morning, now pulled sweat from her pores and burned her skin. She unfastened her cape and hung it over her head, trying to shade her face from the sun. Her bodice was soaked under her arms and her chemise stuck to her back. Thirst drove her to sidetrack westerly, closer to the river, and climb down a steep embankment. She lay across rocks pounded smooth by the rushing waters, cupped her hand, and lifted drink after drink to parched lips, then splashed water on her face and arms even though her cuts and scratches stung.

She thought about soaking her feet in the cool water, but she was afraid once she took her shoes off she'd never get them on again.

She had badly miscalculated the distance to Wickenburg. But she was still sure she'd be there before nightfall. Climbing up the riverbank, she continued walking and distracted herself from the pain in her feet by envisioning her arrival, how she would tell her story to the sheriff, provide accurate descriptions of the outlaws, and identify them when the posse dragged them into town.

She rubbed her chafed wrists.

The people in the street would shake their fists and hurl insults as the criminals paraded past. When they sat chained to the jail tree, dogs would bark and snap at them, and children would taunt them with words and stones.

She pictured the four men swinging from a gallows in front of the town hall. Sam and Eddie, skin blackened, tongues protruding. Dodger and Caleb, faces obscured by their long, greasy hair, feet twitching as they swung slowly around and around.

A horse whinnied from somewhere ahead. She slowed. Sweat burned her eyes as she peered through shimmering heat that rose from the swell of grass, until she saw them. Men barely visible in the distance through cactus and mesquite. Two men or three? They stood beside their horses. The wind shifted, their voices carried, but she couldn't make out the words.

They could be cowboys rounding up strays for some Wickenburg rancher. Or desperados just as bad as the ones she'd escaped. Her father had always said that caution kept brave men alive.

She crouched low and slipped closer. A thorny bush caught her cape and pulled it from her head, but she kept going until she was near enough to see there were two of them. She heard their voices clearly now. Indians!

A callused hand clamped over her mouth. A whisper in her ear. "Don't make a sound."

She nodded.

Caleb pulled her backwards until the men were out of sight. "Wait here." He headed toward the Indians and returned in just a few minutes, leading a horse. "This one'll be easier for you to ride; not as big as that gelding."

She put her foot in the stirrup and swung into the saddle. He held onto the bridle but let her take the reins; they were smeared with blood. She wiped her hand on her skirt.

They came to where he'd left his horse. "Keep those fingernails to yourself now, or I'll tie you up again. I got chains in my saddlebag too, from the jail if need be. Don't try runnin' off."

Just to make sure, he tied the bloody reins to a paloverde tree. He took the canteen from the horse she had ridden the night before, rifled through the saddlebags, then untied it and slapped its rump hard.

"I'll bet you can hang for horse-stealing, even if you turn it loose."

He laughed, watching the horse run off, then threw the canteen to her.

She drank, the water still cool from the night. "All I've had to eat in over a day are those pieces of jerky you threw at me."

"Probably all you're gonna get till we get to Stanton." He took her reins and held on to them as he mounted and nudged his horse to a walk. They rode back the way she had come, rode past the abandoned campsite.

The sun was high in the sky before he reined to a stop. "Let's rest. We'll go on when the sun lowers."

They dismounted on top of a low hill with a clear view of the area except for some bushes on the western edge. A pile of boulders offered a place to sit up off the ground, and she found a flat rock that was almost comfortable. Caleb hobbled the horses, brought the canteens, and knelt in front of her. He lifted her hands, gripping them hard when she tried to pull away. "How can those little fingers be so strong? Untying those ribbons on your hat. That knot must have been pulled tight as can be."

He leaned toward her, hands on either side of her legs, and

looked into her eyes.

"Do you have any idea how I felt when I thought you had fallen or jumped off that cliff? When all I'd been trying to do was protect you?"

"Protect me? Don't make me laugh."

"Things ain't always what they seem. For instance, I know you think your pa is dead. But maybe not, huh? He was alive when I left him."

He was a cruel man playing a cruel game. She held her face expressionless except for the contempt she felt for him.

"I don't believe you." Her gaze locked with his while her hand inched toward the top of her shoe. Her fingers touched shoe leather. She dug in, worked the knife upwards, acting as if she were cocking her head to listen to him.

"You shouldn't have untied the ribbons," he said.

"What?"

"When I fished your hat out of the water, they were gone. You wouldn't have time to do that while you were falling off a cliff. To your death." He smiled up at her. "Ribbons weren't the only thing gone. Seems your father taught you a few tricks of the trade."

"You don't know anything about my father."

He reached into his shirt pocket and pulled out one of her father's business cards. "Found this while I was taking his watch and money belt." He read from the card, "Walt-er H. La-Belle. Texas Ranger back in the day. Wealthy now. Silver mines, gold mines, a hotel in Prescott."

"How do you know all that?"

"Newspapers." He turned his head and spat. "I can read. I ain't stupid."

"You didn't say anything in front of the others."

"They'd want to hold you for ransom. I got other plans for you."

At a slight flicker in his gaze, she paused, fingers touching the carved ivory hilt of her knife.

"You made me think you tried to climb down to the river, and how could you do that with your hands tied so tight? But then I knew how strong your little fingers must be. They untied the rope from your wrists, untied that other rope too." Something flickered again in his eyes. "How else could you have gotten loose?"

Her hand closed on the knife.

He caught her arm, jerking it up. His grip tightened on her wrist until she cried out and the knife dropped. He grabbed it while continuing the agonizing pressure on her wrist, his face close to hers. "I made the mistake of underestimating you. Don't make that mistake about me. Nothing is going to keep me from getting to Hellgate. With you."

He slipped a hand under her skirt, touching her leg. "Anything else hidden in there?"

They struggled for a moment, but he shoved her, hard, and she landed in the dirt beside the rock.

A whoosh of air whistled over her head, a dull thud, and Caleb's pistol fired.

She scrambled behind the rock and Caleb's hand pressed into her shoulder, pinning her down as he continued to shoot. When he stopped, she peered over the top of the rock. An Indian lay at the edge of the clearing near the bushes. Blood spurting from his neck slowed to a trickle. Naked but for a long breechcloth, the man's dead hand clutched a bow near arrows that had spilled from his quiver.

"Stay down!"

She crouched and put her arms over her head while he slowly stood.

"I don't see any others." He sounded breathless. "Must've run off. Yavapai renegades. Jesus, they must be all over the place." His legs folded beneath him, and he sat down hard on the rock. His shirt stained red as blood flowed from beneath the shaft of an arrow buried in his shoulder.

CHAPTER SIX

"It won't go through. It's stuck against something. A bone, I think." Rose wiped her bloodied hands on her skirt. "I can pull it out."

"No!" He pushed her away. He leaned, hung his head over the side of the rock, and vomited. He remained doubled over and, instead of sitting up, slid down the rock until he sat on the ground, resting against the boulder. His words came with great effort between small, pained grunts. "The Yavapai don't tie the arrowhead on—it's just stuck in a little cut on the end of the shaft—if you pull, it'll come off—you have to push again. Push it through." He drew up his knees and waited.

Her father had an arrowhead buried in his back during his Ranger days. He'd explained to her that it had not been removed quickly and the injured tissues swelled. The company doctor tried unsuccessfully to dig it out, and the infection almost killed him. He said it was the closest he had come to death from a wound, and it still pained him when the weather was damp.

She wrapped her hands tight around the shaft and pushed. Her own stomach turned as she felt the arrowhead give a little only to snag again.

"Twist it."

She twisted. She pushed again but her hands slipped on the blood. The muscles and veins of Caleb's neck bulged as he clenched his teeth.

She picked up a rock and hammered the arrow's shaft. It

released. She found the arrowhead where it had ripped through his shirt and pulled it out of his back like a giant splinter. Then she got in front of him, pushed him up, braced one hand against his chest, wrapped the other around the feathered shaft, and, with a hard yank, pulled it out. This time his groan was more like a scream.

The front of his shirt was quickly turning red from the rush of blood. She ripped a ruffle from her petticoat and pressed it against the wound, but he pushed her hand away.

"Let it bleed—it'll clean it out."

"I don't think it needs to be quite that clean." She packed pieces of the ruffle into both sides of the wound.

His breathing slowed, and he leaned back against the rock.

"Do you want something to drink? Some whiskey maybe?" she asked.

Sweat ran down his face. "You have some?"

"No, of course not. I thought you might."

He shook his head, the hope dying from his eyes. His mouth curled up a little on one side. "I'd even settle for some of that snake oil Eddie drinks."

"You need to rest."

He nodded, then dragged his legs up and attempted to stand, but after raising himself a few inches, he fell. He glanced at her, wariness in his eyes, an animal caught in a trap.

"I told you to rest," she said.

"Dodger won't wait forever."

"You'll probably bleed to death, you know, if you try to catch up with them."

"Yeah, well, we'll probably both die if we try to make it to Hellgate on our own. Goddamn Indians."

The horses snorted and shuffled nearby, legs straining against the hobbles. They had never calmed down since Caleb first fired his gun. Most likely the salty-sweet smell of blood, heavy in the air, continued to spook them. She got up, and he grabbed her arm.

"I'm just going to tend to the horses," she said. "I'll be right back."

He rested the pistol on his thigh but cocked the hammer. "Don't try anything smart."

She unfastened Caleb's bedroll and saddlebags, then got the bedroll off her stolen horse. She turned to carry everything back to the rock.

Her instinct was to run, but if the area was full of renegade Yavapai who liked to kill white people, her chances of getting to Wickenburg were slim. She wasn't a good shot with a pistol and there was no rifle. She thought of her father. Was he really alive when they left? If so, they'd left him helpless, to die in that road at the hands of marauding Indians.

She wished her father could advise her. Or Auntie, who always knew how a lady should behave. Be kind. Be helpful. Always make people feel at ease. Which fork to use for which course. She almost laughed. Ladies' rules didn't apply here. Her father would be a better advisor.

He'd tell her do whatever was necessary to survive. Don't go off into the desert alone again with renegades all around. He'd say live to fight another day.

Surely a posse would chase after the outlaws, the rescue of Walter LaBelle's daughter a high priority. No doubt they already tracked them, gaining every day, every hour. Not that she had much choice but, in the meantime, staying with Caleb seemed the best course of action.

She knelt next to him to spread out his bedroll and saw her knife, half buried where he had dropped it near the boulder. She whispered a prayer of thanks to her father, feeling that Papa was looking after her still.

"Here." She touched Caleb's arm. "Get on the blankets. We

have to get that shirt off so I can bind your wound properly."
Once on the blankets, he sat looking up at her with half-opened
eyes, his face ashen.

"Go. I can't stop you."

"No, you can't. And I *should* go. Leave you here for dead like
you left my father."

"Go ahead," he snapped, anger giving his voice strength. He
waved the pistol at her.

"Lift your arm if you can." She helped him, pulled his shirt
out from under him and over his head, and while he was turned
away, she quickly snatched the knife and slid it back into her
shoe. Then she ripped more of her ruffle into bandages and
strips to bind him up. With the flow of blood not yet completely
staunched, she worried about his untimely death. "Try not to
die," she said.

She felt a chill. Darkness was falling, and she thought about
the dead Indian on the other side of the rock. Would others
come looking for him? A fire was out of the question. She lay
down beside Caleb and pulled the blankets up.

Every time she awoke through the night, she found him
awake, pistol in hand, keeping watch. It didn't look like he
would die before dawn.

She prayed that she would be alive, too, come morning.

Chapter Seven

Caleb led her horse along the narrow trail. As the day wore on and the heat increased, even the cicadas fell silent. The dry air held no scents except damp horses and creaking leather. Sweat trickled down Rose's back. White froth hung from her horse's mouth. The high mountains to the north seemed distant, and the land flowed before them in what appeared to be a flat plain, yet they traveled over low, rolling hills. Up and down, up and down on the rocky trail; it was impossible to tell if some danger lurked even a hundred yards away, or if a posse was catching up from behind.

She wondered how far it would be to the rendezvous with Dodger in Stanton. Snatches of conversations between her father and his comrades flashed through her mind, remarks made while discussing how the lawlessness of the territory prevented statehood. The men considered Stanton a problem, outside the law and uncontrollable. So far the sheriffs and marshals just stayed away.

"There's a stage stop coming up, a shelter with some water." Caleb flinched as he removed his hat and drew a sleeve across his sweaty brow. "If there's nobody around, maybe we'll stop and rest for a while. There's a creek, Antelope Creek."

"That's the creek that runs through Stanton."

"No wonder you were so cocky about running off to Wickenburg." He reined his horse to a stop. "You know this country. And I thought you was just a helpless woman, lost in the desert."

"My father mentioned Stanton. It has a bad reputation."

He laughed. "Surely it does."

It seemed an endless trail, and Rose became lost in her thoughts. Daydreams of Arthur coming to her rescue, daydreams of her wedding in Auntie's rose garden come spring. Auntie pleased with the results of all her civilizing efforts as she beamed upon Rose marrying a successful businessman.

But who would walk her down the garden path to where the priest waited under the flower-festooned arbor?

The sun climbed toward the bleached zenith of the midday sky, and for the hundredth time she cursed the futile sacrifice of her hat. Her horse came to a sudden stop, its nose bumping into the hindquarters of Caleb's.

"Why are we stopping here?" she asked. "I don't see any creek."

When he didn't answer, she nudged her horse forward until she was beside him. His chin rested on his chest, and the wide brim of his hat and thick tangle of hair hid his face from her. One hand lay on the saddle horn, the reins loose between his fingers. His horse lowered its head to munch on the tender grasses growing on the side of the trail.

His other hand hung at his side, dripping blood. She leaned closer and touched his leg, and his foot slipped out of the stirrup.

"Caleb!"

He jumped at the sound of her voice, automatically pulling out his pistol. "What is it?" He sat listing to one side, while the weapon hung like an anchor from his bloody hand.

"Put your gun away."

She took the reins from him. The trail had taken them to the wagon road with the deserted stage stop on the far side. She led the horses to it and tied them to a post.

"Get down, for God's sake, before you fall off." She tried to keep the joy from her voice. She just needed to delay them here until a stage arrived, and then she would be saved.

Somehow Caleb managed to swing his leg around and slide off. He hung onto the saddle until Rose helped him into the crude lean-to slapped together from saguaro ribs and ocotillo branches plastered together with dried mud. The only comfort it offered was shade, but that was comfort enough.

She went to the creek, drank, and splashed fresh, clear water on her face, brought Caleb a filled canteen, then led the horses over to the water. After they drank, she left them in the shade by the creek, tied to a palo verde.

"You need to get that shirt off," she said. Dirt, sweat, and the remnants of beans covered it, overlaid with blood, some dried and stiff, some fresh. After rinsing it in the creek, she hung it on a branch to dry and ripped more strips from her petticoats to replace the bandages. She dipped some in the cool creek water for him to press against his hot forehead.

His wound tended, the soft breeze, the shade, and the shushing of the creek lulled them to sleep. Rose dreamed of Auntie's rose garden in full fragrant bloom. She inhaled the perfume of a vivid red variety. Hummingbirds darted among the budding flowers, iridescent feathers gleaming. Meadowlarks sang their flute-like sweet notes, high-pitched and descending in their distinctive song. She pictured a staff, a treble clef, saw the graceful eighth notes arranged to match the meadowlark's call. Dew glistened on rose petals, coppery leaves gleamed in dappled sunshine. Auntie called out that tea was ready. Rose turned toward the house but before she found the end of the path, the garden suddenly grew dark, the air heavy, and a spasm of fear tightened her insides. She could not push herself forward. Thorns stretched toward her, jabbed at her. She dropped the blossoms she'd held cupped in her hand, and the petals turned to a viscous liquid that splashed across her path. The sweet fragrance turned to the stench of a dank root cellar, one filled with decaying meat, and a rough jerk on her wrist pulled her awake, into her real nightmare.

"Quiet."

Caleb held the pistol low between them and cocked the hammer.

With the rattle of wheels along the rough road, the chink of bridles, and the clang of iron shoes against rock, a stagecoach came into view. She watched its approach and felt growing joy. Her chance had come! But as she gathered herself to leap for freedom, Caleb jabbed his pistol into her side. "Move or talk and you're dead. And they'll be next." His hand closed around her arm. The rest had refreshed him—his grip was strong.

The driver reined the big mules to a stop. They snorted and stamped. They shook their heads, whites of their eyes showing they smelled the creek. The stage driver and the guard seated beside him lifted their rifles at the sight of horses tied near the shelter.

Several more men on horseback appeared, all of them weighed down with guns and cartridge belts, rifles in scabbards and additional ones held across their saddles.

They sat their horses and stared into the shelter. They looked more like outlaws than Dodger and his gang. "Make yourself known," one of them said.

Caleb sat up, keeping the gun pressed against her. "Afternoon. We're just resting. Don't mean nobody no harm."

"You people need help?" The driver climbed down and carried two buckets over to the creek, taking in Caleb's bandages and the ripped-up shirt hanging from the bush.

"Looks like you've had some trouble," the guard said from his perch on the coach.

"Indians."

The horsemen tightened reins and looked around.

"Yavapai renegades, I believe," Caleb added.

"You probly shouldn't be out here alone. Been lots of trouble in these parts. More than just renegade Indians," the driver said.

"Oh?"

Rose hoped they would see through the false innocence of Caleb's question. She tensed, poised to make her move—these guards would help her, no matter how rough their appearance.

"Heard a stage was held up outside of Phoenix."

Despite Caleb's threat, she spoke. "What do you hear of—" Caleb's hand squeezed her shoulder. She gasped when the pistol's barrel bored hard into her back.

"Ma'am, we heard the guards and the driver was kilt. One of the passengers was hurt pretty bad. Don't know if he made it or not."

"Oh! Dear God—"

The gun jabbed her ribs so hard, the pain jolted her into silence.

"Don't you worry, honey," Caleb said, keeping the pistol pressed hard. "Nothin's gonna happen to you."

The driver removed his hat and scratched his head. "Well, there musta been a gang of them, to kill that many guards. You don't look like you'd be much able to fight them off by yourself. And, not to scare your woman, but they seem partial to the ladies. Stole one off that stage, they say."

"Well, the area must be crawling with lawmen then," Caleb said. "I reckon we'll be safe enough."

The driver's scratching slowed. "Now you mention it, I ain't seen a single lawman since we left Wickenburg."

Caleb looked at the mounted men beside the stage. "You men ain't the law?"

One of the horsemen laughed. "Law? Hell, no. We been hired to guard this here stage and that's all."

"Besides," another added, "they say those men are with McCabe. We ain't lookin' for no trouble."

"I heard there was lawmen after them stage robbers already," said another rider. "Chasing them after they broke out of jail in Phoenix."

"Those are the ones that came into Wickenburg with the passenger. That's what I heard."

Another said, "No, wait, Harry. I heard there was a bunch of United States marshals in Wickenburg, come down from Prescott. Got there right afore we left."

"There's only one United States marshal up there since Morgan moved to Tombstone."

"Marshals." Another man laughed. "They'll never find the trail. It's been cold for days now."

The driver finished scratching and replaced his hat. He showed brown teeth when he smiled, carrying the buckets to the team. He leaned over and spat. "There you go," he said, nodding at Caleb. "There's your law. Sittin' back in Wickenburg, trying to figger out whether to shit or git off the pot. That's why the stage line hires its own guards."

"A lot of good it did to hire guards for the stage from Phoenix," Rose said.

"Now, honey," Caleb said. "I'll just have to protect you myself."

The guard looked at him. "If you think you're up to it."

"She'll take good care of me. Won't you, honey?"

"Go to hell."

"Got a spunky one, hey?" The driver spat again.

Caleb nodded. "She's got a bit of spunk. Too much sometimes."

"Guess that explains the rope burns on her wrists," the one called Harry said.

"Guess so."

The man held Caleb's gaze.

"Harry, we ain't hired to rescue pissed-off wives." The driver sloshed water from the buckets as he walked from one mule to another, letting them drink.

"Reckon that's so."

"Where you folks headed?" The driver held a bucket for the last mule.

"Stanton," Caleb said.

Rose twisted away from the gun barrel but Caleb's hold on her tightened.

"She's been mad at me for days. She don't want to go to Stanton. Honey, I'm sure that gang is long gone by now. You don't got to worry about them. Don't be stupid about this," he said, the threat clear in his tone.

"Maybe it isn't stupid." Harry was looking at her, and his eyes narrowed.

The driver climbed up to his seat. "No need for any fussin'. Man's got a right to use his woman the way he wants."

They were going to leave! No matter what Caleb said, he wouldn't shoot her in front of all these men. But even if he tried, she was ready to risk getting shot. She pulled free and jumped to her feet. She would make them understand. Instead, a million needles pricked her face as the blood rushed from her head.

Everything went black.

CHAPTER EIGHT

Rose awoke with a start. Ropes tied her legs to the stirrup leathers and her tightly bound hands to the pommel. Faint but raucous music floated from around a bend in the trail. Her horse clopped along behind Caleb, who rode slumped in the saddle, holding her reins. It was night. Distant points of light glowed far below. Antelope Creek wound beside the lights, a black ribbon reflecting tiny stars. The horses clattered down a series of switchbacks. They reached level ground, and the starry lights became lanterns shining through the windows of ramshackle buildings.

"About time you woke up," Caleb said, reining to a stop. "Convenient you fainted when you did. Otherwise you and several other people would be dead now."

He cut the rope that had kept her tied to the saddle. She slid off and fell to the ground. Caleb knelt in front of her, holding a set of chains. He locked the shackles around her waist, wrists, and ankles.

"Those men helped you tie me to the horse?"

"Of course. They couldn't go on their way and leave a hurt man with his wife passed out on the ground, could they? Especially with all the woman-hunting desperados running loose."

Her hand went to close on her locket, as it always did when she was nervous. Before a recital. Before her first ball. Before she gave her answer to Arthur's marriage proposal. But, of course, the locket was gone.

She wished Caleb had bled to death. She would have been better off taking her chances with renegade Indians.

Along the street amber beams of light seeped through windows layered with dirt and grease. The light flickered, broken by the shadows of men coming and going. Each time a door opened, the voices and music grew loud until the door slammed shut again. The buildings, supported by stilts, clung to a hill on one side of the street, the creek flowed on the other. A boardwalk, also on stilts, would accommodate the spring floods. No floods this time of year. They walked on a road packed hard, dry as bone, and climbed the steps to the boardwalk.

He dragged her through the door of the nearest building, into the foyer of a hotel. A few sofas, an abandoned registration counter, a carpeted stairway that led up to rooms. Flocked wallpaper hung in shreds. The stained carpet beneath her feet smelled, a bad smell. Moldy. Maybe vomit. A dusty chandelier dangled above them. The few candles illuminated a woman reclining on one of the sofas. She held a cigarette, intent on the spirals of smoke rising from her mouth and nostrils.

"Emily, darlin'," Caleb said.

The woman glanced up, her gaze running up and down Rose, then Caleb. "What in hell happened to you?"

"You seen Dodger?"

"He's at the mercantile. Him and his two idiots." The gaunt-faced woman wore nothing above the waist but a skimpy corset that barely contained her bulging breasts. A yellow skirt hitched up above the knees fastened behind her into a huge bustle. Drawers with ragged ruffles brushed the tops of tall high-heeled boots. "Who's your friend?"

"I'm takin' her to McCabe."

The woman's expression changed. There was something in her eyes as she turned her gaze on Rose. Fear. Maybe pity.

"She needs to eat," Caleb said. "She tends to faint if she's hungry, and I don't plan to carry her all the way to Hellgate."

Emily pulled open a massive double door, revealing a cavernous room packed with tables, chairs, and loud men. Stale tobacco smoke, dust, and the sour smell of sweat floated on a haze of kerosene fumes. Rose couldn't see more than six feet ahead. Her chains dragged on the floor as she followed Caleb through the crowd. Emily's voice came from behind her. "There's a table in the back. It's always loaded with food."

The long room narrowed at the far end, culminating in a raised platform, lined with hooded lanterns, a staircase at either end. Velvet curtains, covered with dust and cobwebs, hung in tatters across the top and down the sides of the stage. An upright piano had been shoved against a wall.

A piano bench sat in the middle of the stage, occupied by an old man playing a guitar. His lips moved and his head bobbed, but the noise throughout the hall drowned out his song. Dishes, glasses, and silverware clinked. Men talked in loud voices. They laughed and yelled and scraped their chairs across sticky planks. Emily shouted, "I'll save a place for you," and waved toward a table with two empty chairs. Caleb headed for the long table that held the food, Rose clanging along behind him. She filled a plate with biscuits and ribs and fried chicken, then slid into the chair next to Caleb.

Emily emerged from the smoky gloom carrying three mugs of beer, which she put down in front of Caleb, then crawled onto the lap of a pockmarked man. She looked around. "Where's Frank?" Several of the men at the table answered, food spilling from their mouths.

"Dead."

"Dead!"

"Yeah, this afternoon. Went quick, I heard," said a man with a shiny bald head.

"You'd die quick, too, if that many snakes bit ya!" said Pock Marks.

"I heard it weren't so quick," another man said. "Heard he screamed till he foamed at the mouth."

"Snakes?" The chicken leg Rose was about to eat stopped inches from her mouth.

"Look, the little ragamuffin has a voice!" Pock Marks said. "Yes, rattlers. Up in the old mine tunnels. Never gets too cold or too hot in there. Hundreds of 'em. Shit, maybe thousands. They love it in there—lots of mice and rats. They grow real big. Fat." Obviously enjoying Rose's horror, he spread his arms beyond Emily's corseted midriff to show just how big and fat. "You gotta be careful where you put your feet."

Baldy laughed. "Fat snakes," he said. "Whoever heard of a fat snake?"

Another man added, "I heard both his legs and one arm turned black. Swole up and the skin split open before he croaked. Him screaming the whole time."

Rose's chicken leg fell to the plate and she held a hand hard against her mouth.

"What the hell was he doin' in them mines anyway? They's all played out years ago. Everyone knows that." Pock Marks folded his hand of cards with a disgusted grunt.

"What's the matter, honey?" Emily asked. "You look peaked. Caleb said you needed to eat. What're you waitin' for?"

"I don't like thinking about that many snakes in one place."

"Aw, look," Pock Marks said. "The little woman is scared of the snakes."

Baldy pretended to strike at her with his fingers curved like fangs. He hissed at her and laughed, looking around to see who else would laugh with him.

Rose sank lower in her chair while the men at the table stared and made comments. "Fresh meat" and "new pickin's" and the voices grew louder, their hands pawed at her. Emily laughed, no help at all. Caleb had finished two mugs of beer. He was slumped in his chair, eyes glazed, and fresh blood staining his shirt.

Rose jumped up. The chair crashed to the floor behind her. "Don't touch me!"

The men at the next table looked over, annoyed, while those at her table leered and laughed and continued their lewd remarks. The bald man wrapped his hands around her waist, picked her up, and stood her on the table. More eyes turned toward her, expectant now, sensing an interesting incident about to ensue. Pock Marks spun her around so he could look up into her face.

"If you ain't no whore, how come you to be here?" he asked. "You think we just keep women around here to be nice?"

She held up her manacled arms. "I didn't *come* here! I was *dragged* here!"

Others joined in. "You ate our food. How you gonna pay for that?"

"Yeah, you gotta earn your keep in Stanton! You got any money?"

The bristling, sneering faces all looked the same. She kicked at the hands reaching for her ankles.

Pock Marks held up a gold coin. "Em, I give you five dollars for her."

"She's not for sale. She belongs to Caleb, I told you!"

"Okay, three dollars then. Just to rent her. For an hour!"

Rose balanced on the wobbling table, trying to not slip on spilled gravy and puddles of beer.

"I can sing." She cleared her throat and said it louder. "I can sing!"

The men exchanged glances. While they considered her entertainment value, Pock Marks stood up, sliding Emily off his lap. He drew his pistol and shot toward the stage. The old man flew off the piano bench, blood spattering the guitar he still clutched. He sat up for a second with a surprised expression, held a hand over the hole in his chest, then choked as a gout of blood welled up in his mouth. His eyes rolled back and so did he, his head hitting the stage floor with a crack that reverberated through the room's sudden silence.

"I hate that Cajun caterwauling anyway," Pock Marks said.

Heads nodded in agreement. Two men jumped up and dragged the body over to the side of the stage, and another shoved the bench over near the piano.

Pock Marks flung Rose up onto the boards. She slipped in the blood, fell, and slid across the splintered floor. She lay staring at scattered yellowed sheet music covered with rat droppings.

The back wall of the stage, crumbling adobe brick, was pitted with small holes and a couple of larger ones—one broke all the way through the wall and gave a view of the black night beyond. Evidently many entertainers before the old man had displeased this audience. Rose got to her feet.

She dragged her chains to the front of the stage and sang, not for the supper she had just eaten, but for her life.

> *Amazing grace! How sweet the sound*
> *That saved a wretch like me!*

Her voice rang out clear and sweet. Heads turned toward the stage.

> *I once was lost*
> *But now am found.*
> *Was blind but now I see.*

The room hushed, any comment or sound silenced quickly.

She sang on. Here and there men took off their hats, bowing their heads as if they were in church.

> *Through many dangers, toils and snares*
> *I have already come . . .*

The words rang true, filling her heart as they never had before. As she sang, she held out her hands, chains hanging from the shackles around her wrists, beseeching God to make the words true. As if in response, a few tentative chords flowed from the far side of the stage.

A man sat at the piano, his back to her. He wore no hat or coat, and his dark hair curled over a starched white collar. Fingers worked to find her key, and he looked over his shoulder at her with the same icy blue eyes that had challenged Caleb at the stage stop.

She heard the right key and nodded. They began again, at the next verse, together. His bold playing lifted her voice.

> *When we've been there ten thousand years,*
> *Bright shining as the sun,*
> *We've no less days to sing God's praises,*
> *Then when we first begun.*

Her voice hung in the hazy room and the last chords faded. The room's silence gradually filled with snorts and sniffling from the crowd. Then applause—a smattering at first—grew thunderous.

At the table Caleb, either asleep or passed out, sprawled with his head resting on an outstretched arm. Rose bolted from the stage, down the steps on the side opposite the piano, and pushed her way through the cheering crowd. If she could just get to the door, just get to the horses, this time she'd make it to Wickenburg. Only a few yards left to reach the big double doors when they banged apart and three men filled the opening—Dodger, Eddie, and Sam. Eddie's eyes lit up at the sight of her.

She spun around. A window! She would throw herself through the glass! Instead she collided with the piano player. His arms went around her, pinning her.

"Hold on, hold on! This isn't the way to do it." His mouth was close to her ear. Rose fought him. Loud conversations and laughter swallowed the applause, and nobody paid any attention to her. The voice in her ear insisted, "Come with me." She elbowed him, twisted away, turned, and kicked. There was so much noise in the hall, she didn't hear him howl with pain, only saw the surprise on his face, but he doubled over and hit the floor with a thud. Looking for the window, she glanced at Caleb's table and froze; his chair was empty. He suddenly appeared through the smoke, stepped over the fallen piano player, and yanked her to him.

That night Rose devoted many sleepless hours to pondering how you could not prevent your ears from hearing, nor could you then forget what you had heard. Hours of grunting and moaning while the bed shook and creaked. The smell of sweat and unknowable odors as they kicked away the covers, and a blanket landed on her head where she sat chained to the foot of the bed, on the floor of a squalid hotel room that stank of urine and stale beer. She found a few hours of sleep when Caleb finally grew tired of Emily, and his eventual snoring lulled her into oblivion.

They left Stanton before dawn, and although Caleb had removed the chains, she felt no less trapped. Leaving the Stanton town limits, they crossed Antelope Creek and headed north, toward a looming wall of mountains, almost sheer cliff, nothing but rocks, sand, and prickly pear. Dawn turned the hillside golden and they plodded along, single file, back and forth and ever upwards, ascending the steep, barren hillside. A coyote appeared on a boulder, stood blinking as if awakened by their passing, lifted its head to sample the breeze, and was gone.

They crested the hill and picked their own trail through the brush, piñon pines, and juniper, still in a general uphill trend, with Sam bringing up the rear. They headed northwest, deep into the Bradshaws.

Although they rode slowly, Rose sensed a new energy in her captors. Eddie enjoyed a swig from his flask every so often, looking back and leering at Rose until Caleb snarled at him.

Sam, riding behind her, felt free to plague her, his southern drawl quiet and unheard by the others.

"Hey, Rosie Pink. Thought you was gonna escape, huh?" He let out a low laugh. "Sure is nice to have you amongst us. Ah almost forgot how tender you are. Hope your sweet thighs ain't chafin' through them lady britches."

She stared straight ahead.

"Ah'd be happy to soothe them. Ah'd be happy to just soothe your whole body." He rode up closer, his horse crowding hers.

"Get away from me!"

Caleb whirled his horse and drove it between hers and Sam's.

"How many times," he said, jamming a finger into Sam's chest, "do I have to tell you the woman is mine?"

"All right! Enough!" Dodger yelled, reining in his horse. Eddie, mid-swig, crashed into him. Now all the horses shuffled and snorted and everyone fought for control.

"If I've said it once, I said it fifty times! Quit this Goddamn fighting over the woman or I'm gonna get rid of her. Caleb, you keep her next to you if you still want her so bad. Sam, get the hell back there. Your job is to keep an eye out for Indians. Not pester the woman."

"Yes, suh."

They plodded along for several miles, always uphill, into

ponderosa pine country. A carpet of dry needles cushioned the horses' hooves, and an eerie silence hung on the early morning chill. Rose shivered as they splashed through a small stream. Weak sunlight broke through the trees and glinted on patches of ice that skimmed the wet depressions made by other animals' tracks. Deer, elk, mountain lion.

She recognized the terrain—the mountains near Prescott. She closed her eyes as the horse's steady gait rocked her, picturing Auntie's house and the bedroom in the upstairs turret. Her home away from home. She imagined herself at the windows, looking down into the rose garden, pruned and mulched in preparation for the coming winter. She wondered if she would live to see the roses bloom again. Despite the creaking saddle leather and Eddie's spitting, Rose was able to imagine herself snuggled into the big four-poster bed, covered with downy quilts, watching the stars wink over Thumb Butte in the distance.

"Stay away from the edge here, Rosie Pink." Caleb twisted in his saddle so he could see her and pointed to where the trail dropped off. "Keep that horse under control."

They had ridden higher, and gusty winds swept clean the carpet of pine needles, leaving rocky and uneven ground beneath the horses' hooves.

Rose retreated again into her mind. She imagined her father alive, in Prescott with her aunt. In her daydream he organized search parties, contacted his friends and acquaintances in law enforcement, and led them in the quest to find his daughter. She wanted so much to believe her father was alive, but a small, hardening part of her heart told her she couldn't believe anything Caleb said. She had ridden away with them and left her father lying still as death in that dusty road.

She started a different story in her mind to replace her painful thoughts. Now it was Arthur urging lawmen to deputize him so he could participate in the widening search for his—

Sam's horse nudged hers. She yanked on the reins to stay away from the steep drop, and Sam pulled closer, almost beside her.

"Hoo hoo, Rosie Pink," he whispered, reaching for her. "That little bottom of yours must be tired of settin' that horse by now. Let me—"

"Stop that!" she yelled.

Caleb looked over his shoulder.

Sam raised a hand in front of him. "Didn't mean no harm, just tryin' to be nice."

He let the space between them widen again.

Then, moments later, he was back. "Rosie Pink? Hoo hoo, little woman. Wouldn't you like to ride back here with me? Set here on my lap and—"

Caleb reined to a stop and dismounted, strode over to Sam, and dragged him out of his saddle. The two men swung at each other. Clearly Sam would win the fight. Caleb could barely lift his arm and cried out in pain when Sam punched his shoulder. The horses stomped and shuffled and kicked up dust that obscured the narrow trail. Rose fought to keep away from the trail's edge and screamed when her horse stumbled, dropping a hoof off the brink before collecting itself and she could regain control.

Eddie turned in the saddle, looked back, and smirked.

Sam looked to see what Rose had screamed about, and Caleb was able to catch him off balance and knock him to the ground. "Now stay back where you belong." Caleb headed toward Rose, a hand pressed against fresh blood on his shirt, but Sam scrambled to his feet and rushed forward. Caleb stepped to one side. Sam's own bulk worked against him, with help from Caleb, who shoved with his good arm as the big man stumbled past. Screaming, Sam disappeared over the edge, followed by a spray of dislodged stones, snapping branches and dust.

Dodger dismounted and peered over the cliff.

"Oh, for Christ's sake."

Eddie ran up and the three men looked down.

"Get up here," Caleb yelled.

"I can't! I can't move! My legs won't move!"

Rose stayed behind the men but peeked between them. On a wide ledge below, Sam thrashed his arms, flinging rocks and dirt in his struggle to sit up.

"What the fuck." Dodger turned away. He pulled himself into his saddle and trotted off down the trail.

"Don't leave me!"

Rose covered her ears. Eddie took a swig from his flask, grinning like it was all a great joke. Then he hopped onto his horse and followed Dodger.

"Let the buzzards have him," Dodger yelled over his shoulder. "He was a pain in the ass anyway."

"You're not going to just leave him there, are you?" Rose asked.

"Get on your horse." Caleb grabbed the reins for Sam's horse and then swung into his saddle. He motioned for her to ride ahead of him. "Don't worry about him. He ain't gonna last long."

She looked back once as they rode away. A couple of turkey vultures already circled overhead. Sam continued to scream. And behind Caleb, just as they rounded a bend in the trail, she caught a glimpse of a rider. It was that man from the stage stop, the piano player who tried to capture her in Stanton. He was following them. She turned and kept her eyes straight ahead. A minute later a single gunshot echoed through the hills.

"See?" Caleb said. "Sam knew what needed to be done."

CHAPTER NINE

Mary Alice braced herself against the porch railing and fought to maintain her composure. The buggy driver reined the horses to a stop and set the brake on the steep hill. Walter, drawn and pale, climbed down to the street before the driver could help him, but Kimo rushed to assist him up the porch steps.

"Oh, Walter," Mary Alice whispered.

"I'm doing well, dear. Don't fret." He squeezed her hand. "The authorities will soon return our Rose to us. And if they haven't done so in a day or two, I shall go out myself and find her."

Mary Alice dabbed at her eyes and tried to cling to the shred of hope his confident words offered even as she felt the tremor in his grip. "Well, come inside now," she said. "We've prepared the guest room for you. Shall I send for the doctor?"

"I'm quite all right, Mary Alice. Just a little tired and hungry."

"We'll fix you something to eat right away and then you can rest."

The driver carried Walter's luggage into the guest room. Mary Alice thanked him but he said, "Wait, one more thing. I could use a hand." He asked Kimo to help, and they returned with Rose's battered trunk, its broken lock dangling from the hasp.

"Kimo, help him carry it up to Rose's room," Mary Alice said.

With the driver gone and Walter settled in the parlor, Mary Alice climbed the stairs to Rose's room. The turret's three curved-glass windows sparkled above Rose's writing desk, and sunlight filled the room. Kam Le had spent days cleaning—washing windows, dragging rugs outside and beating them until not a speck of dust remained, rubbing turpentine and lemon into the furniture. Mary Alice sat on the freshly made bed and stared at the trunk.

Where was her niece? Who would find her and bring her home? Walter was alive and would recover, but he was in no shape to do anything about this situation. He looked every one of his sixty years, pale and drawn and in pain. Despite what he said, she would send Kimo for the doctor. Despite the brave words in the note he'd sent from Wickenburg, he would not be looking for Rose. At least not any time soon.

The smell of road dust permeated the room. She used her handkerchief to wipe dirt off the trunk, then ran her hand along the top. She imagined Rose's excitement and happiness as she packed her things a few days ago. Looking forward to visiting, to planning her wedding, and choosing a style and embellishments for her wedding gown.

Mary Alice released the latches, pulled the broken padlock from its hasp, and opened the trunk.

The tray was gone. A bolt of torn and dirty silk, no doubt meant for Rose's wedding gown, lay atop a pile of clothing. It looked as if someone had shoved it all into the trunk willy-nilly, everything stained with the red dirt of the wagon road. Everything ruined.

She lowered the lid, rested a hand on it, and bowed her head. "Please God, let her know we are praying for her. Keep her safe, keep her strong, hold her in your loving arms, and bring her back. Oh, please, return her to us."

She made the sign of the cross, and then the tears came.

Kam Le's soft voice came from the doorway. "Missus? May I help you?"

Kam Le brought her a fresh handkerchief and sat beside her. Mary Alice quieted, then thought of Rose. Lost, maybe hurt, held by outlaws. A fresh onslaught of wrenching sobs overcame her. Kam Le's arm went around her. She leaned against the younger woman and wept into Rose's handkerchief until her grief was spent.

She patted Kam Le's hand. "Go on downstairs, dear. Maybe you could make some tea?"

Kam Le nodded, her own cheeks wet. Mary Alice gave her a hug. Both women blew their noses, wiped the tears from their faces, and tried to smile. Kam Le left, padding down the stairs.

Mary Alice stepped onto the raised floor of the turret. She sat at Rose's writing desk and leaned toward the windows. At the bottom of the hill the brick courthouse with its stately clock tower looked solid and civilized. Beyond it, though, Thumb Butte's dome jutted above the mountains, a reminder of the rough wilderness that surrounded the territorial capital.

"Where are you, Rose?"

She so clearly remembered her sister, Leila, as a young mother, holding her precious baby girl. Leila had said, "You have the most delightful rose garden, Mary Alice, but you'll never grow anything like this in your yard."

"No, indeed." Neither knew at the time that Mary Alice would never have children of her own. "Your daughter is the most beautiful rose of all." And so she had been the one to give Rose her name.

Six years later Leila died while giving birth to a stillborn son. How many times had Mary Alice reached for her rosary beads to repent the joy her sister's death eventually meant to her? Because Rose became *her* child, the child she'd never had, spending every summer in Prescott.

She held the memory of the precious little girl in her heart, could almost imagine the sound of the child's feet racing down the hall. Could feel the young Rose jumping into her lap and covering her face with kisses, laughing eyes filled with joy. Her child. Her beloved child.

Where was she?

Mary Alice took a deep breath and one more look at Thumb Butte. Rose was out there, somewhere in that wild land. But her niece was a strong woman now, capable and sensible. For the first time Mary Alice felt gratitude that her brother-in-law had reared the girl on that ranch, raised her more as a boy than a girl. Had taught her how to ride and shoot and be independent. She would survive, and she would come home.

Kimo had set a small table beside the bed in the downstairs guest room, and Walter put his cup upon it when Mary Alice entered the room. She knew her eyes were swollen and her nose red. Well, she would not apologize for crying under these circumstances. "How are you, Walter?"

"I'll be much better once I can sit a horse again. Maybe tomorrow."

"The doctor will come tomorrow. He will be the one to say when you can sit a horse. You'll do no good killing yourself."

"Mary Alice, you are not in charge of me."

"Right now I am."

Walter's face softened. "You're as hard-headed as Rose and just as bossy."

"Thank you for the compliment." Pain had filled Walter's eyes when he spoke his daughter's name. "She'll be found, Walter."

He nodded but looked away. There were lines around his eyes and mouth she had never noticed before.

"She is a resourceful woman," he said. "If there is any way she can escape, she will. And she knows the countryside. She can find her way to us."

"Yes, I'm sure." Mary Alice pulled a chair to the other side of the table and poured herself some tea. "If there's any way, she will find it."

They were each lost in their own thoughts for a while before Mary Alice asked, "Has anyone notified Arthur?"

"Yes." Walter grunted. "I had a telegram sent to him as soon as I was brought to Wickenburg."

"Oh, then I'm sure he'll be here any day as well. I'll have another guest room aired out for him."

"No need."

"Oh?"

"He's already responded. Said he was sure the authorities had everything in hand and it would be best if he stayed in Phoenix."

"You're not happy about that."

Walter slammed his fist on the table. Tea splashed onto the rug. "Who could sit there doing nothing while Rose is lost in the wilds? What kind of man is that?"

"Walter, Arthur is a city man. He's wise enough to know that he'd be of little help. He'd get in everyone's way during a hard search on horseback."

"Don't stick up for the man. Rose will never be able to abide his ways for a lifetime. She'll be sorry if she marries him."

"He might be just what she needs, to calm herself down a little. She is a lady, you know, even though you've brought her up to behave like a common ranch hand. Besides, he can provide very well for her—she'll never want for anything."

"Not for anything but a real man. Is there nothing stronger in this house than tea?"

"Indeed, there is."

Mary Alice hurried to the kitchen and returned with her brandy decanter and two glasses. She handed a glass to Walter and raised her own. "To Rose. Home safe and sound!"

Chapter Ten

The sun fell below the hills ahead, and the sky darkened enough for a few stars to appear above the trees. They finally stopped. Rose slid from the saddle and leaned against it, hanging onto the stirrup strap. Every muscle in her body ached, every bone so chilled she feared she would never be warm again.

She didn't know which was worse—the horrible sounds Sam had made or the silence that had followed that gunshot. And of her choices now, which was worse? To look at Dodger's evil, uncaring face, Caleb's indifference, and Eddie's smirk, or close her eyes only to see images of vultures circling.

Or that man, the piano player, swinging off his horse, wool coat flapping, hat pulled low, and pistol in hand.

"Come on," Caleb said. "Sit over here. We're gonna build a fire." He held out his hand.

"Don't touch me!"

"Jesus Christ, is she still pissed off?" Eddie asked. "She didn't even like Sam."

"No, I didn't! But he was your friend. You don't care he's back there being eaten by buzzards?"

"He weren't no friend of mine."

"He was a person! He was a human being!"

Caleb laughed. "Just barely!"

"Just like you! Barely human!" She wanted to slap every one of them.

"He was already dead," Caleb said. "That bullet just finished it."

"You could have buried him." And stopped the image of circling vultures that plagued her still.

Rose spent the long night propped against the tree he'd chained her to, burrowed into the filthy blanket he'd thrown at her, praying that God would give her strength to get through whatever lay ahead. Unable to sleep, she found comfort in the thought of Arthur heading a posse that would soon catch up to them and close in on Hellgate. Or she would escape and bring all the lawmen in Arizona to capture and hang every one of them.

The next day their steady, uphill ride continued through forests of ponderosa pine. They climbed ever higher along a faint trail. The trees thinned and revealed what appeared to be a ridge looming above them. When they reached the top, a man with a rifle stepped away from a boulder he'd been leaning on. Dodger dismounted and spoke with him. The rest of them sat their horses while another guard appeared and collected the men's pistols and rifles, dug through the saddlebags, and removed half the money stolen from the stage. Rose braced herself for a violent protest, but Dodger and the guard over by the boulder watched quietly. They exchanged a few words and shook hands before Dodger rejoined the gang.

The horses huffed and shook their heads as a putrid stench wafted up from the other side of the steep incline and overpowered the fresh scent of pine and juniper. The men pulled their rags up to cover their noses and mouths. Caleb rode up to her and tied a cloth to cover the bottom half of her face. "You get used to it after a few days."

The guard waved them on, through an opening in the ridge,

and they began their descent into Hellgate. Armed men stood at regular intervals around a rim that encircled a deep depression. Sunlight reflected off their rifle barrels and glinted on fingers of black volcanic rock that snaked down the sides of the steep slopes. The outlaws and their prisoner walked their mounts slowly along switchbacks carved into the barren walls of what Rose recognized as a large crater. Her horse jerked beneath her when her chains clanked, and she felt a shiver of fear that the horse would spook and they'd fall. The jagged cliffs above them formed a natural fortress for the shabby village inhabiting it.

Halfway to the bottom the slope eased; bushes, prickly pear, and stunted juniper lined the widened trail. They reached level ground and rode between a double row of canvas tents, the kind army officers used, the size of small cabins. Men passed by, leading horses, carrying packages. Nobody paid attention to them as they sat their horses. Dodger nodded when Caleb pointed toward the tents. Beyond them a crowd milled around outside a rough wooden building. Rose took it to be a mercantile of some sort, with a corral full of horses to one side, then a barn.

No blacksmith, though. No blazing fire into which he would lower iron, no banging on a forge to shape the heated metal. She looked around—no fires anywhere. No smoke. With all these people around, no scent of sizzling meat, no coffee brewing. November in the mountains yet there were no campfires. It was cold now. What would it be like in another month?

To the east, not more than a mile away, Thumb Butte's dome loomed above the cliffs. McCabe's hideout sat right under the noses of the territorial government, not more than a few miles from Fort Whipple!

They found two empty tents next to each other. Caleb pulled her off the horse. He locked the shackles onto her again. The men pulled bedrolls, saddles, and blankets off the horses before

Eddie led them off toward the corral.

"It stinks worse over here," Dodger said. "The jakes are too close. So's that fence. You know the ditch is right there on the other side."

Caleb was already hauling his belongings into one of the tents. "You want to find another tent, go ahead."

The fence Dodger spoke of was about ten feet from the back of the tent Caleb had chosen. Boards, thorny branches, and small tree trunks still covered with bark, all held together with barbed wire attached to a taller post here and there. One of the wooden slats had broken halfway up, and a shadow moved behind it.

Rose walked closer. Within the enclosure, blanket-covered mounds clustered close together. A blanket flapped, and a young boy, maybe three or four years old, burst out from under it. A woman rose, grabbed the boy, and pulled the blanket over them again.

A child's voice came from near the broken slat.

"My mama made a face like yours once. When she found a dead rat amongst the potatoes in the root cellar."

Rose pressed her cheek against the fence and looked through the opening. A girl huddled on the other side, thin arms wrapped around knees drawn up under a ragged dress. Matted hair fell over bony shoulders, and large eyes in a smudged face returned Rose's stare.

"Hello, little girl."

"I ain't that little. I'm ten, almost eleven."

"What's your name?"

"Sarah." She held up a filthy cloth doll, its porcelain face chipped, bald spots on its head. "This is Mrs. Coppage."

"Are you all alone?"

The girl shook her head.

Rose asked, "Where's your mother?"

Sarah pointed to a woman lying on her side in a muddy spot, her back to them. She lay in the middle of the enclosure and appeared to be asleep. No blankets. A young boy sat next to her squeezing handfuls of mud onto her skirt.

"Is she sleeping? Who is that boy?"

"My brother," Sarah said. "It's okay. Jonathan knows mama don't care no more about being dirty."

"What's wrong with her? Why aren't you all under a blanket like the others?"

"Nothin's wrong with her. She's just a'sleepin'. She come back a little while ago. I guess she don't get much sleep there, up at the house. She's always tired when she comes back."

"What house?"

"The nice house Mr. McCabe lives in."

Rose looked around but could only see tents. From a pocket she pulled out a biscuit she'd saved from breakfast. "I'll bet you're hungry."

Sarah stuck her hand through the fence, snatched the biscuit, and ran toward her brother.

"Who are you talking to?" Caleb asked. He stood beside her and looked over the fence.

"Nobody."

"Get in the tent."

Once inside, he shoved her and told her to sit, but she dove for the bottom of the canvas and was halfway out before he grabbed her feet and dragged her back in.

"Let me go!"

He pinned her down and held her. "You can't escape from here."

"Yes, I can. I can escape, and I'll come back with an army. That'll wipe that smile off your face."

Caleb found extra tent stakes and a mallet someone had thrown in a corner. He dragged her to where he could reach them, then pushed her to the ground. He unlocked the leg irons, pulled them as far as he could from the chains around her waist, and hammered a tent stake through a link. Hammered it deep into the hard-packed dirt, then one on the other side, angled so she'd have no purchase to pull them out. She couldn't even stand up.

"I don't want to have to go looking for you." He dropped the mallet and left.

The canvas walls blocked the sun. Chilled, she inched over, pulled the canvas up a bit, and lay so she could see under it while letting in some light and warmth. Riders passed, followed by about a half-dozen women tied together like a string of horses. The women coughed from the dust, stumbling as the rope pulled their arms ahead of them. Rose saw five women: two emaciated Indians, a woman pleading in Spanish to anyone who glanced her way, and of the remaining three women one who seemed very young. Her light blond hair hung down her back. She turned her head from side to side, eyes wide, mouth open. Rivulets of tears cut through the layers of dust on her face. The men herded her with the others into the stockade as if they were cattle being pushed into a stockyard chute.

Rose let the canvas wall drop.

The bright sunlight left her temporarily blinded, but she sensed motion by the pile of supplies. She dug into the top of her shoe for her knife.

"I'm glad you have something to defend yourself with. Besides kicking, I mean."

She pulled back as far as her chains would allow and raised the knife.

"Don't you think if my intent was to harm you I'd have done it by now?" His quiet voice sounded almost friendly.

Her eyes adjusted. It was that stagecoach guard, the piano player, the one who'd followed them.

"You killed Sam."

He shrugged a shoulder, looking around the tent before turning those ice-blue eyes on her. "My name's Harry Sheldon. That mean anything to you?"

"Do you feature yourself to be some famous outlaw? I've never heard of you." She tightened her grip on the knife and kept it raised. "But the guards let you in this place. That doesn't speak well of you."

"They don't much care who comes in. It's getting out that's a problem."

"What do you want?"

"To get you out."

Something about his expression—intense, determined—made her ask, "And then what?"

"Take you to your father."

She tried to hold the knife steady. "What do you know of my father?"

"I know Walter LaBelle would've protected you with his life."

"He did. He gave his life. He's dead."

"I thought he might have been the passenger they took to Wickenburg."

"I told you. He's dead."

"All the more reason for me to help you. I have—had so much respect for your father. If I can get you out of here—"

"How do you know who he is, who I am?"

"I'm sorry I didn't figure it out at the stage stop. Wasn't until later, when I heard he'd been on that stage, that I put it together. By the time I circled around, you were already on your way to Stanton. And then I realized there was a whole gang."

"So why are you still following me?"

"I told you."

"Then knock these stakes out. The mallet is over in that pile somewhere."

"I can't. You'd run. And you'd get killed." He went to the tent flap. "We need to figure this out."

"Don't leave me here!" She threw dirt at the flap as it closed behind him.

CHAPTER ELEVEN

"Take care, Walter. Watch your step," Mary Alice said. "Please, hold the railing."

Walter descended the porch stairs one at a time, holding the railing as instructed. He'd insisted he did not need to see the doctor and now was going to hire a buggy and driver to take him to Fort Whipple. He would ensure the army quickly sent a scout to search for his daughter. Mary Alice was in favor of the plan, just not with Walter running all over the countryside when he should be resting. He looked frail, not a word she would have thought to ever apply to Walter LaBelle.

She remembered the day he rode into her parents' ranch north of Maricopa Wells, looking for land to acquire and some advice on setting up a ranch in what was then New Mexico Territory. He was tall and good-looking, sat his horse as if he'd been born on one. The fact that he had been a ranger in Texas added to his allure. She and Leila had both smoothed their hair and brushed off their aprons as he spoke with their father. Once they'd made themselves presentable, they emerged from the house. Walter's eyes had lit upon Leila and never strayed.

Walter reached the bottom step, and Mary Alice said, "Kimo, go with him."

"I don't need a nanny, Mary Alice."

"He's not a nanny. He can drive the carriage. Why pay extra for a driver?"

She knew Walter would rather die than admit he needed help.

Because she had presented the idea as frugal, he gave in and allowed the Chinese to accompany him. Kimo would, of course, do more than drive. He would take good care of Walter.

She went inside. "Kam Le, I'm going to rest in my room. Please don't disturb me."

"Not until dinner, Missus."

"I'm not feeling well, dear. I doubt I will want to eat. Maybe later in the evening, if Mr. LaBelle has returned by then." At the girl's worried expression, she added, "I'll let you know if I want tea later on."

She hadn't slept the night before. She'd left her door open so she could hear if Walter got up or needed anything during the night and, as a result, had tossed and turned, starting awake at every cough or snore. That morning she'd had to call Kam Le to button her shoes; her fingers were too stiff and painful to do it.

She closed the door and hung her cane on the footboard of her brass bed. At the window she started to pull aside the heavy drapes and lace panels to see if Walter and Kimo had reached the bottom of the hill, but the sight of the inflamed, swollen knuckles stopped her. She stared at her fingers as if they belonged to someone else. Letting the drapes fall, she sat at her dressing table and opened the drawer where she kept a bottle of sherry and a glass. She pulled the cork out with her teeth and lifted the bottle to her lips.

The vanity mirror reflected an image that was hardly that of a respected widow. Mary Alice was always shocked by the sight of herself—her graying hair, her wrinkles, her sagging skin. She preferred to remember how she looked in years past. The young woman Joseph always said he still saw when he looked at her. Sunlight seeped from the edges of the drapes and cast a harsh light upon her face. Tired, drooping eyes, made worse for her sleepless night, stared back.

She put the bottle down and removed the pins from her hair, wincing at the pressure on her finger joints. A few more sips of sherry and she was able to pick up the brush, but could only pull it through her hair once.

It was so strange, the way time moved through a person. All those summers filled with Rose's visits had passed in the blink of an eye. Yet the months since Joseph died—an eternity. She missed him. He had been a pleasant man, quiet and friendly; everyone liked him. He'd had a kind heart and never grew impatient with her, no matter how impatient she was with herself. He should be here with her now, his soothing presence comforting her. Her heart ached for the touch of his hand, but a part of her was glad he was not suffering this torment. He loved Rose like a daughter, just as she did.

And now where was their little girl? What was she going through? Mary Alice willed her thoughts away from what could be happening, could have already happened, to her precious Rose. But the black images played on the edges of her consciousness, and she could not stop the most awful thought: it might be better if Rose were dead. The tears came and she shook with sobs, her hand pressed to her mouth to keep Kam Le from hearing and rushing into the room.

The mirror displayed a grotesque face—wet with tears, nose running, blood-red eyes. The splotchy face contorted as her hand fell away, revealing an ugly grimace.

She grabbed a handkerchief and wiped her face, then squeezed the damp cloth, pressing her fingers into it, welcoming the stabbing pain. She banged her fist on the table and cried out, and that brought Kam Le running down the hallway.

"Missus?" She knocked and cracked the door.

Mary Alice lowered her head into her hands. "Go away, dear. Please."

The door clicked shut.

What she needed was to lie down, to rest. She started to take off her shoes but her fingers were clumsy. She tried to use the button hook in reverse, to push the buttons through, but that didn't work. She flung the button hook to the floor where it bounced on the carpet. Its quietness enraged her. She threw the empty glass with all her strength at the wall, hitting a drawing, a horse's head drawn by Rose as a child. The glass shattered and the frame itself crashed onto her dresser, knocking over her jewelry box and perfume bottles. She heard Kam Le's feet scuffing across the hardwood floor in the hallway.

"Go away," she shouted.

The girl made no sound, nor did she touch the door. Mary Alice imagined her lurking just outside, waiting to leap into the room. "I said go away!" Footsteps retreated down the hallway.

She picked up Rose's drawing and laid it on the dresser. She sat again at the vanity and looked at the hag in the mirror. Smiling now. Satisfied. She lifted the bottle to her lips, drank deeply, then raised it in a toast, but the face in the mirror dissolved again into tears. "Rose. Oh, Rose. Where are you? Please, God, bring her back to me."

Sometime later a sudden flash of light struck her eyes. She brushed tangled hair from her face and blinked as a lamp flared on the bedside table. She smelled the match's burning sulfur and followed a hand that floated upward to Walter LaBelle's puckered lips. His breath extinguished the match.

"Oh, God." She rolled away from him. "Get out of my room."

Instead he sat on the edge of the bed.

"What the hell happened in here? It smells like a French whorehouse."

"How would you know?" She lifted her arms across her face, all she could do to hide from him. "I couldn't get my shoes off."

He pulled her legs onto his lap and unbuttoned her shoes,

letting them drop to the floor. His hands were strong and gentle. Joseph used to take off her shoes and then rub her feet. At the thought she began to cry again.

"Here, here," Walter said, ignoring her attempts to kick him from the bed, holding her legs down through her skirts. "I shouldn't have left you here alone."

"I'm always alone."

"But not always terrified for your missing niece." He took her shoulders, helping her to sit up and settle against the pillows. He handed over a handkerchief and pushed the hair away from her wet face, then sat again on the edge of the mattress.

"Don't look at me. I must be a fright."

"I don't scare easily."

"You just got home?"

Walter nodded. He picked up a cup and saucer from a tray on the bedside table and held it out to her, but she shook her head. He followed her gaze down to her hands; she didn't mind the look of compassion that came into his eyes. He held the cup to her lips, and she drank. "Raising a girl on your own has gentled you," she said.

"Old age has gentled me. Against my wishes, for the most part."

"The alternative to growing old is a poor one."

"You must miss Joseph very much. But I fear you wore yourself out caring for him his last years."

"I was happy to do what I could." She turned her head away when he offered the teacup again. "Tell me what they said at the fort."

Walter put the teacup down. The bed springs creaked when he stood. At the window he held the lace panels aside and looked out at the night, his angry expression reflected in the glass. "They will increase their patrols and send a scout toward

Wickenburg, as a favor to me. He said it's not a military problem."

"Then you need to talk to the sheriff. Talk to the marshal."

"I did. They were not helpful." He turned to her, his face colorless except for the dark circles beneath his eyes. "I believe it's up to me to find her."

She nodded. If she were able, she'd be on a horse herself—riding through all the countryside between Prescott and Wickenburg until she found her niece. But she was not able, and neither was Walter right now. Although soon enough he would be, and there would be no stopping him.

"Perhaps you should get up now," he said. "I'll have Kam Le come in and clean up this mess."

He helped her up. She went to her dressing table and picked up the brush.

"Here, let me," Walter said.

She closed her eyes as he ran the bristles through her hair, smoothing it and then arranging it into a long braid down her back. "Rose wore her hair in braids until she was almost sixteen."

Mary Alice pushed up from her chair. "I know." Rose must have enjoyed her father's strong fingers running through her hair.

He smiled and gave a small laugh. "She always complained I didn't do it right, after spending her summers with you."

"Let's have some supper. You look tired."

Mary Alice left her cane hanging on the footboard and put her arm through his. Down the hallway, to the dining room, they leaned upon each other.

CHAPTER TWELVE

Rose clutched her knife, listening and waiting, until long after dark. None of the outlaws returned. The noisy activity outside the tent—horses, men's voices, occasionally a woman's cry—had moved to the other side of the crater. Loud voices, an intermittent burst of laughter, some of it high-pitched. Evidently not all the women were in the stockade. Not all were as miserable as she.

After fighting with the tent stakes for hours, she lay exhausted. A feeling of hopelessness had festered since leaving Stanton, but she refused to let it deepen into dread. Caleb had claimed her for himself, had put her in this tent instead of that stockade with the other women. He didn't do it to protect her. He'd made it clear he intended to hand her over to McCabe. He seemed to think she was valuable enough to curry McCabe's favor.

At least she could make sure she wouldn't be such a prize.

She grabbed a long section of tangled hair and held it taught. She raised her knife and sawed through it, dropping the hank of hair onto the ground. She pulled hard, not minding—rather welcoming—the pain at her scalp as handful after handful cut away. Clumps of matted hair lay scattered all around her.

Caleb returned later, carrying a lantern. He looked at her hair. "That was stupid," he said. He twisted her wrist and took the knife away, threw it in the corner, then fixed himself a pallet of blankets and went to sleep.

★ ★ ★ ★ ★

In the morning Caleb pulled the stakes and let her go to the jakes by herself. "I'll be watching." He held the tent flap open.

She gathered up her chains and clanked away. She looked back before pulling open the door, and he was still there. When she came out, she realized it smelled worse outside than inside the outhouse. A ditch carried black water from the stockade. It flowed under the fence and curved past the jakes, ending in a fetid pool near the edge of the compound. The guard stationed there had tied a rag to cover his nose and mouth.

A human arm floated by in the ditch's meandering current. When it reached the pool, it twirled a solemn circle, palm up, slender fingers curled. Rose fell to her knees, retching, and the guard laughed at her. She stumbled to her feet and ran, chains dragging and kicking up dust behind her. Her breath blew clouds into the chill morning air. She stopped at the fence and hung onto it, gasping for breath.

Caleb's boots crunched across the rocky dirt. "Next time you complain about those chains, stop and thank God you're not in there." He nodded toward the women in the stockade while he rolled a cigarette.

She curled her fingers around the top of the fence, digging them into the rough wood. Rats scurried around the blanketed mounds that hid the women and children. Turkey vultures perched on the fence nearest the pool and in the branches of a stunted tree, their bald red heads emerging from hunched black bodies.

Caleb gently pried her hands from the fence. Inside the tent, he again used the mallet to hammer the stakes through the chains. He tossed her a piece of jerky and some hardtack before he left.

"Could I have a blanket? It's cold in here."

"Jesus. Anything else I can do for you?"

He threw a blanket at her. She pulled it over her shoulders, swaddled herself with it, and waited for her shivering to stop. She pulled splinters from the fence out of her fingers with her teeth. The sun climbed toward noon, warming the inside of the tent, and hunger finally moved her to pick the jerky and hardtack out of the dirt and eat. Then she slept.

A sudden whoosh of cooler air and a shaft of sunlight awakened her. Caleb dug his bootheel into the dirt around the stakes and yanked them out.

"Time for you to pay your respects to Mr. McCabe."

He held on to her arm as they walked to the edge of the two rows of tents and turned right. Past the mercantile and corral and barn, a white two-story Victorian house with wraparound porch and turrets, covered with gingerbread trim painted in shades of red and pink, nestled against the sheer cliff of the crater wall, as far from the stockade, the ditch, and the stench as was possible. It shimmered in the bright noonday sun. Guards questioned them at the bottom of the porch stairs before allowing them to pass. Caleb banged on the door. They waited among rocking chairs, wicker davenports, tables, discarded whiskey bottles, and overflowing spittoons.

The door swung open. "Come in, *Señor.*" A Mexican man ushered them inside. Rose stepped onto a gleaming hardwood floor and then a thick wool rug. Flocked wallpaper. Gold velvet draperies, tied back to reveal lacy white panels. Polished mahogany woodwork and furniture gleamed in sunlight streaming through sparkling windows.

A Chinese woman walked by carrying a dust rag. The scent of lemon oil reminded Rose of Auntie's home. She closed her eyes and fought a wave of loss and longing. But McCabe's house overflowed with ugly furniture, tasteless artwork, and tables crowded with knick-knacks. Everything overdone, tawdry, garish. A mockery of Aunt Mary Alice's home.

Servants—Negroes, Chinese men and women—scurried here and there, holding trays or cleaning rags. The sound of rattling pans and clinking dishes carried through a center hallway from which the inviting odors of cinnamon and sugar and coffee wafted.

"Hot coffee," Rose whispered.

"He keeps a Celestial perched up on the roof. He has a fan to wave away the smoke from the chimney," Caleb said. "No cold beans out of a can in this house."

"Why are there no fires?"

"Same reason they took the guns away when we got here. Fort Whipple's only a few miles away, and Prescott just beyond. Smoke and gunfire would no doubt draw the curious."

Delicately carved furniture with horsehair upholstery filled the parlor, and three women sprawled on upholstered chairs and a sofa. Caleb removed his hat. "Afternoon, ladies."

Three sets of heavily lidded eyes above rouged cheeks looked him over, and black-toothed smiles blossomed on painted lips. The women wore nothing more than corsets, corset covers, French pantaloons, and house slippers. Rose looked away from their exposed breasts.

A black lacquered tray, inlaid with mother of pearl, rested on a table in front of the sofa. It held smaller trays, delicately carved wooden boxes with lids, and a collection of metal spoons. The spoons had long, thin handles and small, flattened bowls. One of the women picked up a pipe and held it over a miniature lamp, not more than six inches high. She heated the pipe over the low flame, puffed on it, and passed it to the next woman. They handed it back and forth among the three of them, taking turns inhaling. Sweet smoke floated throughout the room.

Footsteps banged down a stairway and a man burst into the room, talking nonstop with a heavy Irish brogue. He was hardly taller than Rose. Bright blue eyes gleamed behind spectacles balanced on pudgy cheeks. His red hair and beard stuck out every whichaway. He carried a thick stick, almost a club, too short for use as a cane.

"Can you imagine? A whore thinks she can sleep in my soft bed and yet refuse me my pleasures. She can *póg ma thoin.*"

"Speak English," one of the whores on the couch said.

The man walked over and snatched the pipe from her hand, leaned into her face, and shouted, "I said she can kiss my arse. And you'll be next, for not watchin' your tone of voice." He threw the pipe at her and she jumped, brushing at the hot ash that ate into her corset cover. One of the others, keeping her eyes on the man, picked up the pipe and sucked on it.

"Rosie Pink," Caleb said, "meet Mr. McCabe."

Mason turned to Caleb. "And who the hell is this?"

"The girl I told you about."

Caleb pushed Rose toward Mason.

"She don't look like much. Skinny as a stick. What the fuck happened to her hair?" He went to a sideboard and poured himself a drink from a crystal decanter. "No matter. I don't care for brunettes." He waved as if to dismiss the two of them.

"It ain't her looks, Mr. McCabe."

He looked at her again with narrowed eyes. "A *maighdean,* you said." He glared at the whore who had sassed him earlier. "A virgin." He exaggerated the word with a rolling brogue. "Not that the likes of you would remember what that is." He turned to Caleb. "That would add considerably to her value, 'tis true."

"And she can sing."

"Can she now."

"Rosie Pink, sing for Mr. McCabe. Not a fucking hymn, either."

"My name is Rose." She pushed his hand off her arm.

Mason laughed. "Got spirit, too, I see."

He had one of the women get a drink for him and one for Caleb, then pushed a whore off the sofa and sat down, settled back with his boots on the table, and sipped his whiskey.

He motioned to Caleb. "Come and sit by me." He looked giddy with anticipation. "Nothing like a musical interlude to brighten an afternoon."

Rose tried to cough the dust out of her throat. No music came to mind. She just stood there, staring at the floor.

"I said sing for Mr. McCabe." Caleb started to get up from the sofa. "What the hell are you waitin' for?"

Mason laughed. "Now, now, that's no way to get a pretty little bird to sing. Sit down! You must entice it—birds sing when they are happy." He turned twinkling blue eyes on Rose. "What would you like? What would make you happy enough to sing? We have all manner of drinks and opiates. Just say your preference."

Outside, on the far side of the tents, women and children huddled in a fenced enclosure, living in filth beside a trench filled with rotting garbage and feces, crawling with rats and vultures feeding on decaying human bodies. She gagged, pressing her lips shut. This man who had created this nightmare place wanted to know what would make her happy?

Mason issued a loud sigh and banged his boots onto the floor and his glass onto the table. "I've had enough of this. Whores sassing in me own parlor and now this. God knows what else." He stood up and yelled. "Horace! Horace, come get all these women and take every last one of 'em to the stockade. I'm fuckin' sick of the lot of 'em."

The Mexican appeared in the hall. The whores whimpered, crawled to Mason, and grabbed his hands. He shoved them off, pushed past Horace, and headed for the doorway. Rose found her voice.

I'm dreaming now of Hally . . . sweet Hally . . . sweet Hally

. . . I'm dreaming now of Hally . . . For the thought of her is one that never dies; She's sleeping in the valley . . . the valley . . . the valley . . .

Mason motioned Horace away and returned to the sofa.

Listen to the mocking bird, Listen to the mocking bird, the mocking bird still singing o'er her grave; Listen to the mocking bird, Listen to the mocking bird, Still singing where the weeping willows wave . . .

At the final verse, she closed her eyes and let her emotions flow into the words and melody.

When the charms of spring awaken . . . And the mocking bird is singing on the bough, I feel like one forsaken . . . forsaken . . . forsaken . . . I feel like one forsaken . . . Since my Hally is no longer with me now.

She opened her eyes. The women huddled together at one end of the sofa, noses running, dabbing at their eyes between frightened glances at Mason, who pulled a handkerchief from his vest pocket and blew his nose.

"She has the voice of an angel, Mr. Connor. You were surely right. She is worth her weight in gold." He blew his nose again.

Rose wanted very much to slap the smug smile off Caleb's face.

"She can sing at my shindig the night before we head out," Mason said. "The boys'll be talkin' about it all the way to Mexico. We've never had real entertainment. Just makeshift bands of guitars and fiddles. And once a whore knew how to do fancy ballet but someone accidentally shot her halfway through the performance. 'Twas before I made everyone store their guns upstairs. Stupid bastard." He shook his head, smiling at the memory.

"What is he talking about—heading out?" Rose looked at Caleb. "What's this about going to Mexico?"

"Didn't you tell the lass? And here we'll be leaving so soon. Don't look so worried, young lady. Special as you are, you can be assured whoever acquires you will be a man of property and fortune."

Caleb slipped a hand around her arm, a warning to not bolt. "Mr. McCabe goes to Mexico every year for the winter. *Everyone* goes."

"Everyone?" She thought of the women and children in the stockade.

McCabe went to the far side of the parlor and opened carved pocket doors, almost as big as the entire wall, to reveal a music room with a grand piano. "I'll tell you what, Mr. Connor. See if you can find someone to play the piano." He came and patted Rose's cheek as if he were a kindly uncle. "It would enhance the loveliness of her voice."

"I know someone who can play," Caleb said. "I saw him come in not long after we got here."

" 'Tis settled then. Send her and the piano player back tomorrow to practice. We've less than a fortnight before my party." He put his arm around Caleb and ushered them both toward the door. "I'll be sendin' a small token of my appreciation to your quarters, Mr. Connor. And let us stop being so formal. From now on it's Mason." He threw back his head and laughed. "A *maighdean* songbird, indeed. She'll bring a pretty penny in Mexico." He ushered them onto the porch. Before he shut the door, he leaned out and yelled, "Take those Goddamn chains off her before they chafe her skin. She ain't goin' nowhere, are you lassie?"

Caleb removed the chains, which meant he felt obliged to sit in the tent keeping his eyes on her. Rose wished she was still in chains. At least that way she didn't have to look at him. Not a word passed between them, except she said thank you when he gave her an opened can of beans.

As the sun went down, the sounds of revelry grew. Every now and then, Caleb would get up and stand at the tent flap, holding it open, looking toward the house.

"You can go. I'm not going anywhere."

"Right." He shot her a look, and the flap fell shut. He lit the lantern, put it on the ground between them, then sat and stared at her.

"Really. I'm not going anywhere."

He rolled a cigarette and held a match to it.

"Don't you have anything to read in that pile?" She nodded toward the heap of supplies they'd left in the corner.

He laughed at that one. "What'd you have in mind? The Holy Bible?"

She fixed a bed of blankets. She crawled between them and lay quietly except for her mind, which filled with images she didn't want to see. She would not go to Mexico to be sold to "a man of property and fortune." And if all the lawmen were as incompetent as those hired stage guards thought, nobody was going to find her before they all headed south.

She thought for so long, Caleb must have assumed she had fallen asleep. She began to sense that she was alone and, when she threw her blankets off, he was gone. He'd left the lantern burning and quietly slipped out.

A quick search in the pile of supplies provided jerky, a flask of whiskey, and a canteen. And her knife. She could hardly believe her luck when she pulled out a pair of trousers, perhaps cast off by Eddie, as they weren't very long. After quickly removing her skirt and what was left of her petticoat, she pulled on the trousers. She rummaged through the pile one more time.

She found no pistols or rifles but did find a man's blouse and braces.

She slipped out of the tent and walked slowly along the stockade fence. The guard at the gate gave her a quick glance before turning away. She could go up the trail Dodger had led them down, and just walk past the guard. Then run for Prescott.

She picked her way up the rocky trail, stumbled, and fell. She brushed dirt and pebbles from her hands and kept going, but the closer she got to the top, the more nervous she became. It would be a little easier just to stay on the trail and walk past the guard, but it wouldn't be that much more difficult to cut over a hundred yards before she got to him, stay in the brush, and avoid any possible confrontation.

Stepping off the trail, she walked until the ground was too steep, scrambled until the ground gave way to slick rock, then crawled. Searching for toeholds and handholds, she inched her way up. She touched the top of the ridge, pulled herself up, and looked over. Nothing beyond but black sky and stars.

She was sure the mountain ahead of her was Thumb Butte. In the darkness she couldn't see it, but rather the absence of stars in a pattern that seemed to indicate the distinctive dome. She'd hoped to see the lights of Prescott, but the town was either behind the butte or hidden by trees. Or maybe she miscalculated as she had the distance to Wickenburg. No matter. She would make it this time. She reminded herself to be extra careful going down. A quick flash of imagination saw her tumbling down the side of the mountain, landing at the bottom. Dead.

She swung one leg over and something grabbed her other leg, a hand that tightened.

"I knew you'd try something."

Caleb dragged her back to the inner side of the ridge.

He held out a hand. "Give me the knife."

She pulled it quickly from her shoe and tried to stab him, but he was ready for her. He easily wrested the knife away, even laughing as he did so.

"Now sit there. I need to tell you something."

"I don't want to hear anything you have to say."

"Look down there. You see that stockade? The one where he keeps the women and children?"

"Of course I can see it." The prisoners were lost in darkness, but she could see the gate. The guard had a lantern and was playing cards with some other men. She folded her arms across her chest. "What about it?"

"Now you see how the guards are spaced around the edge up here?" His fingers and thumb pressed into her cheeks and he forced her head to turn. When he was satisfied she had looked at each guard post, he let her go. "Now I suppose you're thinking you'd have made it to Prescott—better luck than you had getting to Wickenburg—and come back with the law. A posse, maybe the army. Sure, the guards would pick off some of them, but some might make it through. Mad Mason McCabe and his little hideout would be wiped out."

"And good riddance to everyone in here."

"There's something you don't know. I let you get this far on purpose. So I can make this perfectly clear." He grabbed her face again and made her look down, aiming her eyes at the stockade. "The guards have orders from Mason. If they see any kind of posse, any kind of rescue attempt, coming up these hills, first they are to turn their rifles on that stockade. They are to kill every woman and child within that fence."

He let her go. She rubbed her cheeks where his fingers had pressed and stared at the darkness within the fence, where she knew women and children huddled under blankets trying to keep themselves and their children warm.

"And once they've done that, which would only take a minute

or two, then they turn their rifles down the hillside. I doubt many of your rescuers would make it to the top, and for what?"

He slid to where the slick rock ended and waved at the guard. He walked down the trail, toward the compound. Never even looked back at her. She let herself slide to a rocky area, picked up some stones, and threw them at him, but they fell short.

She returned to an empty tent. She found her knife in the pile of supplies and slipped it into her shoe. After changing into her own clothes, she lay down on the blankets. For a long time she fought the despair that tried to sneak past her seething anger.

Caleb returned late into the night, reeking of whiskey and cigar smoke. He fixed his pile of blankets and soon snored loudly. Peaceful sleep for him, knowing he no longer had to worry about his captive attempting another escape.

Chapter Thirteen

In the morning Rose poked her face out of the flap into cold air. She grabbed a blanket to wrap around herself before going outside. The sun was not yet up, although the sky to the east was beginning to grow lighter.

A whimpering sound drew her to the fence. The little girl again huddled at the broken slat. This time she held her brother close, both of them wrapped in a tattered blanket. Her face was wet with tears and she wiped her running nose with the doll's tattered dress.

Rose knelt by the opening. "Why are you crying?"

"Mama. She's gone."

"What do you mean, gone?"

The little boy said, "She never come back. All day yesterday and not this morning. Sarah, where's Mama?"

Rose reached through the fence and stroked the girl's hair. "Please don't cry. She'll come as soon as she can. I'm sure she doesn't mean to stay away."

"No, she likes it at that house. She don't want to sleep in the dirt with us." Sarah fingered her doll's cloth arm, along a raised ridge of tiny, neat stitches. A loving mother must have repaired that tear in the doll's arm. But the girl said, "Mama don't care about us."

"Sarah, I'm sure that can't be true."

"She likes Mr. McCabe better. 'Cause he used to come down here and talk nice and bring us apples. He'd ask if she weren't tired yet of sleeping outside and wouldn't she like to come and stay in the house. Nobody else got apples. Just us."

This didn't sound like the Mason she had heard of and had now met, that she had seen abusing the whores in the house. Perhaps the man had some kindness in him.

"But Mama wouldn't go. And then he came one time and asked *me* if I wanted to go. He said I could sleep in a nice bed and have all the food I wanted." The girl imitated Mason's Irish brogue. " 'I'll have Mrs. Ling sew some new clothes for your wee dolly.' That's what he said."

Not even Mason, Rose thought. Not even Mad Mason McCabe would take an innocent child to his bed!

"But you're still here."

"That's 'cause Mama started screaming. 'No, God, no don't touch her. Take me, take me, leave the girl here!' And so *Mama* got to go with Mr. McCabe and me and Jonathan have to sleep out here by ourselves. *She* gets to stay in the nice house and eat all the food."

"She brung us food in the mornings when she come back," Jonathan said. "Except for yesterday. And today. I'm hungry."

"When she comes back she walks funny." Sarah wiped a hand beneath her nose. "Her legs spread apart like her bum was hurtin' her."

"Spankings, probly," Jonathan said. "That's what happens when you don't behave."

"I would've behaved," Sarah said. "If I got to stay in the nice house, I would've behaved."

"Shush, shush now." Rose pulled the blanket off her shoulders and stuffed it through the hole. "Here, wrap this around yourselves. Stop crying. I'm going to the house today. I'll look for your mama, okay?"

Rose shivered in the predawn winds. She remembered she was on her way to the jakes. "I'll check on you later. I'll bring you something to eat."

She stopped at the first outhouse, sucked in a breath, cracked the door, and slipped inside. In the darkness she gathered her skirts and pulled her drawers open. She backed up. Instead of the usual cold draft coming up she bumped against something protruding from the hole. Stifling a scream, she flew out the door.

Gathering courage, she creaked the door open until she held it wide, and dim light fell into the interior. Dead eyes stared at her. The whore who had sassed Mason. Her head stuck up at an angle through the opening, chin resting on the edge. Something slid down the side of her wet hair onto the wooden bench.

Rose slammed the door shut, held it closed with both hands, gagged, then threw up and wet herself before falling to her knees. She sat down, leaning against the door, shaking, drenched in a cold sweat. Blowing dust stuck to her face. A man walked by and went into the next outhouse. She drew her knees up and leaned her face against them, whispering a prayer, "Hail Mary, full of grace, the Lord be with thee . . . Oh. God. Help me leave this place. Or kill me."

A bird called from high up on the nearby hill. She lifted her face. Although she reeked of urine and vomit and sat leaning against an outhouse door, she focused on the bird's lilting song, naming the notes in her mind. But then the bird suddenly fell silent and flew away.

Bats. A cloud of bats, flitting and swooping, flew straight at the bush where the bird had been singing. And then they disappeared.

She rolled onto her knees and started to crawl up the hill. If there was a cave in the hillside, maybe it would be a place where she could hide when the time came, when Mason headed for Mexico to sell his stolen goods and his stolen people. A place to hide with those children, where the guards and Mason and Caleb wouldn't find them. Her heart banged in her chest. She climbed higher, keeping her eyes on the bush where the bats had disappeared.

She flattened herself against the hill and crawled under juniper trees and past skunk bush. A flurry of brown dried leaves shook loose, and she froze. She crept forward again, trying to keep her eyes on the exact spot she needed to reach.

A wide buckthorn bush covered with red berries hid a rocky outcropping. She pulled a bough to the side and peered in. She wriggled under the branches and pushed herself through, once again ignoring thorns that caught her clothes and scratched her face and arms. Each time she snapped a twig, she stopped, waited, listened, then continued until she was through the branches and lying in the opening of a cave.

Downhill, far below, the camp was still. The sun had not yet risen over the ridge. She rested and listened. No birds sang, the winds had calmed, no heavy footsteps of guards or Caleb coming to drag her back down the hill. She welcomed the slight breeze blowing over her, drying the perspiration on her face and arms.

Wait! The breeze was warm. Her head shot up and she gasped. The breeze came from inside the cave! She crawled farther in, got on her knees, and ran her hands over the smooth opening. Tools had done this. It was a long-abandoned mine, like the ones in Stanton. Old railroad tracks dipped down below a ledge that ran along one side. She slowly walked with her back against the wall, feeling her way as she descended into pitch blackness, the breeze beckoning her. The tunnel sloped downward, more steeply the deeper she went. Her heart hammered in her chest. A faint glow penetrated the gloom far ahead, coming from around a slight bend in the tunnel like a beacon, glowing with the dawn's growing light. But still so far away, a small patch of light at the end of a long, black tube. She leaned against the wall and tried to control her trembling legs. She had found a way to escape.

She needed a lantern. She needed matches. Food. Water. She had to talk to Sarah. Tell her to be at the fence with Jonathan at nightfall.

As close as she could determine, the tunnel opened to the east, the direction of Prescott. She turned to go, but a movement caught her eye. Light from the tunnel's end crept ever closer, turning the blackness of the tunnel to gray. The ground beneath the ledge seemed to be in motion. Here and there. A rippling movement, shapes writhing between the rails. She pressed herself against the wall.

Rattlesnakes. A hundred. More than a hundred. Rattlesnakes. Coming awake as the warmer air flowed into the shaft with the morning light. They slithered over and under each other, heads lifting, tongues tasting the air. They knew they weren't alone. One by one they began to vibrate, the sound of the rattles filling the passageway.

"I heard it weren't no quick death. They say he screamed till he foamed at the mouth."

The height of the ledge decreased the closer it got to the bend. White bones lay scattered in the trough of vipers. A snake crawled around what looked like a human jawbone and coiled, then rattled. Its tongue flicked in and out. Its head floated back and forth. The mouth opened. Fangs flashed.

She screamed. She flattened herself against the wall of the tunnel. As fast as she could move her legs, she slid sideways, back into the gloom until the entrance appeared, and she threw herself at it and fell into the buckthorn bush. Thrashing her way through, she slid halfway down the hillside before skidding to a stop.

On her back, gasping for breath, she suddenly realized all the noise she'd made, that she was lying in plain sight. She rolled onto her stomach and crawled beneath a juniper. There she lay while her heart and breath slowed, listening for approaching guards or for the rifle shot that would put an end to her nightmare.

After a while she crawled to the bottom of the hillside and, on shaking legs, returned to Caleb's tent.

Caleb sat on his bedroll, pulling on his boots. "Where the hell have you been? God, you stink."

She sank onto the blankets. Caleb stood over her and prodded her with a foot. "You better clean yourself up. You go to the house smellin' like that and Mason'll kill us both." After he left, she heard an outhouse door bang. She wondered which one he'd gone into.

She went out for a bucket of water and washed herself, scrubbing as hard as she could, even though the scratches on her hands and arms and face stung. She removed her bodice and skirt, washed the stained areas, put them back on, and went to sit in the sunshine until the wet places dried.

She was still sitting there when Caleb returned with two women, two of the three who had been in Mason's parlor the day before. They wore men's frock coats, long and dirty, that hung open to reveal the same undergarments they'd had on the day before. They dropped a bundle beside her on their way into the tent.

"Mason wants you to look presentable when you go over there today," Caleb said.

Rose unwrapped the parcel. Polished shoes. Clean stockings and undergarments, a nice town bodice and skirt, a bonnet and shawl. Everything laundered and ironed, folded around a sachet that smelled of lilacs.

Going inside to change her clothes, she found the three of them sprawled on Caleb's pallet, one whore unbuttoning his pants. Rose dressed as fast as she could, threw the shawl over her shoulders, and left. Walking past the corral, her foot twisted in the too-big shoes and she almost fell.

She kept her head down and limped quickly past the corral where men were gathered, Dodger and Eddie among them.

"Hey, look at Caleb's woman, all decked out." Eddie pointed a small brown bottle in her direction and pulled on Dodger's arm. Dodger turned his head, brushed a few greasy strands of hair behind an ear, then looked away, but Eddie ran over and fell in beside her.

"Where you goin', Rosie Pink?"

"Get away from me." She quickened her pace.

"You get an invite to the house? How'd you manage that? Me and Dodger ain't got invited to the house."

She was almost at the porch steps.

"Where's your beau? He let you run loose like this?" He grabbed her arm, but only for a second. One of the guards stepped away from the porch stairs and slammed a rifle butt into Eddie's side.

The guard stood over him while he lay doubled over, squirming in the dirt. "The women belong to McCabe, asshole. Don't touch."

Eddie pointed at Rose. "Not this bitch! She belongs to us. We brung her here and—"

The guard's boot thudded into Eddie's ribs, silencing him. Over at the corral Dodger, who had been watching, turned away again.

Chapter Fourteen

At the house, Mason himself opened the door, greeting her with a bow. The lemon smell of furniture polish again reminded her of Auntie's house, and she fought the tightness that clutched her throat.

" 'Tis good to see you again, young lady. The bonnet is an improvement. Leave it on, darlin.' Please, come in."

"Thank you, Mr. McCabe."

"It's Mason to you. We're to be good friends—no need for formalities."

He put his arm around her and ushered her toward the sofa. A teapot, cups and saucers, and serving plates filled with crustless sandwiches and frosted cakes replaced the opium pipes of the previous day.

He chatted away, taking his place beside her, leaning his shillelagh against the table.

"Would you like some tea?"

He placed a sugar cube in a teacup and poured milk from a small pitcher, then poured the fragrant, steaming brew.

He lifted a delicate bone china saucer in his thick fingers and handed it to her. "I suppose I shouldn't assume that everyone takes their tea the English way. 'Tis the one civilized thing they do, a good tea." He fixed himself a cup, then put a sandwich on a plate and placed it in front of her. "Don't be shy now. Take what you want. What was your name again, darlin'?"

She cleared her throat. "Rose."

"Your family name?"

"LaBelle."

He stared at her for a moment, then sniffed. "French, heh? Well, could be worse. At least you're a Roman Catholic then?" Rose nodded, and Mason smiled. "Good girl, good girl. Drink up! And eat. Don't be turnin' up your nose at me hospitality."

She sipped the tea and took a bite of the sandwich. It stuck in her throat. She drank more tea.

"I used to carry a tune myself, back in the day. Of course, nothin' so cultured and precious as your own choice of song the other day. 'Twas said I had a fair tenor."

He put down his tea, and sat up straight.

> *Well they fought for poor old Ireland,*
> *And full bitter was their fate*
> *Oh! what glorious pride and sorrow*
> *Fill the name of Ninety-Eight.*
> *Yet, thank God, e'en still are beating*
> *Hearts in manhood's burning noon,*
> *Who would follow in their footsteps,*
> *At the risin' of the moon!*
> *At the risin' of the moon, at the risin' of the moon,*
> *Who would follow in their footsteps, at the risin' of*
>   *the moon.*

He stopped, quite pleased with himself. "About fightin' for freedom, that song. And a great betrayal. 'The Risin' of the Moon,' 'tis called." He picked up his tea and slurped. "Now that's when we'll all be headed south to Mexico. At the risin' of the full moon, less than a fortnight hence."

Rose pressed the linen napkin to her knees to stop the sudden shaking in her right leg.

"Did you have a particular song you wanted me to sing, Mr. McCabe? I mean Mason? At your party?"

"Well, darlin', I put some sheet music over by the piano. When the piano player shows up, the two of you can confer on what you think might please the guests."

She put one of the cakes on her plate but couldn't bring herself to taste it.

"He's highly recommended by your Mr. Connor. Now, Mr. Connor, he's a good Irish boy. We chatted a bit when he was here earlier. So many Irish come west, you know, due to being treated like curs in the cities back east. But he came on his own after the war. Not a long time ago, on the orphan train as I did.

"Of course, I was no orphan, you see. The authorities snatched me from my parents' very arms and sent me to an asylum. Hellgate, 'twas called. And a good name for the place, us poor children stolen from the streets of New York and locked up for no sin worse than being the issue of starvin' Irish parents."

"Hellgate? Why did you give *this* place that name? A name you must hate?"

"To remind me. Of what happens to the weak. Of what happens when the authorities decide what is best." He fell silent for a moment. "They sent us west to be raised by Protestants. 'Twas a sin, I say, them tryin' to make us white. I never laid eyes on my beloved *máthair* again." He picked up the napkin and dabbed at his eyes. "Fucking Children's Aid Society. Someday I'll go back there and kill them all."

A knock on the door startled her; some of her tea spilled.

"That would be our piano player." Mason wiped the drops from the table before he went to the door. He came back with Harry Sheldon. "I can see by the look on your face you're not pleased?"

"He tried to assault me in Stanton. And he killed a man on the trail between there and here." She didn't mention that he had refused to help her escape.

"Yes, Stanton! That is where Mr. Connor said he first heard

him play. Lucky for us he's ended up here. Well, you two get busy. There's sheet music on the piano. Choose some lively tunes."

After Mason left, she joined Harry in the music room where he was shuffling through the sheet music. "I promise I won't assault you." The set of his mouth hardened. "If you know I killed that man, you also know why."

"Did you bury him?"

"No."

"Ha. I suspected as much. Left him for the buzzards, just like his so-called friends did."

"I didn't have a shovel." He held the papers still but kept his eyes on them. "I climbed down and covered him with rocks. The animals won't have gotten to him."

"But he was a stranger to you."

"A man. Deserved at least that much." He put the music down and looked toward the tray in the parlor. "Can you share that tea and those sandwiches?"

The teapot was empty. "I'll get some more." Rose carried it toward the sound of pots and pans. In the kitchen, a young Mexican woman was standing with Mason. The other servants had pressed themselves against the far wall, their eyes fear-filled. Tension was thick in the room, and Rose retreated to the hallway.

"Please, *Señor* McCabe. My *niño*—"

He moved closer to the woman, patting her head.

"There, there. Don't be shaking so. Shush, now. No need to be afraid." He placed a finger beneath her chin and raised her face.

His smile sank. "What's this?" He touched the woman's swollen lip and bruised cheek. "Byron? What is this?"

A man stepped forward and cleared his throat. He wiped his hands nervously on his stained apron. "She complained about fetchin' water for the stew, Mr. McCabe. Said if I sent her outside, she'd go straight to the stockade to be with her child."

Mason nodded as if he were considering this information. Rose ducked farther into the hallway, daring only to peek around the doorway.

"D'ya see this stick, woman?"

Byron raised a hand to hide his smirk.

Mason lifted the stick from where he'd held it against his chest and now presented the four-foot rod, its polished head tapered to a narrow metal ferrule. Black bark adhered to the knobby shaft.

"No, no, 'tis not for walkin'." He wrapped his fingers around the knob and bent closer to the woman, as if giving a lesson to a schoolchild. "Some hollow this part out and pour lead in, but no need to load this particular *bata*. 'Tis made of blackthorn; it be hard enough. Now you are like a child to me, and 'tis my job to protect you."

He pulled back his arm and swung the shillelagh. A whoosh and a crack. Rose ducked to avoid the blood and pieces of bone that spattered through the doorway. There was a thud as Byron hit the floor. After a moment, Rose dared to look again. Mason was slapping the bloody knob on his palm while talking to the white-faced, trembling woman.

"And 'tis my job to see that *you* behave." He tapped her shoulder with his *bata* while she shook. A dark red pool inched from beneath Byron's crushed head across the kitchen floor. "You have much to be thankin' me for. A wee one that is yet alive. Perhaps next time, instead of all this snivelin' and carryin' on, you'll be rememberin' that. And just fix my Goddamn supper."

He took a napkin from the sideboard, wiped blood off his stick and his shiny boots, then dropped the cloth on Byron's body. He paid no attention to Rose, flattened against the hallway wall, clutching the empty teapot to her chest, as he stomped out of the kitchen and disappeared into another room down the hall.

CHAPTER FIFTEEN

Walter guided the rented buggy along Marina Street, but Mary Alice felt his gaze upon her. He turned the horse into Gurley, and they headed down the hill into town. Her cheeks still burned with embarrassment every time she thought of Walter finding her disheveled, lying fully clothed on her bed, obviously passed out from drink.

"You must think me a terrible hypocrite," she said, keeping her gaze straight ahead but glancing at him out of the corner of her eye.

He laid his hand on hers where it rested in her lap. Her gloves did not hide the crooked fingers and enlarged joints. "Mary Alice, no one blames you. Your rheumatism . . ."

"That's not always why I drink, and you know it."

He put his hand on the ribbons, giving them a light slap to move the horse a little quicker as they passed Whiskey Row.

"If it helps your rheumatism or your nerves, no need to apologize."

She pressed her gloved hands together to stop their trembling. "Kam Le has been brewing this wonderful tea for me. It has ginger and something called turmeric and other herbs she purchased in Chinatown. I think it's had a helpful effect."

"That young woman is a Godsend. I noticed today you don't have your cane."

"No need for it. Here we are."

Walter reined the horse to a stop in front of the Prescott Free

Academy. In the governor's seldom-used offices on the second floor, the governor's wife used to hold a meeting for the ladies of the town. She came to the school every Friday anyway, to talk to the children about her European travels.

In the beginning the well-to-do wives of businessmen and officers' wives from the fort also enjoyed Mrs. Fremont's stories. When she left to go back east, claiming altitude sickness, the ladies continued to meet every Friday afternoon. The topics gravitated toward how to improve their town, or various territorial political issues such as suffrage and temperance, which they considered to be related.

Temperance was a growing movement. Some women felt that controlling demon rum was the first step in civilizing the country. Eventually sober men would see the sense in allowing women to vote. Mary Alice wondered about the logic of this, but agreed the activity on Whiskey Row was sometimes—no, often!—too wild to bear. So she did not drink on Thursday nights, fearing they would detect the alcohol on her breath the next day. Even so, that little clutch of self-righteous harpies from the fort seemed to give her the evil eye lately.

And poor Walter thought she was being abstinent out of virtue.

"Do you want me to walk you in?" he asked.

"No need."

He set the brake and climbed down. "I will be back in two hours," he said, walking around to her side.

Mary Alice knew better than to let Walter see her concern over his unsteady gait. His full strength had not returned, but that would not stop him from his goal to find Rose.

"That Lieutenant Schiffman had better listen to me this time," he said.

"If anybody can make him, it's you."

He released the step and held out his hand to help her down.

107

The gesture so reminded her of Joseph, she turned her face to keep him from seeing her sudden tears. Funny how grief could just well up out of nowhere, without warning, no matter how much time had passed.

When she could speak, she said, "Be careful around those officers. I think there is something going on with them."

"What?"

"I can't put my finger on it. Several wives from the fort attend the Ladies' Friday Meeting, quite decked out for every gathering. Even though their husbands are officers, I don't see how they can manage such finery on a soldier's pay."

"You suspect graft? But who would be paying off the army? And for what? The Indians don't have any money."

"Perhaps criminals."

"But to what end? The army says crime is a civilian matter."

"Exactly. And why do they say that? When travelers between the centers of civilization are being attacked?"

Walter's frown turned to a look of admiration. "Mary Alice, you are indeed surprising." Then his expression darkened. "If that's the case, and they are refusing to help look for Rose because of payoffs and bribes—"

"Don't go off half-cocked, now. It's just a thought. For all I know, those women come from wealthy families."

"That let their daughters marry soldiers and get dragged off to the frontier?"

"True. But still, you need to be circumspect when you speak with the lieutenant. We need to think this through. We need to know which officers are accepting bribes, if any. We can't go to the commanding officer on the basis of an expensively adorned wife." She straightened her hat and smoothed her gloves. "I'll see what I can discern this afternoon. Even if it means being nice to those witches."

Walter laughed and, to her surprise, leaned down and pressed his lips to her cheek. "I do admire you, Mrs. Bradford." He climbed into the buggy and slapped the reins while she stood like a fool in front of the white picket fence, her hand to her cheek. She felt heat rush to her face. She didn't dare raise her eyes to the second floor window to check if anyone had been watching.

She entered the upstairs meeting room and found the ladies clustered together on the far side of the room, near the tea service, staring at her, their surprise evident.

"Mrs. Bradford," one of the women said. "Where is your cane?"

She smiled in relief. "My rheumatism has been quiet for several days. I didn't think I needed it."

"Why, that's wonderful!"

Alvenia brought her a cup of tea fixed just the way she liked it. "Mary Alice, please have a seat. We're all happy to see this turn of events, but let's not overdo." She pulled out a chair and Mary Alice obediently sat herself down.

Alvenia eased her ample proportions into the seat beside her. "I saw what you did. Rather, what Mr. LaBelle did," she whispered, and laughed quietly. "Don't worry. Your secret is safe with me."

"I'm so glad you don't share information with your husband."

Alvenia laughed. "Wouldn't that be something! To see some of the things you and I talk about posted in *The Miner*."

The others had taken tea and pastries from the sideboard and were settling in around the table. Mrs. Schiffman stood at the head of the table, holding folded pages, half sheets, covered with drawings and text. She put them down and, with a great dramatic flourish, picked up last week's issue of *The Miner*, rolled it up, and banged it against her palm.

"Ladies, please settle down, we have some important business to discuss this afternoon." She opened the newspaper to the editorial page and read:

> The precocity in crime, which is noticeable among the juveniles in our large cities, is said to be directly traceable to the pernicious effects of the flash story papers. If this story be true, it is high time that some censorship should be established over this class of literature. To poison the innocent mind of childhood by familiarity with deeds of blood, to hold up to the admiration of our boys and girls such characters as heroes and heroines in these nasty prints is an irreparable evil to public morals.

She read the entire passage, which railed against the corruption of the youth and strongly encouraged banning the flash stories, then she paused and looked around the table.

Mary Alice had to admire the woman's natural ability to be dramatic. Melodramatic.

"I have here a copy of one of the offending publications." Mrs. Schiffman held the shameful publication by a corner, as if holding a dead mouse by the tail, and handed it to the woman on her right, indicating that she should look at it and pass it around.

Mary Alice watched each face in turn register shock and then disgust as the distasteful publication circled the table until it reached Alvenia, who stood and cleared her throat. "My concern," she said, firmly grasping the story papers and holding them up, "is that if we start censoring this, where do we stop?"

Mary Alice suppressed her smile. That harpy Schiffman wasn't the only one who knew how to use dramatic flair.

Gasps and sudden fervent fan-waving followed Alvenia's question. With considerable stuttering, Mrs. Schiffman managed to squeak out, "But it is *your husband* who wrote this editorial!"

"I'm aware of that." A stunned silence fell upon the gathering. Alvenia continued in a quieter voice. "Ladies, I ask you, what do we talk about during these meetings? Temperance? Suffrage? These are not issues any man is the least concerned with. Why on earth would we deserve the vote if all we ever do is follow the dictates of our husbands?"

Mrs. Schiffman stood, pointing at the flash story papers. "But that is nothing but trash! You can't think that we should just sit back and allow the youth of our city to be corrupted by this?"

"I wouldn't want anybody to be corrupted. But isn't it up to the parents to monitor what their children read, what they choose to spend their money on, and whether or not they have any money to spend to begin with? I had enough trouble raising my own children—I don't need to be responsible for everyone else's."

"That's a deplorable attitude. If everyone felt that way this society would go straight to—why, to—to *heck!*"

In a beautifully histrionic gesture, Mrs. Schiffman flung off her scarf and held a hand to her heart, revealing a brooch of enameled gold, amethyst, and pearl, fastened at her collar.

Although the strident statement caused the meeting to fall into anarchy, everyone speaking at once, nobody paying attention to Mrs. Schiffman's attempts to restore order, Mary Alice heard none of it. She saw none of it. Only the brooch, as if it alone existed, shining within a cloud of evil darkness.

"Mary Alice, are you ill? You've lost all color from your face." Alvenia patted her shoulder, her concerned face appearing as if through a haze.

Mary Alice whispered, "Where did you get that?"

"Get what?" Alvenia asked, but Mary Alice pushed her hand away and stood.

She pointed at Mrs. Schiffman and raised her voice. "Where

did you get that?"

"This?" Mrs. Schiffman's hand covered the brooch. "It was a gift. From my husband."

Mary Alice fell back into her chair. "It's Rose's pendant."

"You must be mistaken," Alvenia whispered close to her ear.

"It is Rose's pendant."

"Somebody send for a carriage," Alvenia said. "Mrs. Bradford is distraught and needs to go home."

"I gave it to her for Christmas last year." Mary Alice couldn't look away from the pendant until Mrs. Schiffman covered it with her scarf.

"You all know her niece is missing—kidnapped on her way to Prescott," Alvenia said. "It's too much of a strain. I'm sure the brooch is similar to one her niece had." She pulled Mary Alice to her feet. "Come, dear. Let's go down and wait for the carriage."

They moved slowly toward the door. Mary Alice was grateful to have her friend to lean on. She was shaken and confused and needed to go home. Several women came to pat Mary Alice on the arm or make soothing noises, commenting on her missing niece and how, of course, it would prey on her nerves.

Mrs. Schiffman gathered up her papers, shaking her head and muttering. "We may as well adjourn. This meeting has become useless."

Mary Alice did not stay to argue that point.

When they arrived at the house, Mary Alice insisted that Alvenia go home. "I'll be fine, dear. I just need to take some medicine and rest. Kam Le will see to it. Thank you so much."

After Alvenia left, Mary Alice paced and waited for Walter to return. As soon as he came in the door, she ran to him. "Mrs. Schiffman has Rose's pendant."

"I went by the school to get you and they said you'd been sent home. Are you all right?" Walter hung his hat on the hall tree and pulled off his coat. "What?"

"She wore it as a brooch. Rose's pendant! The one I gave her for Christmas last year. Something terrible is going on at the fort."

"Who? How can you be sure it is the same—"

"I ordered it from Giuliano's in London. You must remember it: gold with purple stones and pearls, the little tassel at the bottom. Rose loved it."

"I do remember it. But she could have a similar—"

"It was designed by Pasquale Novissimo himself. It's one of a kind!"

"Who wore it?"

"Mrs. Schiffman. One of the wives from the fort."

"The lieutenant's wife. But how could she have come to possess it?"

"Walter! It must have been in Rose's luggage. Somehow there is a connection between the road agents and Fort Whipple and that officer's pockets. We must go to the governor."

To her surprise, Walter said, "No. We will not go to the governor. We need to think about this. We need a plan."

Chapter Sixteen

The old Chinese woman, Mrs. Ling, stepped over the man's body as if it were a log for the fire. She took the tray from Rose and spooned fresh tea into the diffuser, added hot water, and replenished the tray of sandwiches. Two men arrived and dragged Byron out, smearing blood behind them, and the rest of the servants returned to their tasks as if nothing had happened. The young Mexican woman knelt and began to scrub the blood from the floor.

Rose carried the tray to the parlor and put it on the table in front of the sofa. Harry had one sandwich in his mouth and another in his hand before he looked at her. He stopped chewing. "What's wrong?"

"McCabe killed the cook. Bashed his head in with that club he carries around."

Fearing her shaking legs would not hold her up much longer, she sat heavily on the sofa. Harry came to sit beside her and tried to put an arm around her shoulders.

She shoved him away. "Don't touch me."

"I'm sorry—I was just trying—"

"He killed that man for touching one of the women."

She locked her hands together and kept them in her lap so they wouldn't shake. So this man wouldn't see them shake.

She had seen her own father killed. He had charged the outlaws with his pistol drawn. It's possible they wouldn't have shot him if he had not done that. But McCabe killed the way others would swat flies. And as callous as Dodger and his gang had been, leaving her father dead or dying, that did not compare to the indifference of the servants in the kitchen.

Harry nudged her arm. She opened her eyes. He held a flask in front of her. She took it and drank.

Harry went to the piano and sat on the bench. His hands hovered over the keys. He flexed his fingers, then hit a few chords and banged out enough notes to determine the piano was in tune before launching into a complicated classical piece, playing several bars. When he stopped, the vibrations of the last notes dispersed their energy into the room.

"That's from Beethoven's Fourth, for the piano." Rose came to stand beside him. "You played it beautifully."

"Beautiful, indeed!" Mason appeared, stood beside the piano bench, and slapped Harry on the back. "Indeed! I'm thinkin' this year will be the best entertainment ever. You and the lass together, and then perhaps each separate. Or the other way around. 'Twill be extraordinary. Something to warm our hearts on the long trek south." He made a show of applauding the performance, then waved at the pile of sheet music spread across the top of the piano's closed lid. "You work it out amongst yourselves. I'll leave you to your practice."

He left the house, talking to himself the whole time. His voice faded away as he clomped down the porch steps, and Rose exhaled.

Harry leafed through an assortment of popular songs from the last decade. Rose had heard many of them at concerts held in the Prescott Opera House during summers with Auntie. He suggested she pick a few and put the sheets in order on the music rack. She sat beside him, and they began to work on their performance. He was not as familiar with the songs as she and stumbled over the melodies and chords, but his playing quickly smoothed. He paced himself to her voice as she ran through the lyrics, humming and singing while he picked through the notes. Only when Mrs. Ling came in and padded around the room lighting lamps and candles did they realize how much time had passed.

"McCabe will be coming home for his supper," Harry said.

Rose went to the window. Men sat on the corral fence. Against the bloody sunset sky their silhouettes looked like ravens perching. They waved their hats and raised bottles of whiskey, bouncing until the fence rails sagged. A bucking horse raced past them; a rider disappeared in the billowing dust. The tents glowed with lamplight.

Harry came up beside her, pulling the lace panel aside so he could look. She watched his reflection in the glass. He was looking down at her.

"Why don't you join them?" she said. "We can practice again tomorrow." Once he was gone, she could quickly look through the house for any sign of Sarah's mother while the servants were busy preparing Mason's supper.

His eyes were dark in the candlelight. "You really don't know who I am, do you?"

"A soldier in Mason's little army of killers. That's all I need to know. Oh, and you play the piano. A cultured killer."

"That piece I played earlier. You recognized it."

"Of course. Everyone recognizes Beethoven."

"That's not what I mean. You *knew* it."

She looked away. She did *know* that music; it haunted her. But she wasn't going to talk to one of Mason's minions about it.

"It was your mother's favorite piece."

She turned to face him. "How dare you speak of my mother?" But he was right; it had been her mother's favorite music, her favorite piece to teach her students who came from town and—

"She taught me to play it."

116

A memory, an image, formed within a wave of sadness as she saw herself standing by her mother's grave. The smell of flowers and freshly turned dirt. Her father's rough hand enfolding her small one. The last of the people to leave the gravesite, her father's favorite employee, had tears on his tanned face. He'd removed his hat and she stared at his forehead's white skin. Elbert Sheldon. He could barely get his words out to give his condolences. Beside him stood his son. A gangly boy, with dark, curling hair. And the eyes. Icy blue.

For weeks following her mother's death, her father had closed himself off in his room. On the rare occasion when he emerged, he smelled of whiskey and stale clothes. He frightened her when he picked her up with shaking hands and hugged her. He held her too tightly. His wet, stubbled face scratched, and she squirmed until he lowered her to the floor. Then he quickly, wordlessly, retreated into the darkness of his room.

One day she'd been sitting on the porch and the boy, Mr. Sheldon's boy, walked over and sat on the top step. He opened a book and began to read aloud. Every day he sat on the steps and read. She began to look forward to his visits, eventually leaving her chair to sit on the step beside him. He read with a quiet voice. His long fingers turned the pages. Her mother had spoken many times of the boy's hands, of his talent.

"What was the book you read from?"

"The essays of Ralph Waldo Emerson. Was the only book I owned at the time."

"No wonder I didn't understand any of it." But knowing that he cared about her had comforted her more than words ever could. He was more an adult than a boy to her child's eyes, and the only one she could depend upon.

For a long time Mr. Sheldon's son read to her, every day until after her father stopped drinking, went back to running the ranch, and became himself again. Became her father again.

"Where did you go?"

"East. Joined the army. Went to war."

He turned his face away but she could see his lips were a grim line, jaw clenched.

"And now you've ended up here." She hated to think that her childhood friend, that adolescent boy, had become a criminal. Yet here he was. "Quite a letdown, don't you think? For someone who once played classical music and read Emerson."

"I didn't *end up* here, as you put it. I *came* here because I wanted to."

"Who *wants* to come here? Is this your idea of a holiday?"

He turned toward her, the grim line now a sardonic half-smile. He shook his head. "I'm telling you I'm not an outlaw. Do you really think I've been robbing banks? Killing people?"

"Then what have you been doing? The war ended fifteen years ago."

"Perhaps you were too young to remember that my father died not long after I left, so there was no reason for me to return to your father's ranch. I worked at some ranches in Texas, New Mexico. Then came this way and got that job with the stage line." He started to touch her arm, thought better of it. "I'm just sorry I didn't recognize you right away."

She remembered now those kind eyes, that look of compassion. Remembered how safe he'd made her feel, let her forget her mother was dead, her father drunk. She remembered Harry Sheldon, Elbert Sheldon's son, from the saddest time of her life.

"Eighteen years ago," she said. "My mother died eighteen years ago."

"You've changed." He gave a quiet laugh. "That's why I didn't realize it was you until I put two and two together. You're all grown up."

He'd changed too. He'd be thirty-four now. She'd seen other

men who had been in the war. They'd aged. They came back embittered and angry. Harry had been compassionate and kind-hearted to begin with, and there was no bitterness in his eyes or the set of his mouth now.

The smell of roasting meat from the kitchen reminded her that Mason would soon be home. "I'm looking for a woman Mason is keeping here. She has children in the stockade. I promised them I would find their mother."

"You go upstairs. I'll check down here, and if McCabe comes I'll keep him distracted."

She hurried to the end of the hall and up the stairs. Closed doors lined a long hallway lit by wall sconces. She wondered if each whore got her own bedroom. She tried the knob on the first door, pushing it open. There was just enough light from the hall for her to see it held crates of ammunition. The weapons Mason confiscated from the outlaws were piled on the floor, pistols and rifles and shotguns.

The next door opened onto a library. Book-filled shelves lined all the walls; a leather over-stuffed chair sat by the window. At the next room a woman in a white, ruffled nightdress jumped up from a chair when Rose pushed the door open. Her sunken eyes were fear-filled. She had the same silvery-blond hair as Sarah and Jonathan.

"Do you have children here?" Rose asked.

"No, thank God."

"I'm sorry I disturbed you." Rose pulled the door closed.

The next room was empty. She stopped at the door across the hall and tried the knob, opening it a crack. A putrid stench, like the jakes, like the ditch, gusted from the room. She held her breath and was about to close the door when something, whimpering, moved on the bed.

She forced herself to go inside, move closer, and see if it was the children's mother. A woman lay with limbs spread apart, wrists and ankles tied to the bed frame. She turned a bruised and swollen face toward Rose. "Please. Help me."

"Are you Sarah's mother?"

The woman spoke in a dry, harsh croak. "Sarah." She sucked in several shallow breaths. "Jonathan." Her eyes rolled up until only the whites showed.

Rose got her knife and sawed on the ropes that held the woman. She had freed one skeletal arm when Harry rushed into the room.

"What are—"

"Be quiet! Just help me."

He quickly cut the remaining ropes with his buck knife, then wrapped a blanket around the woman and picked her up. At the bottom of the stairs, he nodded toward a doorway on the right. "There's a back door off the butler's pantry."

Rose rushed ahead to hold the door open, and then they were outside. The crowd at the corral had dispersed. In the moonlight a body lay crushed, abandoned in the middle of the corral while a horse circled, snorting.

She led Harry to the tent. He ducked through the flap and laid the woman down.

"She has children," Rose said. "In the stockade. I promised the little girl I would find her mother."

"Come on. You need to point her out."

She showed him the broken section in the fence. "They're usually around here." She shook the fence a little. "Sarah!" she called quietly. The girl's small face appeared at the opening. "Where's your brother?" Rose asked.

"Right here."

Sarah pulled the boy to the opening. He looked up with half-closed eyes, lower lip trembling.

"The guard's not looking," Rose said. "Be quick."

Harry hauled the boy out of the stockade, then the girl, her doll hanging from her hand, and carried them into the tent.

"Sit over there." Rose pointed to the corner farthest from where their mother lay groaning.

"Did you find Mama?" the girl asked. Both children stared with wide eyes and chins quivering.

"Yes, but she's not feeling well. You'll have to stay right here while we try to help her."

Harry found a length of rope, strung it across the tent, then hung a blanket from it. The makeshift wall divided the tent and concealed the woman from her children.

Rose gave them jerky and biscuits and put the bucket Caleb used for drinking water next to them. Sarah lunged for the ladle and drank, then handed it to her brother.

Rose gave them a blanket, then went for more water; she brought the bucket and some rags to Harry, then the washbowl, soap, and towels that she and Caleb used.

Harry removed the blanket he'd wrapped around the woman. He soaked a rag, lathered it, and began to wash her. The lamp on the ground beside him cast a harsh yellow light across her nakedness.

Harry worked the rag over her prominent collarbone and ribs. As he got closer to her distended abdomen, she moaned, then gasped, and Harry jerked his hand away. He resumed the bathing in a different place, and the woman quieted. Rose tied a cloth over her own mouth and nose, then grabbed a rag and knelt on the other side of the woman, drying her face, shoulders, and arms.

The woman cried out when Harry touched her stomach again. She tried to push him away, but she had no strength to do so. Harry continued to bathe her, moving gently down her body. Rose stole one look between the woman's legs, then did not look again. Blood, feces, and pus stained Caleb's bedroll.

This woman had a raging infection deep within. She would not live.

Harry asked for more clean rags. On the other side of the blanket the children slept, scraps of food clutched in their dirty hands. Rose found a sheet that appeared clean. She and Harry tore it into strips, and he packed them into the woman's torn and oozing private places. Blood and excrement seeped from the woman's ravaged innards, quickly staining the clean bandages. Harry washed her legs, her feet. Rose helped him put what was left of the sheet under the woman, and they covered her with blankets.

"He's a monster," Harry said. "Worse than—I don't even know . . ." He shook his head.

"How long?" Rose asked.

"You should bring the children in."

"I had hoped to rescue them. Just this morning I thought I had found a way."

She told him about the tunnel, then about the snakes.

"Still," he said, his voice growing excited, "it's colder each night. They'd be more sluggish. We can take the children through, then get help."

"No. We can't."

"I could come back with a posse. With the army."

The woman woke up and groaned. She turned on her side, drew up her legs, and wrapped her arms around her stomach. She rocked and whimpered through clenched jaws, shivering, and Harry pulled another blanket over her, spoke soothing words, but still the woman moaned.

"Oh, dear God, is there no stopping the pain she's in?" Rose asked, hoping the children would not be awakened.

"It won't go on much longer." Harry pulled a flask from his shirt and held it to the woman's lips. She drank, coughed, then opened her mouth for more. He poured it in until it was running down her chin and her head fell back and she lay panting.

"Get the children. They can say goodbye to their mother before we take them out of here. We'll go to the fort. Get soldiers to raid this place. With any luck, I can lead them here tomorrow and rescue the rest of the prisoners."

"No! Listen to me. It won't work."

"Of course it will. We can get past a few snakes."

"If anyone tries to attack this place, the guards have orders. From Mason. They're to shoot the women and children even before they defend the ridge. Caleb says before anyone can reach the top of the hills and get in here—"

"Before who can get in here?" Caleb pulled the blanket back. "What the fuck is going on in here, Rosie Pink?"

Harry jumped to his feet, pulling Rose up beside him. Caleb picked the lantern up and held it over the woman. He leaned over her, letting the light shine on her face.

"Patience?"

"You know her?" Rose asked.

He fell to his knees beside the woman. "She's my sister."

The blanket pulled back and Sarah and Jonathan appeared. "Are you our Uncle Caleb?" Sarah asked. "Is Mama gonna die?"

CHAPTER SEVENTEEN

Mary Alice unfastened her cape and let it fall over the back of her chair. She wondered why the lieutenant failed to break a sweat, sitting there in his woolen uniform next to the blasting heat from the stove. She wanted to stuff him into the stove. *He* was in charge. *He* was the acting commanding officer. The lieutenant slouched sideways in the real commanding officer's chair, his insolent gaze directed at Walter. He extended his long legs beyond the end of the desk, his high boots crossed at the ankle, and sat back, as if the conversation had come to its conclusion. But Walter sat rigidly beside her.

Perhaps the desk, pushed so close to the stove it was charred, would burst into flames. What would the commanding officer have to say about that, assuming he ever returned to his post? Of course things had been slow with the Indians of late, but there were plenty of other problems, and since when did the governor need a military escort every time he went to Washington? Which happened way too often, with the taxpayers of the territory paying the freight. As the tense silence between the two men continued, Mary Alice also wondered why nobody ever seemed to notice the way Walter's teeth would clench just before he lost his temper. She supposed the way the rest of his face didn't change expression, not even his eyes, kept the imminent explosion from detection. Only a slight protrusion in front of his ears indicated the tightened muscles and clamped jawbones.

Walter put his hat on and pushed up from his chair. The lieutenant looked relieved, but only for a second, because when Walter stood over the desk his fist crashed down. Even though Mary Alice had been expecting an outburst, she also jumped, a hand going to her heart.

"No, I do *not* understand *your* problem. I understand *my* problem. My daughter has been missing for a week now."

The lieutenant composed his expression, gathered his legs, and leaned back in his chair. "It is not a military matter. I don't know how many ways I can state that."

"The incident did not happen within any city marshal's jurisdiction, but between Phoenix and Wickenburg. The county sheriff refuses to help. How many ways do I need to state that?"

The lieutenant stood. "Then get the U.S. marshal to look into it."

"He is in Tucson, as you damn well know, and won't be back until possibly next week at the soonest."

"He has deputies. Send for one. I have no more to offer, sir."

Mary Alice put a hand on Walter's arm. She was about to say something, but Walter gave an almost imperceptible shake of his head, placing his hand over hers and squeezing. He helped her up from her chair, but she was not ready to leave, nor was she ready to be silenced.

She put her face as close to the lieutenant's as she could with the desk between them. "No more to offer? Outlaws have dragged off my niece, no doubt planning to deliver her to that Mad Mason person! She must be found and brought home before something even more terrible happens to her." She cursed the unbidden tears that welled up, cursed the waver in her voice, but she continued. "You are here to keep us safe!"

"You *are* safe, ma'am."

She pried her arm free of Walter's grip, leaned across the desk, and slapped the officer's face. "I would gladly trade myself for Rose. It is *her* safety that brings us here, begging like suppliants for you to help us. And you refuse? How dare you!"

Lieutenant Schiffman stood with a hand to his cheek, his mouth agape. Walter hustled Mary Alice out the door.

In the buggy and headed for home, Walter cracked the ribbons to hurry the horse. He kept glancing at her out of the corner of his eye.

"You don't have to look so nervous," Mary Alice said. "I'm not going to slap *your* face." But her anger had barely cooled. "That son of a bitch. I'm sorry, Walter, but that's what he is! I wish you had been the one to hit him. He wouldn't have been standing when we left."

"Now, Mary Alice, don't get worked up again."

He turned the buggy onto Cortez and then up the hill toward Marina Street and home.

"You never mentioned his wife's jewelry," she said.

"Didn't want to show our hand. There's something wrong when a soldier is that indifferent to a citizen's plight."

"Will you speak with the city marshal again?"

"That, or gather up my own troops. There are men in this town who can be hired."

Mary Alice was thinking how fortunate they were that they could hire people to do what the government officials refused to do, thinking how money can buy anything—even an army—even a sheriff, or a marshal, or an army officer . . .

"Walter, do you think someone is paying the officers of the law to look the other way?"

The buggy stopped in front of the house, but Walter remained still, staring straight ahead. Finally, he said, "I would hate to think that."

"I would too, but Kam Le mentioned the other day that she had seen Lieutenant Schiffman in the U.S. marshal's office. She saw him through the window, saw the lieutenant hand an envelope to one of the deputies."

"That doesn't mean anything."

"Maybe not, but she said the deputy looked very nervous and quickly put the envelope in a desk drawer. It was enough to make her curious. Make her mention it to me."

Walter set the brake and came around to help her down.

"Kam Le looked back when she reached the corner and saw the lieutenant leaving. He stopped in the doorway, she said, and looked around before he left, as if to ensure nobody saw him."

"Did he see her?"

"No. She lowered her parasol before their eyes could meet. When she raised it, he was gone."

"This is very troubling."

"*Now* do you think we should go to the governor?"

"I think we should not. More than ever. We still have no proof, only suspicions, and I fear dire consequences if we speak too soon or to the wrong person. Although I will now be more circumspect in hiring men to help. Only those I know. Only those I can trust."

He took her elbow and escorted her into the house.

This was not the world Mary Alice wanted to know about. She was not blind to the dangers of renegade Indians or highwaymen but had always felt safe living in town. There were institutions designed to protect the citizenry. She'd always respected the authorities, had never questioned their motives or intentions—until she saw Rose's brooch on Mrs. Schiffman's bosom. Piece by piece, her unshakable faith in the order of things was crumbling beneath growing evidence that something criminal was going on among them all.

"If you cannot trust the military, if you cannot trust the local law enforcement, who can we trust?" Mary Alice asked. "Nobody is safe."

She hung her hat and cape in the hallway. In the parlor Walter poured two glasses of brandy and handed her one as soon as she entered.

"I know you're trying to abstain, but I do think your nerves require some soothing," he said.

They sat by the fireplace and sipped the drinks. Mary Alice wanted nothing more than to down hers quickly and have another, but she forced herself to match Walter's pace. They finished their drinks and Walter refilled the glasses.

"I'm sorry you're so distraught."

"Walter, I trust you will find Rose and bring her home. All of this intrigue is secondary to that. Just be careful. You're still not well. Be careful! I can count on no one but you!" She finished her brandy. Calming herself, she spoke quietly. "I apologize for my outburst."

"Don't apologize. You have every reason to be agitated."

"Perhaps. But I have no reason to raise my voice." She stood and handed her empty glass to Walter. "Now we still have to eat, so I shall check on the dinner preparations." When she turned to go, she stumbled and fell against Walter's chair. He twisted and caught her before she could fall to the floor, then stood and helped her up.

She gave an embarrassed laugh. "I'm all right, Walter."

But he continued to hold her by her arms. "No, you're not. I should not have given you the brandy. I'm sorry."

"I'm just tired."

"Mary Alice, I'm afraid you've lost your tolerance for drink. You've tried to abstain. Now I'm afraid I must insist upon it."

"Yes, yes, of course." She pulled away from him. "Stop worrying. I'm fine. And I still need to check on dinner."

But instead of going to the kitchen she went straight to her room. Straight to her vanity table and opened the drawer.

Just the act of pulling the cork from the bottle eased the tension from her body. This was something she could always count on, she thought, as she swallowed the amber liquid.

CHAPTER EIGHTEEN

Rose sat outside the tent, a child tucked under each arm. Harry positioned himself to block any sight of the children from the gate guard. Foot traffic and noise on the other side of the tent grew as night deepened and the heavy drinking began. She imagined the usual thugs gathered around Mason's porch, waiting in hopes he'd allow a whore to join them. A woman's sudden laugh, then cheers. Their dreams fulfilled, Rose thought. How nice for them. Music followed—accordion, banjo, a fiddle—quite the party they were having. Too busy, all of them, to care what went on in this tent where Caleb's quiet voice apologized over and over to his sister.

He had run to the mercantile and come back with an armful of bottles—quinine, laudanum, whiskey—enough to quiet her screams. He'd been by her side since then, dispensing painkillers and begging her forgiveness.

Harry rolled a cigarette and crouched beside Rose, smoking and fidgeting. "Here," he said, and pulled the covers up over the children's shoulders. He tucked the little boy's arm under a blanket. "We have to get them out of here."

She looked down at their matted hair, silver in the moonlight. Just a few more nights and it would all be over. The prisoners, all the women and children, including herself, rounded up and dragged down to Mexico. Women sold into slavery, the children likely sent to work in mines. Or worse. Her arm tightened around Sarah's bony shoulders.

"There's no way out," she said.

"There's that tunnel. Show me where it is. We can take the children and come back with help before Mason breaks camp."

"Their mother needs them here." She checked to see if the children were sleeping. "Maybe tomorrow night." She didn't know what to do. Mason's armed guards ringed the perimeter. All she could think of was Caleb's warning. She pictured the guards aiming their rifles into the stockade, picking off the women and children before turning quickly to stop the rescuers struggling to get up the steep sides of the mountain.

She repeated Caleb's story to Harry. "Now do you see? If we go tonight with the children, we couldn't say where this place is. We couldn't send anybody to rescue the rest of them. It would only cause their deaths."

The children shifted and she tightened her arms around them. "But we do know when they are leaving for Mexico. Maybe a rescue attempt then would work. When they're all out in the open."

Harry took a long drag on his cigarette, blowing a stream of smoke. "When his sister dies, Caleb will kill Mason. What do you suppose will happen then? Who will protect Mason's investment in all those women?"

Rose remembered the guard at the porch steps. *The women belong to McCabe.* Harry was right. Without Mason to control them, the other men would set upon the women like wild animals. "God help us."

"We'll take the children. We'll go tonight. We can't save everyone. If this is the best we can do, you and the children will be enough."

The low moans from inside the tent grew louder.

Harry tossed his cigarette to the ground and stood.

"Where are you going?" she asked.

"To the house. Caleb will be going there soon to get his

revenge." He adjusted the sheath holding his knife so it would be within easy reach. "If Caleb wants McCabe dead, I can at least watch his back. God knows that monster needs killing. When it all breaks loose, I'll come for you."

What if they were both killed and Mason lived? "Please be careful. I can't take the children through that tunnel by myself."

"You won't have to."

After Harry left, Rose eased out from between the children, settled them, and slipped into the tent. Light from the lantern limned the hanging blanket, and she stood next to it, holding a rag over her mouth and nose, until she was able to tolerate the stench. She peered into the makeshift sick room. Caleb sat cross-legged on the ground beside his sister, stroking her forehead, continuing the words, almost a chant, he had spoken all evening and into the night. "I'm so sorry. I didn't know."

Patience moaned, "Children. My children."

"Don't worry about the children," Caleb said. "I'll see to them. They'll be taken care of. They'll be all right."

"Apples. We was out in the orchard eating apples." Patience smiled at her brother. "The sunlight was so pretty comin' through the leaves. Sarah and Jonathan, their hair all shiny and juice runnin' down their chins. John was so proud. First year of apples."

"Shush. Don't talk anymore."

"We heard horses. John looked to see who was coming and then—and then—" She began to sob, and tears ran down her face.

Caleb tried to take her hand but she cried out and rolled over, pulling up her legs and pressing her arms into her sides. She turned her face away from him and her groans, although weak, continued.

She lifted her head. "I want to see my children."

Rose couldn't bear to watch any more. Then the woman made

a different sound, almost as if she were laughing, but it turned into an awful keening.

"—a good mother," Caleb was saying, speaking softly even as the hideous noise grew louder. "Nobody could've done more. Nobody."

Rose heard no more words over the horrible noise the woman made and turned away from the contorted face and thrashing legs as a black gush poured through bandages and soaked the bedding.

The wailing suddenly faded to faint sounds, muffled grunts. Caleb's whispered words, *don't fight it, just let go, don't fight*— Rose pulled the blanket aside as Caleb lifted his hand from his sister's face. White marks across her nose and mouth stood out against the ashen gray of the rest of her skin.

Rose crawled backwards until she was outside, past the sleeping children still curled under their blankets.

She used the fence to pull herself up, and when faintness threatened, she clung to it until the feeling passed. In the darkness of the stockade, black boulders formed a circle, except boulders wouldn't cough or snore or whimper. They slept that way, the woman did, in a circle. Now that it had turned cold, Mason allowed a few small fires—not until after dark—and the children, encircled by the women, slept nearest the heat. Soft clouds of steam rose from the ditch that flowed around the edges of the stockade. Circles. The fire, the children, the women, the ditch, the fence.

Moonlight flashed off a rifle barrel high up on the cliffs. They were all in the middle of one big bull's-eye.

Some of the tents glowed yellow with lantern light, but most were dark. The men were up at the house, which shone so brightly from all the lanterns and lamps and candles that the light reflected off the cliff behind it, and she could see its glow from where she stood. Loud voices and women's laughter rose above the general clamor.

Cold night air began to cut through her clothes, and Rose was about to go inside and get a blanket for herself when Caleb pushed through the tent flap and stepped over the children. The stink of death and decay clung to him. He stared into the stockade, wiping his eyes with his shirt sleeve.

"I'm sorry," she said.

"Yeah, we're all sorry. We're a sorry lot, and that's a fact."

The black lumps inside the stockade cast distinct shadows on the dirt, under the three-quarter moon. Caleb stared at them for a long time.

She put a hand on his arm. He very deliberately removed it. She saw his tears had dried, and she saw the look on his face.

"You won't get away with it," she said. "Even if you succeed, you'll be dead before you can leave the house. You promised her you'd take care of the children."

"I wouldn't make much of a parent, would I? I only promised I'd see they are taken care of."

"If you kill Mason, all the hostages will be fair game. The men will have nothing to keep them away from the women. They'll all end up like your sister."

"You expect me to let him get away with what he did to her?"

"Let me get the children out of here first. Then you can do whatever you want to Mason."

"You won't get past the guards."

"I know a way. Harry will help me."

Caleb leaned against the fence, sank until he was sitting on the ground, and buried his hands in his hair. "How did everything get so fucked up?"

Laughter erupted from Mason's porch, followed by a woman's voice and gleeful shouts. The door opened to a burst of loud voices and piano music, then the door slammed shut again. Harry was there, at the piano, entertaining Mason while he waited to help Caleb commit murder. She caught a whiff of woodsmoke. Mason must have the fireplaces blazing.

She dared to touch Caleb's shoulder, and this time he didn't push her hand away. "What happened to your sister wasn't your fault."

The children stirred. Jonathan woke and, seeing his uncle, went to him. Caleb pulled the boy into his arms. He held him, the boy's face pressed against his chest.

Sarah propped herself on an elbow, her pale face peering out from a huddle of blankets. "Is Mama dead?"

"Yes," Rose said. "I'm so sorry, Sarah."

"At least she won't be screaming no more." The child pulled her doll close and lay down. Jonathan began to whimper, and Sarah's voice came from under the blankets. "Who will take care of us now?"

"This lady will," Caleb said. "And her friend, Harry."

CHAPTER NINETEEN

Rose cleaned up the tent and pulled a sheet over Patience, leaving only her face exposed. There wasn't much she could do about the smell except prop open some spaces along the bottom of the canvas walls to let the night air in. It helped a little.

She went outside to where the children waited. "Come and say goodbye to your mother." She led them into the tent and behind the blanket. The three of them looked down at the dead woman. "Do you know any prayers?"

Sarah nodded.

"Maybe you could say them."

The two children knelt next to each other and said their prayers. They said amen, and the girl pressed her lips together, her chin quivering. Rose made each child kiss their mother's cheek, then she covered the woman's face with the sheet.

Her father had done the same—made her kneel by the bed, say a prayer, kiss her dead mother goodbye.

"Come on," she said. She pulled the children to their feet and ushered them to the other side of the tent. "We have to get ready. We're leaving here tonight."

She gathered canteens and jerky and candles and matches, all the time listening to the sounds from the house. Loud, cheerful voices. Women's laughter. Music, not piano. Nobody was playing the piano. A door slammed.

She waited for an uproar, for a riot to break out. Surely something would have erupted when Caleb killed Mason. A sick feeling came over her as she realized Caleb must be the one who died. Dead at Mason's hand, tossed down the porch steps and left to lie there until someone pushed him into a ditch or the turkey vultures cleaned off his bones.

Her hands shook as she gathered supplies.

What of Harry?

No sooner had she thought of him, it seemed, than he pushed through the tent flap. She kept her voice low so the children couldn't hear her question. "Caleb's dead? Mason killed him?"

Harry shook his head. "He's drinking with McCabe. Acting like they're best friends."

She brushed her hands on her skirt. "What?"

"He's not going to kill him. I don't know what he's up to."

"Not kill him?" There had been murder in his eyes out by the fence, not an hour ago.

"It doesn't change anything. We have to go, get those children out of here."

"No, this is different. It does change things. It changes everything." She looked at the children. Bedraggled waifs clinging to each other, Mrs. Coppage hanging from Sarah's hand. "You have to go without me."

Harry grabbed her arm. "No."

"Listen to me. If I'm gone, Mason will notice. He'll sound an alarm as soon as I don't show up to practice for his party."

The candlelight behind Harry cast his face in shadow. She couldn't see his expression but his whole body tensed, and his grip tightened on her arm. "I'll not leave you here."

"No, wait, listen. When I said I would go, I thought Mason would be dead. The others would have gone after the women and there'd be no way to stop the slaughter. I was ready to run. But if Mason is still alive, once he realizes I'm gone, he'll know he's finished here. It's over. He'll expect me to come back with lawmen. He'll either kill the women and children or leave for

Mexico right away. We can't let that happen. We have to try to save them."

"All of them? How? We can't take fifty women and children through that tunnel without the guards seeing!"

"No, but what if just a few at a time—" Her breath came as fast as her thoughts. "You go tonight and take the children. Wait! Listen to me! Then, on the night of the party, come with the soldiers. Come before moonrise. Sneak in through the tunnel, a few at a time, and then take the women out a few at a time."

Harry shook his head. "It won't work. The guards will see the soldiers. You can't hide a regiment. Come on, let's go." He started to pull her toward the flap.

"No! You have to listen to me. The men can hide under the blankets, like the women do at night. Don't you see? They will trade places, a few at a time, and stay hidden under the blankets. When all the women are safe, the soldiers can rise up. Rise up and capture or kill all of them!"

Harry looked into her eyes for what seemed a long time. "No. You come with me now, and I'll bring the soldiers tomorrow."

"Please, Harry! Wait until the night of the party. The guards will be distracted. Nobody will be paying attention."

"They'll start paying attention when an army regiment rides up to the base of the mountain."

"Tell them to leave their horses in the trees. They'll have to sneak in, just a few at a time. If they come before moonrise, the darkness would help conceal them."

"There's no way I can make you come with me?"

"It's a good plan. We can do it. Save all the women and end this place."

His hand fell from her arm. "It might work."

The usual party noises came from the house as they each

became lost in their own thoughts. Now that Harry had accepted her idea, a million ways it could go wrong occurred to Rose. Anxiety gripped her, tightened her throat so she couldn't have spoken if she'd wanted to. But she would not share her fear or doubt with Harry. It would be up to him to make the plan work. And it *would* work.

"Very well, I'll take them. I'll bring them to your auntie; I'll go to the fort and lay out the plan; I'll show them where the tunnel is." He held her shoulders. "But then I'll be back. Tomorrow. I'll not leave you here alone."

They tied dark rags over the children's silvery-blond hair and draped gray blankets over their shoulders. Sarah tucked Mrs. Coppage inside her coat, and the doll's face at her collar looked like a second smaller head.

"Jesus!" Harry said, when he saw the spectral face protruding from under Sarah's chin. Then he adjusted Sarah's coat collar and buttons to make sure the doll was secure.

"Let's go," he said.

Harry held the tent flap aside, checked the compound for guards, and motioned them out. Rose hurried toward the jakes, the children at her heels, Harry bringing up the rear. At the last privy, Rose gathered everyone in the deep shadows behind it.

"We have to crawl now so the guards won't see us." She got on her hands and knees and started up the hill, trying to picture in her mind exactly where the opening was. She cut her hand on a thorny branch, stifled a cry, and continued crawling, trying to keep beneath the cover of brush and stunted junipers. The children were close behind. Far above them a flash of moonlight glinted off steel, a rifle barrel at the top of the ridge. She froze, waiting for the guard to turn away. When she crawled again, she forced herself to go slowly, quietly, although her muscles thrummed with tension. Breathe in—go slow. Breathe out—be quiet. Jonathan sniffed, then whimpered.

Rose stopped. "Shush," she said. "We'll be there soon." They continued in silence. She felt rock beneath her stinging fingers, pushed forward and upward, into the same thorny bush as before, felt for the ledge, and crawled under the buckthorn. She reached for Jonathan. "Come on. Crawl. Keep your head down." She held the branches up and guided him through.

"Sit right there. Don't go in. Wait," she whispered, then reached for Sarah's hand.

With both children inside the tunnel, she scanned the black silhouettes of the guards while Harry climbed up. They all crouched inside the opening.

Rose pointed into the tunnel. "The ledge is on that side of the tunnel."

"Come with us."

"I can't." She touched the rough wool of his coat, found his hand, and squeezed it. "Whatever you do, don't step off that ledge. And keep the candle burning so you can see what's ahead of you." She didn't want to say any more in front of the children. "You need to go. Be careful. Please."

She handed him a scrap of paper. "This is Auntie's address. Mrs. Mary Alice Bradford."

"I remember her. She used to visit at your father's place."

"When you get to Prescott, take Sarah and Jonathan to her. She'll look after them." She hugged each child. "Remember you must be quiet. Mr. Sheldon will tell my aunt who made the least noise, and that child will get a cookie. Okay?"

Harry tucked the paper into his vest pocket. Rose hung the canteens from Harry's shoulder, the straps across his chest, and pressed the candles and matches into his hand, which she held in both of hers for a moment. Then he helped Jonathan climb onto his back. The little boy wrapped his legs around Harry's waist, and wound his arms around his neck.

"Don't worry," he said. "We'll be all right." He shifted Jonathan so the child was higher up on his back. "Sarah, reach up under my coat and hold on to my cartridge belt. Can you do that?" They started into the tunnel. He stopped and looked over his shoulder. "I'll see you tomorrow."

The blackness of the tunnel swallowed them.

Their shuffling footsteps faded. Rose made the sign of the cross and prayed for God to protect them. The faint glow of a candle appeared from the depths of the tunnel. She took it as an answer to her prayer.

CHAPTER TWENTY

The sky above the steep walls of rock sparkled with stars. Moonlight glinted on rifle barrels all around the rim, and Rose imagined soldiers rising up in the stockade, throwing their blankets aside and opening fire on the outlaws. The fearsome guards falling to their deaths. The vision helped her maintain a slow pace as she descended the steep hillside. After an eternity, a whiff of the jakes seemed as sweet as fine perfume since it meant she was almost at the bottom. Within minutes she reached level ground. She got up and walked to the tent, safe now that she was in the compound proper. Safe from every man but one.

A small red glow and the smell of tobacco told her Caleb awaited her. He sat on the ground outside the tent, and she was within ten feet of him before he looked up.

"Where are they?"

She tried to gauge the tone of his voice but couldn't tell if he was angry or concerned or just asking because he was supposed to. "They're on their way to Prescott. Harry took them."

He motioned her to come and sit beside him. "You should've gone with them."

"I wanted to."

Tossing his cigarette aside, he picked up a whiskey bottle, took a few swallows, then handed it to her. She held the opening to her nose before wiping it with her sleeve. She sipped and let the warmth seep past her throat toward her stomach. She took another sip. Her shoulders loosened a little.

"I thought Mason had killed you."

"Ha! Sorry to disappoint you."

"Why didn't you kill him?"

"Not yet."

He rolled another cigarette, took another drink, and wedged the bottle between his legs.

"Harry said you were friendly with Mason."

"I want to take everything he has. Everything. And I want him to know I took it. Then I'll kill him. So don't worry about it."

"I do worry."

"About me? Is that why you didn't go with Harry and the children?"

He searched her eyes, as if expecting her to say she cared what happened to him. She did care. She wanted to see him hanging from a scaffolding in Prescott, right next to Eddie and Dodger and Mason. But when she looked into his eyes, saw the question there, she thought instead of him by his dying sister's side. She thought of him coming out of the tent, his face wet with tears. She thought of him holding Jonathan, comforting him. She had to look away from those eyes. "About those women and children. I worry about Sarah and Jonathan."

"They have each other, just like Patience and I had each other."

She touched his hand but he snatched it away and took another drink. He handed her the bottle and went inside. She drank what was left of the whiskey. Inside the tent a shovel blade bit into hard dirt, and she dozed to the rhythm of the digging, jerking awake when the sound stopped. The empty bottle rolled away when she tried to get up. She managed to stand up and lift the tent flap. A candle on the ground made Caleb's shadow huge. It wavered on the canvas behind him. The shovel lay by his feet.

"I couldn't throw her in the ditch. And I can't let Mason know she's my sister. He'd be expecting me to get revenge."

The rectangle of freshly dug dirt was almost level; the woman's ravaged body displaced no more than a few inches of earth. Rose crossed herself, bowed her head, and prayed for the woman buried there. "Amen."

"Thank you." Caleb kicked the shovel into the corner and pushed past her.

She sank to the ground by the grave. She continued to pray— prayed that Harry would make it safely through the tunnel and that the children were already on their way to Prescott and Auntie. She prayed her plan would work. And then she prayed to God to give her strength for whatever lay ahead. A dark well of terror grew in her gut. A picture of Harry and the children crept into her mind. They lay in the bottom of the tunnel, snakes crawling over their bodies; dead white eyes accused her. She pulled up her knees and tucked her head down, rocked, reminded herself she was Walter LaBelle's daughter. She would do what she needed to do. She would do what was right.

Sometime later a touch on her shoulder awakened her. She scrambled away, still half asleep.

"It's me," Caleb said. "Come away from there."

He ushered her to the other side of the tent where a lantern burned. He unrolled some blankets, and she crawled to them, curling on her side. He stretched out behind her and pulled the covers over them.

"Go to sleep," he said. "I won't let anything happen to you. I'll get you out of here safe, I promise."

She didn't need Caleb to watch over her. Harry would come back. He would help her get out. Or, if need be, she'd get herself out.

Chapter Twenty-One

Mary Alice sank into the wingback chair by the fireplace. The logs cracked and hissed and threw a flickering light across Walter's face. He looked tired. They nursed their brandies in silence.

Following yesterday's meeting with the lieutenant, her anger had faded to despair so deep she had spent the afternoon in her room, laudanum soothing her nerves until she slept. And today had been no better.

Walter cleared his throat. "I believe the ones who don't have jurisdiction, the local police. They *can't* help us. It's all political. There are elections, and they want to keep their jobs. So they are afraid to be seen as overstepping their authority."

"And the others?"

"I don't know. The U.S. marshal is gone, and the deputies won't help. I guess we now know, thanks to Kam Le, why. They're in Schiffman's pocket. And that damned city marshal Duval isn't stepping up. Probably taking a payoff as well. God knows he acts like he's terrified every time I question him about any of this." He slugged back his brandy and got up to refill his glass. "Excuse my language."

"Don't apologize. If they are buying and selling stolen goods—" Mary Alice's voice rose and cracked as she thought of Rose's pendant.

"I don't know that they are. And even if true, that is not my concern. Not right now, anyway."

Of course. His concern was for Rose. *Please God, let her still be alive. I don't care what has happened to her. Let her be alive.* She wished Walter would just be quiet. She wanted to go to her room.

"The men I hired today know the goal. We'll search until we find Rose or the men who took her."

Or the men? What did he mean by that? He might not find Rose? "When will you go?"

"First light tomorrow."

Tomorrow would be a long day. She said goodnight. At the door to her room, she rested her hand on the knob and looked across the hall. The glow of embers deepened the shadows of Walter's craggy face as he sat staring into his glass.

Mary Alice opened one eye to the light creeping around the edges of her heavy draperies. That dim trickle was enough to set off a headache. She shut her eye but swung her legs out of bed, hands searching for her robe. After a moment, she drew enough courage to open both eyes. Kam Le had already been in. A pot of tea in its cozy had replaced the empty whiskey bottle. It sat next to her favorite teacup, the one with yellow roses on it, and a small pitcher of milk, a bowl of sugar cubes, and tongs. She slipped her feet into her house shoes, tied the sash of her robe, and got the laudanum out of her dresser. Several drops fell into her teacup, followed by four sugar cubes and some milk. She poured the tea, sat on the edge of the bed, and let the hot drink revive her while more light seeped in around the drapes.

Dawn. Walter would be getting ready to search for Rose.

She found him at the dining room table. Platters of eggs, ham, biscuits, grits with bacon pieces, and butter. A carafe of hot coffee sat beside a steaming mug.

"Don't get up," she said, and sat across from him. "I'm sure Kam Le will fix you some food to take with you as well. You won't be out overnight, will you?"

He swallowed. "Depends." He gulped down half the mug's contents. "I'll not come back without her."

"Amen."

Walter went back to his breakfast, his mind on things other than a morning conversation with his sister-in-law, she was sure. Her own mind had trouble holding onto a coherent thought, between the lingering headache and the effects of laudanum so early in the day. She needed to quit taking so much. It clouded her thinking. But even though her thoughts were not clear, unambiguous anxiety and fear twisted throughout her body. She wished Walter would hurry with his meal and be on his way. This would be a good day to go back to bed.

But if he finds Rose . . . her niece would need her. How would she feel if she were unable to give Rose the care she'd surely need, due to over-imbibing?

"Kam Le? Could you please bring me a mug? I will have coffee."

Today she would be strong. And sober.

Walter sopped up egg yolk with the last piece of biscuit and pushed his chair back.

"Walter, what is your plan?"

He ticked off each task on a finger. "The men I hired are meeting me in front of the Palace Saloon at seven. We shall ride out toward Thumb Butte, possibly down toward Skull Valley. We'll look for anything out of the ordinary. Talk to any ranchers or farmers along the way to see if they noticed anything unusual a week ago."

"Good. You are taking action. More than we can say of the marshal or the army." She needed to get up, to move around, to dispel the anxiety that was growing within her. "I'll get your scarf and lined gloves. It's cold out there now, and will be again at night should you be out after sunset."

"Mary Alice, sit down and stop fussing over me. I have everything already packed in my saddlebags. Mr. Nason from the livery is bringing a good mount for me. He should be here any minute."

Walter grunted as he rose from the chair and held the edge of the table to push himself to his feet.

"You're not healed," Mary Alice said. "You're not recovered enough to be riding all over the countryside like this."

"Then who will do it?"

She wondered if Rose was warm and sheltered. Or was she out somewhere, freezing and suffering, sleeping on the ground? Tears sprang to her eyes.

"You're distraught. You should go back to bed." Walter's eyes held such kindness and concern. He didn't understand the last thing she needed was to retire to her room today, where the laudanum in its shiny bottle and the honey-colored whiskey waited. And no eyes to see her.

"I think I'll call on Mrs. Pumfrey. I haven't thanked her yet for her kindness to me last week. I'll give her a jar of the lotion Kam Le makes with the rose petals from the garden. I think there are still a few unopened. Well, you'll know where to send for me if you're home early."

"A splendid idea. Give her my regards. Now I must be off."

The front door closed and his heavy boots thudded down the porch steps. Kam Le came in to clear away Walter's dishes and, as soon as she left the room, Mary Alice got her whiskey and poured some into her coffee. It was a chilly day. The whiskey would keep her warm.

Mary Alice stepped onto the porch to wait for Kimo to return with a carriage, the packaged jar of rose-petal lotion under her arm. She pulled her cape close around her neck and was considering going in for a scarf when she heard pounding hooves approaching. Walter came galloping around the corner, a wagon careening behind him up the hill. At least a dozen riders followed close behind. The driver reined to a hard stop and set the brake while the horses huffed out white vapor and tossed their heads, making the tack jangle and creak. Two men jumped from their mounts and helped the driver pull someone from the wagon bed.

Walter hurried up the steps to hold the door open.

"Walter, what—"

"Not now! Isn't the doctor here yet?"

She stepped back out of the way. They carried a man, his face twisted with pain, into the house. His pant leg hung ripped from his knee to his bare foot, exposing a horribly swollen leg.

"On the right," Walter directed. "In the room with the piano. Lay him on the sofa. And someone get that doctor, God damn it!" He followed them inside and let the door slam behind him.

A young girl, draped in a man's coat, climbed from the wagon. She held up her arms and helped a little boy down. A coat hung from him too; its hem dragged in the street. The children held hands, ignored by the men who had dismounted and were milling around the street. The gaunt boy, white-faced except for bloody scratches and dark shadows beneath his large eyes, and the girl, forehead and one cheek caked with blood, looked as if they had just woken up.

"Children!" She waved at them. "Come up here, children. Get out of the street!"

They climbed the stairs and stood backed against the railing.

"Don't be afraid. Tell me, what happened to your father?"

"He ain't our pa," the boy said. He looked at the girl and rolled his eyes. "Why does everyone think he's our pa?"

"Not everyone. She's just the second or third person."

"Can you tell me your names?"

The girl eyed Mary Alice with suspicion. "I'm Sarah. This

here's my brother, Jonathan." She pulled a broken-faced, half-bald doll from somewhere within the coat. "And this is Mrs. Coppage."

"Oh, my!" Mary Alice held out her arms and motioned the children closer. Walter needed to tell her who these children were and what she was supposed to do with them. "Well, would you like to come inside? And perhaps have something to eat?"

At the mention of food, the children took a step toward her. She hoped she displayed a friendly smile and not the horror in her heart. "You may call me Auntie."

"*You're* the auntie?" Sarah asked. "We didn't know you was so old."

"I get the cookie," Jonathan said. "I was the quietest, because she kept yelling at me to shut up."

Dr. Dugan rode up, dismounted, and threw his reins on the picket fence. Mary Alice nudged the children away from the door so the doctor, leaning to one side with the weight of his medicine case, could rush into the house.

Then Kimo drove up with the carriage, and Mary Alice asked him to please go by Mrs. Pumfrey's. "Tell her I won't be visiting today, but thank her so much for her kindness. Tell her I hope to see her soon. And give her this, please." She handed Kimo the lotion. "Hurry back."

Alone in the kitchen with the two little ragamuffins and not a word of explanation from Walter, she wondered what to do next.

"My hand hurts," the boy said.

Mary Alice unbuttoned the coat to check his hand and arm. "I think your wrist may be broken, child. We'll have the doctor look at it before he leaves." The girl had a long cut on the side of her head, not deep, but clearly the source of dried blood on her face and in her hair. "What on earth happened to you children?"

The girl's eyes filled. When the boy saw that, he started crying.

Mary Alice hugged them. "There, there. Everything is going
to be all right now."

"No, it ain't," the girl yelled. "Pa's dead and Mama's dead,
and now Mr. Sheldon's gonna die too." She pushed her brother.
"It's your fault. All that wiggling around. You made him fall."

"Did not!" The boy shot an angry look at his sister, then
lifted a tear-stained face to Mary Alice. "My arm hurts worse
now she pushed it." He resumed crying, only louder.

"Hush now, hush. Come." She herded the children into the
parlor, to Joseph's big chair near the fire.

"What about my cookie?" the boy asked.

"In a minute. You can both rest here while I see what's going
on. I'll be right back."

She tucked the afghan around them and pushed her way past
the crowd of men in the doorway to the music room. Walter
knelt on one knee, listening intently to the injured man while
the doctor cut the torn trouser leg away.

"What the hell is this?" the doctor asked. When he untied a
makeshift bandage a stone, the size and thickness of a half eagle,
fell to the rug.

"Snake stone," one of the men said. "Sucks the poison out."

Walter looked up. "Mary Alice, do you have the children?
Bring them in here. He's asking for them."

She ushered the children up to the sofa so the man could see
them.

"I'm sorry!" The boy sobbed. He fell to his knees and hid his
face in the sofa cushion. "I'm sorry!"

The man, teeth clenched against the pain he must have been
in, put a hand on the boy's head. "It wasn't your fault."

The boy lifted his wet face, nose dripping. "I don't want you
to die."

The man closed his eyes. The doctor moved his leg and the man sucked in air, keeping his lips pressed shut to keep from crying out. Walter quickly pushed the children toward Mary Alice and she took them to the kitchen.

She helped them out of the heavy coats and had them sit on kitchen stools. "Hold still," she said as she checked the boy's injury. A towel wrapped around his arm would do until the doctor could take a look. "How did you two get hurt? Did that man do this to you?"

"No! Mr. Sheldon is nice," Sarah said.

"We fell out of the end of the tunnel," the boy said. "When we woke up, he was trying to get that snake off his leg." His eyes filled again, his downturned lips quivering.

"He was saving us." The girl tilted her face so Mary Alice could wash away the dried blood. "Miss Rose said they had to save the children. That was us."

Mary Alice held the cloth in midair. Had she heard correctly?

The boy pulled on her sleeve. "Are we saved now?"

"Miss Rose? Did you say Rose?" Mary Alice braced herself against the countertop as a wave of relief washed over her. Just then Walter rushed into the kitchen, holding a scrap of paper in one hand, wiping his eyes with the other, a huge smile on his face.

"Rose is alive! He had this note in his vest pocket."

The note was in Rose's handwriting. Mary Alice sobbed, clutching the note to her bosom.

Walter handed her his handkerchief.

"She was with these children and that man last night," Walter said. "Before they escaped."

"Then where is she?"

"I don't know. I have many questions. And few answers. The tunnel he speaks of can't be far. We found them in that meadow near the base of Thumb Butte. Him with a dead rattlesnake hanging from his boot."

Mary Alice gasped. "She's out there somewhere dying of snake bite!"

"No, no, that's not the case!" Walter wrapped an arm around her. "She stayed behind. The children said it, and so did he. She gave him that note so he could find us."

"Then she's alive! Oh, thank God. Thank God. But stayed behind where?"

The doctor called out, "Mr. LaBelle, could you come, please."

Mary Alice followed Walter into the music room. The man's inflamed leg was an ugly red. An even uglier darkness surrounded a gash that split the skin below his knee.

"I see you cut the skin. Tried to suck the poison out? I doubt your efforts or that snake stone were useful," the doctor said. "Too much time has passed."

The man's damp hair stained her silk pillow, which someone had placed under his head. A fine sheen of perspiration covered his gray-tinged face.

"Will he live?" Walter asked.

"Snake bite can vary. I can only find one fang mark."

"Yes, the other was caught in the top of his boot. Does that mean less venom?"

"Might. Hard to tell." The doctor shrugged. "He's passed out. Might wake up. Might not. The venom will work its way out of his system. Or kill him. We'll just have to wait and see if the treatment works."

"What treatment? Whiskey?" Kam Le asked.

"That is the prescribed treatment for snake bite." The doctor turned to see who had spoken so disrespectfully. "Someone get that Oriental out of here," he said. But Kam Le was already on her way out, pushing past the curious men who lingered in the music room doorway.

"You men go on home now. I'll send word when I want to

search again." Walter turned to Mary Alice. "I'll sit here with him. If he awakens I'll get him to tell me where Hellgate is."

"Hellgate? That's where my Rose is? Hellgate?"

"Mary Alice, please. Go take care of those children."

Mary Alice returned to the kitchen. She heard the men in the hallway and then the front door slammed shut. Steam hissed from the kettle. Kimo, fixing sandwiches and coffee, had cracked the window a bit. Beyond its fogged panes came men's voices, creaking leather, jangling bits, and hoofbeats fading down the street.

Mary Alice leaned against the counter top, dazed as if someone had struck her.

Hellgate?

Kam Le finished washing the children's hands and faces, bandaged the little girl's head, and put the boy's thin little arm in a sling, his wrist wrapped up in linen strips. Her voice penetrated Mary Alice's fog.

"They are not hurt, Missus. The wrist is sprained, a small cut on the head. We do not need that doctor to say maybe they'll get better, maybe not." She put a hand on the girl's matted hair. "I could not get the comb through."

The two women put plates of buttered biscuits, left over from breakfast, in front of the children, who stuffed them into their mouths. "Wait, children. Here." Mary Alice put little pots of jam and honey on the counter, and soon both had smeared their hands and faces. Starving. Dirty. Their clothes in tatters. What had they been through? And they had come from the place where Rose remained.

"Kam Le, please get some money out of my reticule. Go into town and buy these children some clothes."

"Yes, Missus."

Mary Alice sat next to the children.

"Sarah? Can you tell me about Rose?"

Sarah nodded, swallowed, and wiped the back of her hand across her mouth. "Yes, ma'am. She's the nice lady who helped us. She had Mr. Sheldon lift us over the fence. They was takin' care of Mama." The girl picked up her doll and hugged it. "Mama died. Then he took us away."

Mary Alice picked up a napkin and wiped the girl's face. "Mr. Sheldon." The name seemed vaguely familiar, but there were no Sheldons in Prescott. "Mr. Sheldon took you away, but my Rose stayed behind. Do you know why?"

"She was scared of the snakes," Jonathan said.

"No, that weren't it. I heard her say Mr. McCabe would do something bad if she left."

"Maybe she thinks Mr. McCabe likes her. I don't know why he would." Jonathan took another biscuit. "She was funny-looking."

"Shut up, Jonathan! You're making the lady cry. Sorry, ma'am. He's just sayin' that 'cause her hair was all cut off."

These children had seen Rose, could testify that she was alive. They had spoken to her. They had been with her. Despite the jam and crumbs and spilled tea, Mary Alice scooped the children into her arms and hugged them until they squealed.

"She looks like a boy," Jonathan said, settling onto his stool. "Her hair looks stupid, all chopped off, and it sticks up too."

Sarah shoved an elbow into him.

"Ow!"

Mary Alice didn't care if Rose were bald. As long as she breathed and walked and would someday, somehow, come home.

That night Mary Alice sat by the fire, in Joseph's chair, in a soft brandy-induced haze. She'd sneaked into her room and drunk enough that the story she'd heard was manageable. Some of it had come in rare lucid moments from Mr. Sheldon, the rest from the children or Walter. While she didn't dare think about the trip through some kind of tunnel, a tunnel crawling with rattlesnakes, she could envision only too clearly their desperate leap at the end of it, tumbling down the mountainside, how Sarah had searched, terrified, for her brother. When they found Mr. Sheldon, the writhing and rattling snake hanging from his leg, they thought he was dead. But he'd sat up and killed the snake with his knife and tried to pull it off, but one fang was stuck in his boot. Then he tried to saw the snake's head off but gave up.

Without a word, he'd started walking. The children had to run to keep up. He'd limped steadily along until they reached that meadow, lights from the town shining through the trees on the other side, and then he had fallen. They'd spent the rest of the night in the wet grass, huddled close to Mr. Sheldon.

That's where Walter found them a little after dawn. In the meadow. The man seemed near death but spoke one word. Hellgate. That was enough to tell Walter the lair was nearby. And so, perhaps, was his daughter. And now they knew that was the case.

Walter expected Mr. Sheldon to recover enough to direct his search party to Hellgate. Mary Alice was not convinced. For all she knew, the man had forced Rose to write that note. Had abandoned her in that horrible place and stolen these children. The children wouldn't know they'd been kidnapped. It was natural for them to think they had been saved. Well, time would tell. If he woke up asking for ransom money . . .

The drone of mumbled prayers came from the music room. The doctor had sent for two nuns from the Sacred Heart Church to sit with the patient for the night. They prayed the rosary. Mary Alice suspected they were also standing guard to keep Kam Le away. The doctor thought all Chinese were heathens and thieves and had often lectured Mary Alice about allowing them in her home.

Walter had made Kimo set up a bed in the music room, pushing the piano and sofa to the far end. They'd replaced Mr. Sheldon's torn, damp clothes with one of Joseph's old nightshirts. The doctor spent most of the day pouring whiskey into the man. Nothing they did seemed to matter. The man was in an awful state, barely conscious, in terrible pain.

The fire, the praying, the brandy. Mary Alice let her chin sink to her chest. She was drifting in a pleasant haze until sudden loud boots on the stairs and a banging on the front door shook the house. Her head came up, and Walter bolted out of his chair.

Lieutenant Schiffman stood on the porch barking orders, and Walter's angry response pulled Mary Alice from her chair. She went out to the hall just as Kimo handed a shotgun to Walter and positioned himself beside him, a second rifle cradled in his arm.

"You are harboring a criminal from Hellgate. I'm here to take him into my custody. The hospital at the fort will see to his medical needs. And my wife will take care of the children he kidnapped." Schiffman tried to push his way into the house, but Walter held the shotgun's barrels across the doorway.

"You are not welcome in this house."

"I'll be happy to lock you in the guardhouse, if that's what you want. Do not stand in my way."

Soldiers waited at the bottom of the porch stairs. Mary Alice couldn't see how many, but there were more than Walter and Kimo could keep at bay. At a signal from the lieutenant, they approached.

Walter stood firm in the doorway.

Kimo raised his rifle and moved closer to the door. Walter's jaw clenched. For a moment the only sound was an occasional moan from the music room. The nuns were in the parlor, clutching their rosary beads, eyes big in faces as white as their wimples.

"I thought Hellgate was a *civilian* matter," Walter said. "What would be your interest in the children? You had no interest in *my* kidnapped daughter."

The soldiers started up the stairs. Mary Alice stepped forward and took satisfaction in the flash of recognition on the lieutenant's face. "Don't you dare enter my home," she said. "This is out of your *jurisdiction.*"

Civilian men suddenly appeared from the shadows and surrounded the soldiers. They came from across the street, from the side yard, from the other side of the porch. The men Walter had hired. They had not left as directed, but had only moved their horses. They had stayed behind, standing guard all this time.

The lieutenant, realizing he and his men were outnumbered, stomped down the stairs, shoving through the cluster of soldiers. After they rode away, Walter stepped out onto the porch. He looked around at the men who had shown such loyalty and thanked them.

"We figured he'd show up," one of the men said.

"Walter?" Mary Alice stepped out onto the porch. "How did he know to come here?"

"The lieutenant and some of his men—same men he had with him just now—were out near Thumb Butte this morning. They stopped us from going in that direction, and that's when we noticed Mr. Sheldon and the children."

"Stopped you? Stopped you from searching for Rose? But why?"

"He said there were renegade Indians in the area. That it wasn't safe."

"I can hardly believe how brazen he is."

"If you'd seen the way his head twisted around when Mr. Sheldon said 'Hellgate' and the children mentioned a tunnel."

Walter spoke to the assembled men. "I don't think he'll return. Come back in the morning and we'll go out again. Hard to believe Hellgate is so close. He won't keep me from finding it."

"Mr. LaBelle? A few of us will stay behind if you don't mind. We'll just be out here on the porch."

"Very well. I appreciate it."

The nuns returned to their praying in the music room. Walter and Mary Alice settled into their chairs, raising their glasses.

"I will leave some men here tomorrow, too. In case the lieutenant comes back or sends soldiers. I hope Mr. Sheldon is able to give us some direction by morning."

Mary Alice hoped so, too. And more than that, she hoped her Rose would soon be home.

CHAPTER TWENTY-TWO

Rose awoke at first light with Caleb's arm heavy on her shoulder, his breath hot against her cheek. Her head throbbed from last night's drinking, and she didn't remember falling asleep next to Caleb. The image of Harry and the children, bloated and milky-eyed with snakes crawling over their bodies, had haunted her dreams and now that image persisted into daylight. If they were dead, they had died for nothing, and it was her fault.

Harry promised he would be back today. He had to be. Otherwise there would be no way to know the children were safe, that the plan was in place. No way to know that her nightmares about the tunnel were not real.

Crawling from under Caleb's arm, she sat in a corner and ate a can of beans while he snored. What would Arthur think of all the nights she'd spent with this man? She felt a flush of shame, realizing she hadn't given Arthur a thought in several days. Well, not since Harry had shown up. Harry, who had managed to find her—trailed her and got into Hellgate. Done what she had expected Arthur to do.

Now Harry would help to make her plan work. Harry would arrange everything, and he would come back. She saw herself riding triumphantly into Prescott with the soldiers, all of the criminals tied up or in chains—she had some chains they could use—headed for the gallows.

"What brings that smile to your face?" Caleb's sleepy voice

came from the pile of bedding.

"I'm thinking of the song I will sing for Mason on the night of the full moon."

Caleb stretched. "Oh. And who's gonna play the piano?"

"Harry will."

"He ain't comin' back. He's probably sold those kids to some mine owner and is on his way to San Francisco." He propped himself on an elbow.

His sly, hateful expression made her nervous. "I can accompany myself if need be."

"And what are you going to tell Mason about Harry? When you show up all by yourself to practice today? Now that he's run off with those kids. *My* kids."

"Stop it." In fact, she hadn't thought about what to tell Mason because she'd expected Harry to be back before it was time to practice. That was stupid. They didn't even know positively how far it was to Prescott. He might not make it back until late. Or tomorrow. "I'll just say I don't know where he is. Men come and go in this place all the time."

"And what if Mason goes looking for Sarah?"

"He wouldn't! She's just a child."

"You don't know Mason."

"Well, he won't find her, will he." Not a question but a statement that raised her spirits. "I'll tell the women in the stockade that the children died. Caught a chill from sleeping on the ground and died."

"You've got it all figured out."

"That's right. Now get out so I can change. Mason likes me to look nice."

"Oh, yes. We can't upset Mr. McCabe, can we?"

The coldness in his voice startled her. She knelt in front of him.

"Please, I beg you. Don't try to kill him."

The murderous look in his eyes gave way to surprise, then suspicion. "You're afraid he'll kill me, aren't you?" He brushed her hair away from her face, and his hand lingered, his expression softened.

It was the very opposite she feared—that he would succeed and they would all pay the price, too high a price, no matter how much she wanted McCabe dead. She lowered her head so he wouldn't see the truth in her eyes. "Caleb, I'm engaged to be married."

He threw the covers aside and got up. "I'll leave you to your dressing. I'll be outside waiting."

Caleb fell in beside her and walked with her to the house. From beneath the brim of her fancy bonnet, she scanned the hillside for signs of the tunnel but couldn't locate it. They had been careful enough then, had not disturbed the bushes that hid the opening. Caleb took her arm as they passed the guards and climbed the steps to Mason's door. Horace waved them into the parlor.

Too early in the day for whores and outlaws, faint sounds came from the kitchen. Dishes and silverware clinked, water splashed, a pot scraped across a stove top, and voices murmured.

Caleb settled himself in a carved rosewood chair and rolled a cigarette. Rose went into the music room, sat at the piano, and looked through the pile of sheet music for the ones she and Harry had been practicing. She played a few chords, and it was as if the music conjured Mason. His booming voice grew louder as he stomped down the hall and into the room.

"Ah, my performers have arrived!" He came to stand by the piano, beaming down at her. "What? The songbird also plays the piano?" He looked around the room. "Where is your accompanist? Drank too much last night, did he?"

Caleb spoke up before Rose could offer any explanation. "He

left. Last night." She felt her heart pounding. What else would he say?

Mason's expression darkened. "Now why would he be doing that, knowin' as he does my dependence upon him?"

Rose stared at the keyboard, forcing her hands to be still. *God damn you, Caleb.*

"I threatened to kill him," Caleb said, and Rose closed her eyes and exhaled. "He was thinking his business with Rose was more than playing the piano."

"Would you be sayin' he's not aware of the rules about the women?"

Caleb shrugged.

Mason's elbow and arm rested on the piano. A mother-of-pearl cuff link secured the sleeve of his spotless linen shirt. The rough hand that protruded, knuckles bruised and swollen, was all the more crude in comparison. She felt his gaze upon her but kept her eyes on the piano keys.

"And here I was looking forward to seeing—what was his name?"

"Harry," Rose said.

"Harry the piano player. As I was sayin', I was looking forward to seein' him. I heard 'twas he removed that stinkin' half-dead whore from my bed chamber. I intended to thank him this morning. Lucky for me there was another yellow-haired lass available. I hope she proves to be more . . . durable."

Rose waited for the blow, for Mason to fall to the rug, dead. But when nothing happened, she looked up, and Mason smiled expectantly at her. "Play somethin', darlin'! Don't be shy." He waved at the keys where her hands had frozen in midair. She turned to look at Caleb. Not a hint of emotion showed on the man's face. He remained seated, smoking his cigarette.

"I'm sure Harry will be back," she said. "You can thank him then."

"Sometimes they come back, sometimes they don't. 'Tis the way of things around here," Mason said. He clapped an arm around Caleb's shoulders. "Come and have breakfast with me, while the young lady practices. Now she must learn all those chords herself." He ushered Caleb toward the hallway. "I'll send you some refreshments, dear."

Her trembling fingers pressed the keys. Voices came from the dining room, conversational tones. Caleb's ability to hide his feelings amazed her. Dishonesty and manipulation—qualities she now admired, aspired to.

The Chinese woman brought her a tray of scones and tea, leaving it on the table in front of the sofa. She helped herself to a scone, slathered it with peach preserves, and wiped her hands on the embroidered napkin. Through the sheer panels at the windows, ghostlike shapes moved in the awakening compound. Men emerged from tents, horses milled in the corrals, servants hurried back and forth, busy at assigned chores. She carried her teacup and saucer to the window, hoping to see Harry walking toward the house.

Instead of that comforting sight, she overheard the conversation coming from the dining room.

"The business location in Mexico is changed every year or so. Keeps these louts from thinkin' they can take any advantage, you see. They can't go without me, even if they were there last year."

"So everyone from Hellgate goes to Mexico?"

"Well, the prisoners of course. And whatever men wish to join me. I hope that will include you this year. Most will come. I keep a separate home down there as well. Dealing with the *federales* is more complicated than 'tis here. They can be difficult, but I have several trusted associates that remain in Sonora, to take care of . . . my business interests.

"They're charged with finding a suitable base of operations. I don't even know myself where it is, but I'll know soon enough. A courier always arrives before the November full moon. He brings a map, you see."

Rose placed her cup in the saucer. Mason lowered his voice. "I probably should not have told you that."

Rose winced, expecting to hear the whoosh of the shillelagh and see Caleb's brains spatter through the doorway. Instead, Mason laughed. She went to the table and put her rattling teacup and saucer down and sank onto the sofa.

Mason's voice reverberated through the house. "You know I trust you as a son! I've been meanin' to talk with you about a partnership. You're not like these others around here, just brutes out for a quick dollar. I see a lot of myself in you, seen it from the first day you arrived here. A planner—always lookin' ahead."

"A partnership?"

"I'm growing older. 'Tis hard to produce an heir when the women just don't last that long. And by now I might not live to see any heirs of mine reach adulthood! I ain't gettin' no younger." He laughed again. "In the meantime, I'd like to spend more time enjoyin' the rewards I've reaped, more time in my lovely *hacienda* down south. I could use some help riding herd on the operations up here. Someone I can trust. And you have looked out for my interests all along. Bringin' me the lass for entertainment, and now lookin' after her, keeping that randy piano player from overstepping' the boundaries." Silverware clinked against dishes, and he yelled for someone to come and clear the table. "I see you are overwhelmed by my generosity. We can talk more another time. We've still a few days before leavin'."

That afternoon Rose leaned on the stockade fence, watching the women bound for slavery in Mexico. They didn't know what was in store for them. Maybe they thought there was some reason to stay alive, some reason to hope, that loved ones would pay a ransom or rescue them. She wanted to tell them about the plan, but Harry had not yet returned. She wasn't sure if there still was a plan.

Someone touched her shoulder.

"You spend a lot of time hangin' by this fence."

Dodger, as sickly pale as ever, maybe more so, brushed stringy hair from his stubbled face. He tucked it behind an ear, its crevices and whorls black with embedded grime.

"How would you know how I spend my time?"

"I been watching. Not much else to do around here."

She forced herself to stay calm. What had he seen? "Why do you stay then? If you're so bored?"

He coughed, a deep wracking cough, then spat. "Nobody bothers me here. Don't have to look over my shoulder. No law chasing me. That's why we're *all* here."

"There are other ways to keep the law from chasing you."

Dodger's laughter ended in another spell of hacking and wheezing and spitting into the dirt. He wiped his mouth, leaving a smear of pink across the back of his hand.

"Give up my life of crime? Don't get stuff like this that way." He stuck his hand in his trouser pocket and pulled out her locket, dangling it before her face from his smoke-stained fingertips. Dirt, as black as his fingernails, filled the intricate silver carvings, and the clasp was broken. Everything these men touched turned to trash. She tried to snatch it, but he was quicker. His yellowed teeth showed, and the whiskered crevices that framed his mouth deepened in what must have been a smile.

"Maybe if you was to tell me who gave you this little treasure, someone who'd be willing to pay to get you back, I might think it worth my while to help you get out of this place."

"I don't need your help to—"

Dodger laughed. "So you think your beau Caleb's gonna help you escape? He ain't nothin' but a toady to McCabe. He's got nothin' on his mind but making lots of money."

"You don't know what you're talking about."

Dodger ran a finger, rough as sandpaper, along her jawline until she slapped his hand away.

"You're right. I don't." He shoved the locket deep in his pocket. "I guess I'll just cash this here jewelry in when I get to Mexico. I hear we're leaving next week. My head ain't stopped hurting in a month. Maybe spending the winter in a warm, sunny climate will cure me."

"A noose around your neck will be your cure."

"You're probly right again. How'd you get so smart?" He turned to go. "I'd keep an eye out if I was you. Not everybody here understands the women belong to McCabe."

Gunfire—one shot—startled them both. Rose ran toward the house, Dodger at her heels.

"Hey, hey! Calm down!" he said. "You almost knocked me over!" He grabbed her arms as the house came into view.

Horace threw the front door open and hurried out of the way, flattening himself against the house. The guards on the stairs jumped aside as Mason's angry Gaelic bellowing grew louder. He appeared at the door and pushed his way through, carrying a limp body. The woman from upstairs—Rose recognized the ruffled nightdress and the few strands of yellow hair not covered in blood.

Mason carried her across the compound to the ditch and flung her in. Her arms flew up as if she were still alive and surprised to find herself airborne. Fabric billowed. A thick splash signaled the end of her flight and the vultures hissed and grunted from the far side of the ditch. Mason stomped away, returned to his house, and slammed the door shut.

Dodger let go of Rose's arms and she fell to the ground, to

her knees. She sank her hands into her hair and pulled. She pulled as hard as she could to keep herself from screaming.

Then Caleb was there. He took her hands and held onto them. "Come on, get up." He pushed Dodger out of the way. "Get the fuck outta here."

Caleb pulled her to her feet, and she ran to the tent. When they were both inside, she asked, "Why? Why did he kill her?"

Caleb let the tent flap fall, closing out the light.

"He didn't. She killed herself. He's got a room up there full of guns and boxes of ammunition. After the gunshot, we ran upstairs and found her in there."

Caleb's voice seethed with restrained rage. "He was angry she'd made a mess of the rug. It was expensive, he said. She could've set off the whole place. That's what he said. Just the saints looking after him that the bullet didn't hit a box of gunpowder. He's mad."

"We knew that."

He wrapped an arm around her and pulled her close, forcing her cheek against his chest. "Don't worry, Rose. He'll pay for what he's done."

"There's not payment enough. Not in this world."

"Don't be so sure."

CHAPTER TWENTY-THREE

Mary Alice had sent the nuns away. Their flowing habits and constant, murmured prayers unnerved her. She and Kam Le would sit with the patient until he recovered. She sat by the bed and hoped the fluttering eyelids didn't mean Mr. Sheldon was about to awaken. When the man was asleep or unconscious, he thrashed and moaned, but when he awoke, he lay still. He clutched the bedding until his knuckles turned white. Sometimes he would throw his head back, eyes squeezed shut, and did not breathe at all. The muscles and veins of his neck stood out until the spasm of pain passed, and a shuddering breath would whoosh from between clenched teeth. Mary Alice wanted to tell him to go ahead and scream; maybe it would help. But she was glad he did not, as it would no doubt terrify the children, especially the little boy, who felt to blame for the man's condition. No, Mr. Sheldon's quiet suffering was frightening enough, silent unless someone touched his leg. Then he did cry out or, mercifully, passed out.

Earlier that afternoon, the doctor had come and Mary Alice retreated to the parlor. She looked up from her embroidery to see the doctor standing in the doorway between the parlor and the music room. He held the remains of a green-tinged poultice, which he shook at her. "Dandelion leaves? She put dandelion leaves on his leg? And God knows what she spooned into him!" He returned to the sick room and rinsed his hands in the wash pan, leaving a raft of green debris floating on the gray water.

Kam Le scampered into the parlor, carrying a bowl and spoon. Although she kept her eyes lowered, she muttered, "Not just dandelion. Honeysuckle, skullcap, forsythia, toad venom for heart—"

Dr. Dugan dried his hands on a towel, which he then flapped at Kam Le. "I'll not have this heathen poisoning my patient."

Mary Alice put down her needlework and leaned on her cane to rise from the chair. A bad day for her rheumatism, with pain in several joints, but she would not complain, given what others were enduring.

The doctor leaned over the bed and lifted one of Mr. Sheldon's eyelids, making a big show of peering into his eye. Then he listened to his heartbeat through a stethoscope. "I believe he is resting comfortably. I don't know how you can have those people in your home. Goddamned pagans."

"And to what do you attribute his comfortable rest, Doctor?" Mary Alice asked. "Since you were absent most of the day?"

The doctor huffed and packed his stethoscope into his medical box. "I believe I'll go into town and check on my other patients. Which is what I did during my absence." He pulled on his coat and scarf and gloves and yanked his derby down on his head until his ears bent. "I trust my medical instruments and supplies will be safe here until my return?"

"You won't be needing them to check on your other patients?" Mary Alice knew the other patients could be located at the bottom of a whiskey bottle at the Palace Saloon. The doctor's reputation as a drunk was well known. He yanked the door wide open, shooting a blast of cold air into the house before he slammed it shut again.

Mary Alice threw more logs on the fire and, when she straightened up, she found Kam Le had returned to the music room.

"You didn't bring another poultice, did you?"

"No, Missus. But I should."

"Help me with the children."

She asked one of Walter's men, Mr. Boysie, to come inside and sit with Mr. Sheldon in case he awakened and said something useful in the search for Rose.

She chased the other men out of the kitchen, and she and Kam Le heated pots of water and filled the big copper washtub, keeping it as close to the woodstove as they could so the children would be warm. They bathed each one, washing their hair with eggs to get the tangles out, then dressed them in Rose's childhood flannel nightgowns and settled them at the table. The children ate a hot supper while their hair dried, and Mary Alice combed Sarah's into braids just as she used to do, years ago, with Rose.

Kam Le took the children upstairs to tuck them into bed, and Mary Alice checked on Mr. Sheldon.

"He's been waking up, ma'am," Boysie said, offering her the chair. "I been givin' him the whiskey the doc left but it don't seem to help for long."

"Thank you, Mr. Boysie."

Perspiration covered Mr. Sheldon's face and neck, and every few seconds his hands twitched. Soon he would be in terrible pain.

"Kimo," she called out. "Please go to Whiskey Row to find the doctor."

"That doctor is good for nothing."

"Kimo!"

She heard him go out and slam the door. Mr. Sheldon was watching her with eyes so icy blue, they belied the heat of the fever raging behind them.

"Would you like some whiskey?" But Mr. Boysie had evidently emptied the doctor's bottle, whether into the patient or himself she wasn't sure. She got a bottle from a chest of drawers by the window. She held it to his lips and let him swallow a few times. "They say whiskey is the best treatment for snake bite."

There was so much she wanted to ask, but his eyes closed. By the time Kimo returned with the doctor, Mr. Sheldon was half awake, mumbling incoherently, trying to push the covers away, crying out if anybody touched him.

The doctor, reeking of alcohol, pushed past her to the bedside. "He needs more whiskey."

"We've been giving him whiskey all afternoon! He can't drink any more."

"We could do an enema—"

"Dear God. If that's all you can suggest, I give you leave to go home."

"I know what you're thinking. I'll not have that Chink touching him! Good lord, woman, have you lost your mind?" He opened his medical case. "Get me more light."

Mary Alice brought a lamp from the dresser and turned up the wick. The doctor rolled up Mr. Sheldon's sleeve and tied a cloth above his elbow. "See if you can hold his arm still, please."

She sat on the edge of the bed and took Mr. Sheldon's hand. She patted his arm. "Try to be still, Mr. Sheldon." He squeezed her hand. Pain shot through her joints but she bore it. It was nothing compared to what this man was suffering.

The doctor filled a syringe from a vial he took from his case. He held the needle up, flicking it with his finger. A small air bubble floated to the top, and he pushed the plunger until drops formed at the tip of the long needle. "Keep him still now. I want to get this into a vein."

Mary Alice held on tight, watching as the doctor stuck the needle into the man's arm and pushed the plunger. He waited a few seconds, then pulled the syringe out and dropped it into his case. Within seconds Mr. Sheldon's death grip on her hand loosened. He seemed to be sleeping.

"Morphine," the doctor said. "It should last until I come back." He untied the strip of cloth and stood. "I'm going home to have my supper." He saw Kam Le in the doorway. "God damn it, keep that Celestial away from him."

Mary Alice sat by the bed and watched Mr. Sheldon sleep, watched him breathe, willed him to stay alive so they'd be able to find Rose. She wondered about the children's parents—the little girl had said they were dead—and how the children had come to be in Hellgate. Then her thoughts turned to Walter, searching for Rose. He'd been gone all day. The men he'd left to keep the army from stealing Mr. Sheldon were in the kitchen, probably sleeping with their heads on the table by now.

A voice came from the kitchen and she jumped. They were awake after all. She'd been on edge all day, fearing a visit from Lieutenant Schiffman, waiting for Walter to show up with news or with Rose, listening to Mr. Sheldon's anguished groans. Her niece was alive, but that didn't mean she was safe. Mary Alice had the fleeting thought, not for the first time, that death might be the best alternative for Rose, but she knew her niece's strengths. Whatever she had endured, she would overcome.

It would all be over soon.

Another voice came from the kitchen. The woodstove creaked open and then clanged shut. The smell of fresh coffee filled the house.

Mr. Sheldon remained quiet. She left him, picked up a bottle from her bedroom, and went upstairs to check on the children, sleeping in a guest room. She pulled the quilts up over their shoulders.

She knelt by their bed, watched them in the candlelight coming from the dresser, wondered about Rose, then wished Walter would come home. She uncorked her whiskey bottle. After a while she rested her head on the covers, just for a moment. A sound in the hallway jolted her, and she realized she must have slept.

Kam Le spoke from the doorway. "Mr. Sheldon is awake."

Mary Alice, stiff from kneeling, held onto the banister and hobbled downstairs into the music room. The injection had worn off. The doctor had not returned. She thought about sending for him, but he'd be passed out by now in some saloon.

Mr. Sheldon's leg appeared swollen from the foot all the way up to his hip; she could see the outline of it through the sheet. It hurt to watch him; she had known pain in her life but nothing so unrelenting.

She helped him rise up enough to take a few swallows of whiskey. He fell back onto the pillow, clutching the bottle in a shaking hand.

She had so many questions. This man lay in a soft bed, warm, cared for, no matter how miserable he was at present. But if it were true that Rose chose to stay behind, Mary Alice wanted to know why. He shouldn't have left her in that place, no matter what Rose had decided.

His gaze followed her hand as she unclasped the doctor's case, following the bottle of morphine as she placed it on the table and the needle next to it. "Is this what you want?" she asked. He nodded, his eyes still on the vial.

She tied the strip of cloth around his arm as she had seen the doctor do it. She leaned closer. "First you must tell me how you could leave my Rose behind in that place."

Startled, he looked up at her. In a voice barely audible, he said, "I tried to make her leave."

She filled the syringe, held it up, flicked it, watched the air bubble rise to the top, then squeezed the plunger as the doctor had done. A few precious drops clung to the needle's tip.

"You *tried*?"

He moaned, taking time to gather enough strength to speak.

"She wouldn't leave. The other women." He banged a fist into the mattress. "We have a plan . . . she had to stay . . . the plan—"

"You had a plan? That required you to leave and Rose to stay?" Mary Alice lowered the needle, acting as if she would drop it into the case. "Why should I believe you? A criminal from Hellgate."

His eyes begged for the morphine. His need for it brought strength to his voice. "You know me!"

"I've never seen you before in my life. I don't associate with—"

"My pa. He worked for Mr. LaBelle. Years ago. Elbert—"

"*Elbert* Sheldon? You're his son?" That's why he looked familiar. She remembered Elbert's son. Her sister, Leila, always spoke highly of young Harry and his musical talent. "Oh, what a terrible shame. You had such potential and look how you ended up."

"Oh, God."

His expression of pained frustration evoked a sense of shame in Mary Alice. The man was helpless, probably dying. And she was taunting him. She inserted the needle into his arm and slowly pushed the plunger. Within seconds Mr. Sheldon's breath eased. His eyelids fluttered. He sighed as she pulled the needle from his arm.

"Elbert was a good man. A hard worker. I don't know how his son would end up at such a horrible place, but I hope you at least looked after Rose and kept her safe."

He whispered, "She is unharmed."

Unharmed. The word had hardly any weight when spoken, just a puff of air, but it was dense with meaning.

"That stuff is bad," Kam Le said over Mary Alice's shoulder. "It won't make him better."

"You're right. We need him well enough to tell us how to get to Rose. That doctor is a useless drunk. Do what you can."

"Thank you, Missus. I must go to town to get medicine."

Mary Alice stared at the syringe still in her hand. What a look of relief, almost bliss, had appeared on the man's face. She placed the needle and vial of morphine in the medicine case, and went into the kitchen.

One of the men slept with his face resting on the table. A strand of drool hung from his mouth and pooled beside his cheek. She spoke to the other two, whose eyes drooped, but at least they were awake. "I need one of you to accompany Kam Le to Chinatown. No funny business! She has some items to acquire and then come straight back. Understood?"

"Yes, ma'am," Mr. Boysie said.

Mary Alice returned to the music room. Mr. Sheldon lay still as death, his face serene. The gaping medicine case sat by the chair next to the bed. Someone could easily help himself to those vials.

Staccato thoughts arose in a swirl of nervous anxiety. Walter needed her. A sick man in the music room. Soon—she prayed it was true—her Rose would be coming home. She would need her Aunt Mary Alice's care and comfort. So many people needed her. So many people depended upon her. Who would take care of those children if Kam Le was nursing this man? But she was just a sick old lady. She had pains of her own.

She went to close the medical case and put it away somewhere safe. Mr. Sheldon lay deep in his drugged, heavy sleep. There was no need for her to sit by him; Kam Le would be back soon enough.

Later, in her room, through a gossamer fog, Walter's voice floated down the hall. He spoke with the men in the kitchen. Strange voices replied. Mary Alice sank into her pillows, and the syringe fell from her slack hand to the carpet.

CHAPTER TWENTY-FOUR

Mary Alice sipped her laudanum-laced tea and thought, *another day of this nightmare*. Sun streaming through the sheer panels at her bedroom window augured a pleasant autumn day, but she felt no joy. For days now, that man lay suffering in the music room, keeping the house mired in a miasma of impending death. Kam Le's pungent potions had simmered in the kitchen. The acrid smells of bleach and lye soap rose from boiling kettles of sheets, bandages, and nightclothes. The stench of the sick room, hushed voices, groans from the patient, and worried faces—just like those last horrible months of Joseph's lingering illness.

This morning, Walter skipped breakfast and remained ensconced in a chair next to the sickbed, drinking coffee and smoking cigars, waiting for those moments when Mr. Sheldon opened his eyes. Then Walter would pepper the man with questions until those eyes closed again, leaving Walter frustrated and anxious. Mr. Sheldon was going to have to get up out of that bed and *show* Walter how to get to Hellgate, if it even existed other than in the minds of a delirious man and two small children.

The children. Always lurking on the edges—frail waifs, easily startled. Mary Alice could understand their attachment to the man who had carried them from that awful place to safety at such great cost to himself. Sarah had told them enough about the escape for them all to imagine that long, black tunnel, its floor writhing with deadly serpents.

Mary Alice wondered if each time the children caught a glimpse of Mr. Sheldon's leg, they realized that could have happened to them. Whenever they heard the sick man moan, the children reached for each other's hands and the girl clutched that shabby doll closer to her chest. Kam Le tended the patient, so Mary Alice tried to befriend the children and take care of them. She fed them, washed them up, offered to read to them, cajoled them to go outside and take in the fresh air. She even sent Kimo into the attic to retrieve a trunk with doll clothes from Rose's childhood and offered a whole new wardrobe for Mrs. Coppage. But all the children wanted to do was huddle together near Mr. Sheldon. This morning she'd left them there and returned to her own room.

A gentle knock at the door interrupted her thoughts. She sat up, swung her legs off the bed, and slipped the bottle of laudanum into the bedside table. "Come in."

Walter opened the door a crack and peeked in, as if afraid of what he might see. At the sight of her sitting up in her dressing robe, smoothing her neatly braided hair, he smiled and pushed the door open. "Kam Le said you were resting." He kissed her on the cheek before lowering his bulky frame onto the chair between the window and her dressing table. He hesitated halfway down. "It will hold?"

She gave a small laugh. "Yes, Joseph often sat right there while I brushed my hair." She raised a handkerchief to her eyes.

"My dear, why are you crying?"

"It's nothing. Oh, it's just that man has brought back such awful memories. Joseph suffered so at the end."

"I'm sorry." Walter rested his elbow on the arm of the chair and stroked his mustache. "I didn't think. I should have had Harry brought to the doctor's office."

"Good God, no. He'd be dead by now for sure."

"Mr. Sheldon does seem to be improving under Kam Le's

care. I think he will pull through."

"Has he been able to speak to you?"

Walter nodded. "A little. It seems Rose stayed behind as part of a plan they had worked out. To save all the women and children being held captive. But he can't tell me much. He seems determined that the army will help. I haven't the heart to tell him that's not going to happen."

"Rose is so brave. I wish she were not."

Walter's small smile was rueful. "I wish we could find the place, or this tunnel they all speak of. But when I told Harry of our search, he became agitated. He says we'll endanger the captives."

"Perhaps you should leave him alone and let him gain strength."

"Perhaps."

"Are you going out today to search?"

"I think not. Lieutenant Schiffman's troops effectively trampled away any sign from where we found them, so we can't follow their tracks. And we've covered all the ground around Thumb Butte. We need Mr. Sheldon to show us the tunnel."

"It is so frustrating!"

"Indeed. Do you think the entire hideout could be underground?"

Mary Alice eyed the drawer in the bedside table. She didn't feel like getting into another speculative conversation, but it didn't look like Walter would be taking his leave quickly. "Walter, I do need my medicine."

"Of course. I'll get you a glass of water." He heaved himself up from the chair.

"No need." She opened the drawer, pulled out the bottle with shaking hands, uncorked it and took a swig, then dabbed at her mouth with her handkerchief. "And there's no need to look so concerned. It's medicine, not whiskey."

Walter put his large hand on her shoulder and squeezed lightly. "I can't help but be worried. You've run yourself ragged looking after those children, and now I realize how hard it has been for you, having Harry here in the house in his condition. Isn't it Friday?"

"Yes, why?"

"I think you should get dressed and go to your ladies' meeting. 'Twould do you good to get out in the fresh air and spend some time with your friend, Mrs. Pumfrey."

Mary Alice pushed him away. She pretended to brush lint from her robe. "I don't know. That Mrs. Schiffman will be there."

"Just stay away from her. Don't speak with her."

"Surely her husband told her what I did."

To her surprise, Walter laughed heartily. "Well, I would think that would make her wary of you, rather than the other way around!"

Mary Alice had to smile. "I'll think about it." She put the laudanum in the drawer. "You weren't at breakfast this morning. Go get yourself some biscuits. We left some in a pan close to the stove so they'll be warm. I'll be along shortly."

"Thank you. I am a little hungry."

He must have been hungry, because his hand was already on the doorknob. "Kam Le's been so attentive to Mr. Sheldon, and here you are making sure I eat. The two of you are always thinking of others first."

Such unwarranted admiration embarrassed and shamed her. And despite Walter's mirth over her slapping the lieutenant, the thought of being face-to-face with his wife, that snobbish piece of baggage, made Mary Alice anxious. She worried that Mrs. Schiffman had told the other officers' wives about the confrontation, as if they didn't have enough to gossip about. Then she had the horrible thought that Lieutenant Schiffman might accompany his wife to the meeting. What if he intended to press charges against her? She went to her dressing table and took out the bottle of whiskey, raising it to her lips. Only three small swallows emptied it.

She thought of the morphine, of that pleasant rush of relief the needle provided. But she needed to be sparing in its use and only indulged in the evenings. It helped her sleep.

The doctor had returned on Wednesday morning and thrown a conniption fit when he discovered the Celestial heathen had been caring for his patient. He announced with great drama that he would no longer treat the man under any circumstance and that, when Mr. Sheldon died, it would be on their heads. He'd retrieved his medicine case and stormed out. She wished she'd taken more vials when she'd had the chance, but one and the needle would have to do.

At least Mr. Sheldon was better. His periods of being lucid, although short, came more often, and he was in less pain. He seemed, at times, to be sleeping peacefully rather than unconscious. Whatever his condition, it appeared more restful. It was probably just as well that most of the time he was not awake, though, because one look at his leg would have given him a seizure. While the swelling had noticeably retreated, skin was sloughing off around the area where the snake's fang had penetrated. Thank God for Kam Le who, always unperturbed, kept the ugly area covered with a poultice of some ancient Chinese concoction. She cut off the dead skin and put on fresh compresses. So far she had staved off any infection. Whenever Mr. Sheldon awoke, she made him drink a potion she had brewed and tried to keep Walter away from him.

"My patient needs rest," she would say.

Yes, it was good that Kam Le's attentions were successful because the doctor would not be returning with more precious vials of morphine. Mary Alice doubted the doctor would even notice the missing syringe and vial, which she had secreted in her vanity drawer.

Leaving the empty whiskey bottle on the vanity, she took out one of her nicer skirts and bodices to dress for the meeting, all the while thinking about the bottle secreted in a kitchen cupboard, but she wasn't sure how much was in it—she had been pouring it into her breakfast coffee and not paying attention to how much. Had she run out of whiskey?

After dressing, she grabbed her knitting bag and put a ball of yarn and two needles in it. She stopped in the kitchen and asked Kimo to run to the livery and hire a buggy and driver for her. Alone, she retrieved the last bottle of whiskey and finished off the few ounces it held.

She found Walter settled in the chair by the bed in the music room, eating his biscuits and drinking coffee. The children sat side-by-side on the floor under the window, watching Kam Le change the dressing on Mr. Sheldon's leg. Mr. Sheldon's sunken cheeks seemed to have some color to them. She tapped Walter's shoulder and told him she had decided to go to the meeting. He followed her into the hallway.

"I'll get a buggy and drive you."

"No need. I already sent Kimo to the livery for a carriage and a driver. I know you want to stay by Mr. Sheldon's side. He looks improved."

"Yes, thank the good Lord."

Mary Alice thought of the agony Mr. Sheldon had been in under the doctor's care. "And Kam Le."

"Let me get that for you." Walter took the knitting bag from her with one hand and helped her with her cape. She put on her hat and was pulling on her gloves when he said, "I'm surprised you're taking knitting with you. Is this to keep your hands busy? So you don't slap Mrs. Schiffman?"

She pretended to punch his arm and laughed, perhaps a little too loudly. Mr. Sheldon stirred in his bed and Kam Le shot her a look. Mary Alice put her hand over her mouth and spoke from between her fingers. "I hadn't that in mind. I just thought sometimes the meetings are a little boring."

"I always imagined that would be the case, though it surprises me to hear you say so."

He held the door and they went out on the porch. A driver from the livery turned the buggy at the corner onto Marina Street and pulled up in front of the steps. Kimo jumped down, and Walter helped Mary Alice up to the seat.

"Don't stab her with a knitting needle!" Walter called as they drove away.

The driver reined to a stop at the Prescott Free Academy.

"Now you be here in two hours," she said. "Don't forget your assignment!"

"Yes, ma'am." He tucked the knitting bag between his boots and let her climb down on her own. "Don't you worry."

Well, no need to worry! No, not worried about anything. She wasn't even embarrassed when she tripped over the threshold going into the meeting, but laughed, quite a cheery laugh, instead.

Alvenia rushed to her side. "Mary Alice, are you all right?" She sniffed a couple of times.

"What are you doing? Get your nose out of my face."

"Oh, I'm sorry. Is that a new cologne you're wearing?" She directed Mary Alice to a table at the back of the room. "Sit here and rest, dear. I'll get you some tea."

"I don't need to rest. What is wrong with you? I have things to tell you!"

But Alvenia was off to the front of the room, piling sandwiches and desserts on a tray and pouring tea, and all the while Mrs. Schiffman directed dirty looks toward Mary Alice from her customary spot at the front table. Were there more looks than usual? Mary Alice smiled and nodded, and Mrs. Schiffman huffed and turned away.

Alvenia returned with a tray piled high, and Mary Alice had to admit the food looked good. She'd had no appetite since yesterday, attributing it to nerves.

She thought wistfully of the syringe hidden in the vanity drawer. She knew what she had done was disgraceful. She was not a dope fiend, but she was acting like one. Her rheumatism wasn't even bothering her lately. She just wanted some peace, wanted to attain that alluring look of bliss the needle had brought to Mr. Sheldon's face. But Kam Le had been right. It didn't make him better. The drug had worn off within hours leaving him suffering again. As was she.

Laudanum and alcohol sent her into a hazy world devoid of problems or responsibilities, but her muddled thoughts still returned to the relief that needle had brought, no matter how short-lived. She wondered if morphine were available in China-town.

"You seem distracted." Alvenia filled a plate with food from the tray and slid it in front of her. "Mary Alice! I think you should eat something."

"Mrs. Pumfrey, did I tell you we have a house guest?"

"No, dear. A relative?"

"An escapee. From Hellgate," Mary Alice whispered, almost falling off her chair as she leaned closer.

It took her a long time to tell the story, because Alvenia kept shushing her, as were other ladies in the group. "We are trying to listen to Mrs. Schiffman," the annoyed faces said. Who would want to listen to that harpy—still ranting about the story papers being a bad influence? Didn't they cover that topic last week? Why not move on to organizing a temperance union? But the effects of the morning's laudanum and whiskey consumption lingered, and Mary Alice realized it might not be in her best interests to close down all the saloons. She stopped talking and gave that some thought.

She jumped when Alvenia touched her arm and realized she must have dozed off in her chair.

"Mary Alice, dear, let me get you some more tea."

The meeting was over and the usual groups had gathered, standing around the refreshment table or over by the window, their heads together, whispering and gossiping. Of course, there were looks aimed her way. She lifted her chin and pretended not to notice.

When Alvenia returned with more food and another hot cup of tea, Mary Alice continued her conversation as if she had not fallen asleep, but no longer whispered. "Yes, that's right," she said loudly. "Walter knows where Hellgate is. He's going to bring all those criminals to justice. It seems the place is located not far outside of Prescott! Within walking distance." She noted with satisfaction that the cluster of army wives now looked her way, and she raised her voice even more. "In all this time, the United States Army has not been able to discover that horrible den of murderers and kidnappers. Right under our noses the whole time! But Walter will be bringing them all to justice within a few days. Mark my words!"

Alvenia pushed the plate of desserts toward her, encouraging her to eat, but she wasn't through talking. "And my precious Rose will be rescued and returned to me!" At this she stared at Mrs. Schiffman, who was not wearing her brooch—the one made from Rose's pendant—but only her natural look of haughty disdain. "Yes, that's right. Walter told me there is a plan to invade the Hellgate complex." She rose from her chair for emphasis. "They shall release the hostages held there and bring the evildoers to justice. Before our next meeting, God willing!"

"Now, now, Mrs. Bradford. Please don't excite yourself." Alvenia patted her arm with increasing force and then pulled hard, trying to get her to sit down.

Mary Alice didn't mind being directed to her chair because, truth be told, she was beginning to feel a little queasy and light-headed, and a horrific headache was blossoming behind her eyes.

"Mrs. Pumfrey, would you be a dear and look out the window to see if my carriage has returned yet?"

Alvenia did so, then helped Mary Alice down the stairs, and the driver gave her a hand up onto the buggy seat. "Your knittin' bag is by my feet, ma'am," he said, and winked.

"Just take me home, please."

The buggy lurched. Alvenia disappeared from sight, replaced by a whirring street and a blur of buildings until they reached the house. The driver stopped and set the brake. "You'd best wait, ma'am, and let me help you. You ain't lookin' too good." He jumped to the street and helped her down, then went back for the knitting bag.

"Thank you. I can manage from here." She gave him a generous tip. She held the bag tight against her chest to keep the bottles from clinking as she went inside.

Walter called a greeting from the music room when he heard her in the hallway.

"I'm under the weather, Walter. I'm going to lie down." She heard his chair scrape the floor. "No, no," she called out. "Stay with Mr. Sheldon. I'll be fine." She had Kimo take the bag to her room and summoned Kam Le to help her undress. In her nightgown and house robe, she stretched out on the bed, clutching the bottle she had opened as soon as she'd reached her room.

"There is no need to mention my drinking to anyone. I need it for my nerves, but Walter worries about it. He has enough worries so we will be silent about this. Do you understand?"

Kam Le spread an afghan over Mary Alice's legs. "The children are having supper in the kitchen," she said.

"How is Mr. Sheldon?"

Kam Le shook her head and waved her hand, as she often did when trying to find words. But the waving hand made Mary Alice dizzy. "Please stop that. Just tell me, is he ever going to be able to get out of that bed and take Walter to Hellgate?"

Kam Le found some words, but they were lost in a soft, amber cloud that carried Mary Alice to a dream of her niece as a young child, walking in sunshine in the yard, bending to smell the roses.

CHAPTER TWENTY-FIVE

Rays from the gibbous moon outlined the perimeter of the tent's dirt floor. Its creeping light served only to increase the darkness inside Rose, who awaited with dread a moon soon to be full and all that would mean to her and the captive women and children. Another sleepless night beckoned, filled with fear slicing through her mind, tightening her stomach, and amplifying the noise from the ceaseless nightly party at Mason's house.

She had never felt so alone.

Abandoned.

Her father—dead. Harry—gone. Arthur—where?

She'd trusted Harry. She'd given the children to him. That was five days ago. Why hadn't he come back unless all three lay dead in the tunnel, their bodies rotting under those slithering snakes? Or maybe Caleb was right. Perhaps she had misjudged Harry, swayed by the sweet memories of a six-year-old, and he had sold the children and run off somewhere.

She curled into a ball. Her head ached. At some point, Caleb came in and lay beside her. His arm went over her waist and she shoved it roughly away.

"Don't touch me."

He grunted and turned his back to her. Eventually sleep found her.

Rose awoke to Mason's voice coming from the stockade. She threw the blankets aside and crawled out to see what was going on. The cluster of women on the far side, near the gate, blocked her view of Mason. She sought the higher ground near the jakes, and now could see Mason, red-faced, brandishing his shillelagh at the women.

"Bring me that white-haired *cailín beag*," he roared.

But the women only crowded closer together.

Mason's voice rose with exasperation. "The little girl! Bring her to me!"

The women reached for each other but neither spoke nor cowered. Rose admired their defiance at the same time she feared for them. Mason shoved them aside until he uncovered five children huddled together. Two boys and three girls, Jonathan's age or younger, held up little hands as if to ward off blows, crying. Mason held his arms away from his sides, ready to block any woman who came near. He stood over the children, then turned and faced the women. No longer yelling, he spoke in a low voice.

"Where is the wee lass with the long yellow tresses?"

He lunged like a snake at the nearest woman, pulled her close, and grabbed a handful of her hair, turning her head until she faced the children, and Rose saw her face. The woman was Evelyn Duval, the city marshal's wife! "All of you are darkhaired. What the fuck is the problem here! If there be no suitable women, I want the *cailín*." He jerked the woman's head and she cried out.

"Where is she?" His roar drowned out the woman's whimpering. He gave her arm a vicious twist. Rose felt the cracking in her own arm as Mason pulled Mrs. Duval's shoulder asunder and tossed her to the ground where she lay unconscious.

A man came out of the jakes, letting the door slam behind him. He stood next to Rose and buttoned his trousers while he watched the activity in the stockade. The man spoke with an Irish brogue, although not as pronounced as Mason's. "Fuckin' crazy, he is." He walked away, tucking in his shirt and pulling up his braces.

Mason grabbed another woman. He braced her neck with his shillelagh, put a hand on her head, and snapped her spine. Her body dropped to the ground like a doll. A child shrieked. "Mama! Mama!"

Rose stumbled backwards until she leaned against the outhouse wall. Was he going to kill them all?

A woman yelled, "We ain't seen her! Not for days. We heard she died, her and the boy. Right after their ma passed."

Mason turned his head toward the ditch. The vultures had taken flight at the commotion and circled above. Mason raised his eyes to them, put his hands on his hips, and tapped a foot while he watched them swoop and glide. Then he went to the woman who had spoken up and put an arm around her shoulders. She shrank from his touch, crossing her arms across her chest and turning her face away from him.

"Now, now. I know that was hard for you, to give me such bad news. But I thank you for being forthcoming and helpful." He patted her cheek and let her go, then left the stockade, head hanging.

Rose stumbled down the hill. By the time she reached her tent, two guards had picked up the women and carried them out of the stockade to the end of the ditch where it pooled near the jakes. They tossed the women in. The whomp whomp whomp of wings followed the heavy splash as vultures landed to flap and mill around the pool's edge. They jostled each other, wings raised and spread. A splash turned their blood-colored heads and their dead, black eyes toward a hand that emerged where the ditch flowed into the pool. Mrs. Duval pulled herself up the slimy bank. She stood wobbling for a moment, covered in dark slime. When she saw Rose running toward her, a hopeful look spread across her face. "Miss LaBelle!" she cried and lifted her arm, but with a sudden jolt flew backward into the ditch, leaving a spray of bloody dust hanging in the air. The rifle shot echoed through the compound, and the vultures rushed to where the woman lay partially exposed at the pool's edge. Their hideous hisses and grunts mixed with the children's screaming, and Mason returned to yell at the guard.

"There was no need for shooting! You could have easily just knocked her back in with the stock." He grabbed the man's rifle and demonstrated. Mason walked away, mumbling to himself about incompetent hired hands, while the guard crawled out of the ditch, shrieking and swinging at the vultures attacking his head and shoulders.

Rose ran for the tent and rummaged through the supplies until she found a bottle of brandy. She pulled the cork with her teeth and drank until the hard knot in her stomach eased just a little, then she crawled to the pallet and buried herself under the blankets, where she stayed for the rest of the day, drinking herself back to oblivion any time she happened to awaken.

The next morning she awoke later than usual. Alone in the tent, she pulled herself out of the blankets, her dry mouth tasting like a dead animal had spent the night in it, head throbbing. She dressed in the nice clothes and headed over to the house.

No more than ten yards from the tent, Eddie appeared at her side, eyes glassy and hands twitching. He tried to put an arm around her but she shoved him away.

"Don't be so high and mighty. You ain't nothin' but one of McCabe's whores."

"You smell like a jake."

His beady eyes turned hard. He grabbed her, glancing toward the guards at the house and then at her. "And you smell like a whore."

"What's the matter? Run out of your supply of little bottles?"

He pulled back as if to hit her, but stopped himself, then stood there twitching and sniffing. "I lost my money in a card game. I need money to buy more." He snatched at her reticule but she was faster.

"All I have to do is scream and those guards will—"

"You don't have to tell me what the fucking guards will do." He stepped away from her. "Where's your beau?"

She walked away from him. He fell in beside her.

"Where is he? Caleb will give me some money."

"No, he won't."

"I gotta leave then. I gotta get some." He scratched his head, then his beard. "I don't wanna miss the trip to Mexico. Fuck."

"Just go on. Go on and find some poor soul to rob or kill. Why not?"

"Oh, now, Rosie Pink. I don't wanna rob or kill you. I wanna do something else to you."

He disappeared as she approached the house.

Once inside, memories of Auntie's home in Prescott haunted her. The sun streaming in the sparkling windows, the smell of lemon oil, the Chinese woman, Mrs. Ling, an older version of Kam Le. Rose hung her hat and shawl on the coatrack by the door and went to the piano.

She expected Mason to appear at any moment and question her about not showing up to practice yesterday. She prepared several excuses, depending on how angry he seemed, but he never entered the music room. She could hear voices coming from the dining room and assumed he was busy with a visitor.

She played the songs she and Harry had selected, sang along softly, and wondered, with a sick feeling, what had happened to him. She worried about the children, and she missed her father. Every moment, every second, she fought despair and terror that threatened to suck her down and swallow her.

She practiced until Mrs. Ling brought in the tray. Another

large steak. There'd been a lot of meat lately. Mason must not want to herd the few resident cows down to Mexico. She took her time eating. Mrs. Ling had brought a piece of cake and Rose went to pour more tea but the pot was empty. She was on her way to the kitchen when Horace rushed past to answer a knock at the door.

Harry?

A uniformed man strode into the foyer, military boots banging across the polished hardwood floor. She recognized the man as Lieutenant Schiffman from the fort. The army had found Hellgate! She would be rescued!

He had not noticed her leaning against the hallway wall. He'd turned the other way, and she realized he was not on a rescue mission. He pulled a rolled paper from inside his uniform coat, then went into the dining room.

Mason's voice welcomed the officer and the lieutenant answered, but she couldn't discern the words. She started toward the kitchen, but Mason's low voice and the note of annoyance in it stopped her.

"I've told you not to come here, to send a messenger with the map. Somebody not in a fuckin' uniform."

She moved closer to the dining room.

"Things have gone wrong. It was necessary that I come myself."

Mason banged the table. Dishes rattled.

"What is it then!"

"My wife overheard a conversation at the—"

"Get to the point, God damn it. My dinner is getting cold."

"There are men in Prescott who claim to know that Hellgate is nearby. It seems there is a plan afoot to conduct a raid. Capture all the criminals. And free the prisoners, of course."

Mason laughed. "I've got you guardin' the area, and the city marshal knows we'll kill the hostages should anyone venture near."

Marshal Duval would not know his wife was no longer among the hostages. The image of her covered in black slime, smiling at her, turned Rose's stomach.

"These men seem determined," the lieutenant said. "I don't know if I can keep them at bay."

"And what makes you say these things?"

"There was a man found outside of town. He spoke the word 'Hellgate.' I heard him say it. He was afoot, so they know this place is close by and are searching for it. They are not lawmen; they're civilians."

"Civilians! Jesus Christ. Who is this man they found?"

"I don't know. They took him away. He seemed badly injured. I expect he's dead by now."

Mrs. Ling came from the kitchen. She spoke Chinese and gestured that Rose should return to the parlor. Rose lifted the lid to show the pot was empty. The woman smiled and bowed and took the pot to the kitchen. Rose pressed a hand against the wall to steady herself and inched closer to the dining room door.

"We'll double the guards around the rim, just in case. But 'tis your job to keep them away. Ain't that what I've been payin' you for all these years, for Christ's sake? About time you earned your keep." Mason called to Horace to bring another bottle of wine. "A shame, truly a shame. If they are indeed determined to unearth my lovely hamlet, I guess that's the end of it. I'll have to find another place when I come back in the spring. Just when I have this house the way I want it."

The talk went to other topics, army schedules in the southern portion of the territory, the weather on the coast of Sonora. Rose backed down the hallway and into the parlor. She grabbed her hat and shawl and gloves and hurried to the door. As she was pulling it shut, Mrs. Ling returned with a fresh pot of tea and stood in the middle of the room, looking around.

Rose ran to the tent. The man they spoke of had to be Harry. She tried to puzzle out what she had heard, but no matter how she looked at it, one thing was evident. Lieutenant Schiffman worked for Mason.

The army would not be coming.

Civilians could attempt a raid, but Mason had been warned. He'd be ready, watching.

And Harry was dead.

She wrapped her arms around her waist and rocked back and forth. Schiffman had mentioned no children. Where were they? Had they made it through the tunnel? Wherever they were, this world or the next, they were in a better place. At least she could take comfort in knowing little Sarah hadn't been in the stockade when Mason went looking for another yellow-haired victim.

CHAPTER TWENTY-SIX

Rose found that even in the most hellish of circumstances, one's daily activities could still fall into a routine. This morning she looked forward to practice, knowing the concentration required would help chase thoughts away, thoughts that trampled through her mind like a herd of javelinas, running in circles, ripping out a bite here and a bite there, each ragged hole revealing an ugly memory.

Her father dying in the bloody road by the stage.

Vultures circling the bellowing Sam.

The whore's face in the privy hole.

Patience screaming in agony.

Caleb, lifting his hand from his dead sister's face.

Harry, glancing at her over his shoulder before he disappeared into the darkness of that tunnel with the frail, trusting children hanging on to him.

Nightmare thoughts.

Sometimes her thoughts turned to Arthur, and a seething rage replaced the terror. She'd been an idiot to fancy him a savior. The very reasons she had agreed to marry him—he was respectable, he was a town person, he worked in an office and made money, his hands were always clean—made it unlikely he would be riding to her rescue. She wasn't even sure he knew how to ride! He always drove a buggy, and for that he wore gloves so his hands wouldn't be callused. She looked at her own scratched and chapped hands, stared at the sun-freckled skin, made a fist, dug her ragged nails into her palms, and knocked on Mason's door.

Mason himself opened it.

"I wasn't expectin' you today, darlin'. 'Tis the Sabbath." He pulled her inside and put her arm through his. "But now you're here, so you will join us!" He escorted her into the dining room and sat her at the lace-covered table filled with platters of bacon, steak, and fried eggs. Molded balls of butter, floral designs imprinted, surrounded a plate of biscuits. Mason poured her coffee from a steaming pot on the sideboard and brought her a pitcher of cream and a sugar bowl.

The two dark-haired whores—wearing proper dresses—sat among the men at the table, who hunched over overflowing plates, forking food into their mouths. None of them looked at her except Dodger, who gave a nod and winked.

Mason had seated her between himself and Caleb. He beamed his approval as she ate everything on her plate. He reached for platters and refilled her plate himself. "I like a lass with a good appetite!" His laugh was low and suggestive, and he patted her cheek. The leering men at the table appraised her through lowered eyelids.

When the meal was over, Mason said, "Dearest Rose, 'twould be lovely if you would do us the honor of singin' a hymn."

They all followed her into the parlor and took seats or leaned against the wall. Mason settled on the sofa between the two whores, put his feet up on the table, and lit a cigar.

She sat at the piano and thought of Harry playing in the hall in Stanton. She believed now he *had* been trying to rescue her. And that now he had given his life trying to save those children.

She played the opening chords of a hymn she'd sung many a Sunday at summer church services in Prescott.

> *Before Jehovah's awesome throne,*
> *All nations, bow with sacred joy;*

Know that the Lord is God alone;
He can create, and he destroy—
He can create, and he destroy . . .

God and Mason, she thought.

Mason made the sign of the cross and leaped to his feet when she struck the final note. He lifted her from the piano bench and swung her around. "Ah, darlin'! You have the voice of an angel." He released her and walked her to the door. "Go and rest yourself today. But be sure to come for practice tomorrow! Time is growin' short." He lifted her hand and pressed his lips to it before he opened the door.

At the tent she changed into her regular clothes. The morning's clouds lifted, and she sat in the sunlight, relishing the sun's warmth on her skin and the warmth whiskey brought to her stomach.

Children's voices came from the stockade. Praying. The women must be holding some kind of Sunday service. Soon enough, the time for praying would be over, as if prayers were of any use at all.

They didn't need prayers. What they needed was a way out.

Rose sat for a long time, listening to the women in the stockade, then got up and went over to the fence. One of the women looked her way, and she waved at her to come closer.

The woman hesitated. She glanced toward the guard at the stockade gate, then at Rose. She shook her head. Rose waved more insistently. The woman looked again toward the guard, whispered something to another prisoner standing next to her, and the two of them approached.

The first woman came close to the fence. The other stood with her back to them and kept an eye on the guard, who was leaning on the gate, his face turned to the sun.

"What's your name?" Rose asked.

"Bertha."

Rose whispered, "I know a way out of here."

Bertha, who already looked nervous, narrowed her eyes and took a small step back.

"No, don't run. And don't speak. There is a way out. I know of somebody who made it out of here." She didn't mention he died soon after. "Please listen. We can save those children."

She explained about the tunnel, warning her about the snakes but assuring her it was safe. "Just stay on the ledge above them."

"What happens when we get to the other side?"

"My aunt lives in Prescott. I'll give you directions to her house. But only mothers with children go first, half tonight, half tomorrow night. Any more would draw attention."

"What about the rest of us?"

"Mason is having a big party. Tuesday night. All the men will be at the house. Fewer eyes to see you go. Just pile rocks or logs or anything beneath the blankets. They won't realize you're gone until it's too late."

"I don't know. It sounds dangerous." She started to walk away. "We should just wait for someone to rescue us."

"No! Listen to me. In three days McCabe is moving everybody and everything here to Mexico. He'll sell you into slavery."

Bertha's eyes glazed as the alternatives sank in. "Oh, God."

"Please! Keep your voice down." They both glanced at the gate. The guard was talking to someone and had not heard Bertha's outburst. "Remember, just half of the children and their mothers tonight. I'll wait for you at the entrance. Go just beyond the last jake and then head straight uphill. Can you see that bush?" Rose was afraid to point. "Halfway up. There's a small rocky ridge and a bush. There's an opening behind it. Do you see it?" Bertha nodded. "I'll be in the opening. I'll shake the bush a little when you get close. Wait until it's full dark and go slowly and quietly."

"What of yourself?" Bertha asked.

"We have to get the children out of here first. If I can go with the rest of you the night of the party, I will."

Bertha nodded. She and the other woman held a whispered conference. They seemed agitated. Bertha took the other woman's arm, then whispered urgently in her ear. But the woman broke free and bolted for the fence. Somehow she managed to climb up and throw herself over it. She fell to the ground on the other side, bringing part of the fence with her, then got up and ran for the jakes. Two other women, seeing nothing but the open fence and a chance for freedom, ran after her.

Rose screamed. "No! Go back! Go back!"

At the jakes, the first woman stopped, hopping back and forth, shading her eyes and looking up the hill as the other two ran toward her.

Terrified, Rose realized that if they ran to the entrance now, they would reveal it to the guards. She'd have to stop them somehow. But then the woman's head exploded, spattering blood against the wall of the outhouse as a rifle shot rang out. Two more shots, followed by screams from the stockade. Rose looked up to see three rim guards lever their rifles, eject spent shells, and turn to resume their watch on the outer slope.

Men came to carry the three women to the ditch. "Goddamn buzzards are eatin' better than we are these days," one of them said.

Rose stared at Bertha, still standing by herself in the middle of the stockade. That dazed look had left her eyes. She nodded at Rose and turned away. She would be at the tunnel that night.

Rose crawled back to her pile of blankets and her whiskey bottle.

Mason hadn't even come out to yell about the noise this time. He allowed no piano practice on the Sabbath, but murdering women received special dispensation.

★ ★ ★ ★ ★

That night, at the tunnel entrance, Rose strained to hear the rustle of a bush or the scrape of a shoe. She hoped Bertha was able to convince the mothers to make the attempt, but feared the afternoon's killings might have frightened them too much.

A thick cloud cover obscured the moon's light. She couldn't see the rim or the sentries. Any sound from above made her jump, as she half expected the guards to notice the women coming, turn their guns downward, and start shooting. Then she realized that if she could barely see her hand, held inches from her face, the guards probably wouldn't see the women.

She hoped they could find their way.

She put her cold hands in her coat pockets and calmed her nerves by touching the candles and matches. It had turned so cold she doubted the snakes were moving at all. A thought of Harry and the children unleashed an ache deep inside that was becoming familiar. She could no longer tell the difference between sadness, fear, or despair. Just a gut-wrenching twisted discomfort that doubled her over.

Rustling leaves nearby shook her from her pain.

"Over here," she whispered. She shook the bush gently, and the scraping sounds grew closer. She lay on the ledge and thrust her arm out, waving around until someone brushed against it and let out a stifled cry. "This way. Climb up. Be quiet."

She helped Bertha up onto the ledge and pushed her toward the entrance to the tunnel. "Wait there. Don't go in yet." Two more women and three children followed. She waited until they were all inside the mouth of the tunnel, then gave each mother a candle and matches.

"Stay near the wall. Don't light the candles right away. Go about a hundred yards until you're far enough in the light won't reach the entrance. You'll feel the tunnel going downhill. Just keep going, no matter how long it seems to take. You'll come to a bend near the end. Go straight east toward the town and keep going. I think you'll see lights coming from Prescott."

"You *think*?" The woman's voice quivered. "Bertha, I thought you said she knew the way!"

"I do! I saw light coming through from the other end. I'm just not sure of the distances. But Prescott is a big city. Just head east and you'll see lights. I'm sure of it." She handed one of them a paper with Auntie's address.

She was glad she couldn't see their faces. They were afraid, but they would go. Bertha had convinced them it was the only way to save their children, so they shuffled into the tunnel in a line, all holding hands.

Rose and Bertha waited for a long time before crawling downhill to the jakes. By the time they reached the bottom, the clouds had thinned. Bertha wriggled through the shoddy repairs in the fence and joined the other women, and Rose returned to the tent.

Candlelight glowed through the canvas.

"Where were you?" Caleb asked as soon as she came through the flap. He sat cross-legged on the blankets.

"I was at the jakes, not that it's any of your business."

"Are you sick? Nobody stays at the jakes that long."

"Yes. I'm sick. Sick of Mad Mason McCabe. Sick of this place. Sick of you."

He ran a hand through his hair. "It won't be much longer."

"I know that. The day after tomorrow is his big party, and the next day we'll all be off to Mexico. I'll be sold to the highest bidder."

"I won't let that happen."

"You can't stop it." She pulled the pile of blankets away from him, and sat down. "He killed three more women today. That's five. Plus the poor woman who killed herself. What's that—twenty percent of his profits?"

Caleb stepped over her. "Go to sleep. I'm going up to the house."

She blew out the candle and burrowed into the blankets. She made the sign of the cross and tried to pray. She couldn't remember the words.

CHAPTER TWENTY-SEVEN

The next night, the weather took a turn and warmed up. The snakes might be more active. She stuffed the candles and matches in her pockets and grabbed the mallet. If need be, they could use it to kill a snake, a thought that made her shudder.

Standing in the deeper darkness behind the first privy, she looked up. There had been more guards than usual since the lieutenant's visit, but all faced away from the compound, watching down the hillsides. Expecting a possible assault. There was no guard at the stockade gate. Or maybe he was sitting down—sleeping, drunk? A few men talked outside the mercantile and lingered at the corrals; nobody near the jakes. The usual sounds came from Mason's nightly party at the house. She crossed to where the ground sloped upward, found the heaviest concentration of brush, and started crawling. There was practically a trail worn into the hillside. The thought gave her a fright—what if the guards found it—then she realized it wouldn't matter after tonight.

In the clear night, the brightness of the moon rising over the ridge made her nervous. It would cast shadows, make any movement obvious. Staying under the bushes as much as possible, she hunched down and ran through the open spaces. She reached the tunnel, panting from the exertion but without raising any alarms.

Waiting for Bertha and the women, she sat on the ledge with knees pulled up, arms wrapped around her legs, while her breath gradually slowed. A movement below caught her eye. A woman crept across open ground between two bushes. Rose hoped the higher angle of the guards kept them from seeing the shadow following the woman across the hillside.

Soon Bertha crawled onto the ledge and, behind her, two little girls. Bertha and Rose guided them into the mouth of the tunnel. Another woman crawled in behind them. "She's this one's mother," Bertha said, putting a hand on one little girl's head. "The other child has none."

Rose winced, remembering a snapping neck and a child's cry as a woman's body thudded to the ground.

The mother, fragile looking and emaciated, huddled in the opening. The children clung to her. Rose whispered to Bertha, "She can't go through with two children on her own. You'll have to go with her."

Bertha shook her head. "I have to lead the rest of the women out tomorrow night."

"No, you must go tonight. Look at her. She can't manage two children by herself. They're too little. She'll have to hold their hands. Who will hold the candle?"

"Margaret can," the woman said, pulling her daughter close. "Let Bertha stay and help the others." The woman gave a candle to the little girl, not more than five years old from the looks of her.

"No," Rose said. "Bertha will go."

"Then let me go and tell one of them how to find the tunnel. Otherwise . . ."

As risky as it would be to let Bertha go back to the stockade and then return, Rose knew she could be condemning the remaining women to death otherwise. She told Bertha to hurry and settled down to wait with the mother and two children.

While the woman jumped at every sound, pulling the children close, Rose found herself feeling buoyant. Sarah and Jonathan were safe, at least she felt in her heart that they were. There had been no alarms sounded over the previous night's escapees. They were probably drinking hot tea and enjoying a good meal at Auntie's at this very moment.

Soon Bertha, this woman, and two more children would be on their way to safety.

Rose had thumbed her nose at McCabe. She smiled in the darkness.

Bushes rattled, scraping sounds were heard, and then Bertha pulled herself into the opening. "It is taken care of. Let us go. Now."

Rose gave the women the supplies she'd brought. "Stay along the wall. Don't look down into the bottom of the tunnel. Just keep going. When you come out the other end, remember! There are guards at the top of the hill. You have to be quiet, and you have to be careful."

She hugged each of them. "Go now. When you get out, don't trust any soldiers or anybody in a uniform. Do you hear me? Get into town and go to Mary Alice Bradford." She slipped them the address. "She'll look after you until I get there."

They moved into the darkness. Rose watched them go with a great sense of hope. All the children were safe now, and tomorrow night the remaining women would be gone and she'd be free to run for it. After she sang, she'd have her chance. McCabe would lose interest in her once her performance was over.

The women lit their candles, and the slight glow from far within the tunnel eased her mind even more. She watched until it faded away. When she turned to leave, her hand touched the mallet on the ground where she'd laid it. She thought about going after the women, but she had no candle. And Caleb might be waiting for her again. She'd been gone a long time. Best to get back.

She eased herself off the ledge. A few yards down the hillside, her foot caught on something. She kicked against the sudden pressure on her shoe and tried to crawl away, but rough hands grabbed her legs and dragged her into the bushes. A man fell on top of her, lay heavy on her chest, his hand clamped over her mouth. She kicked and squirmed until she heard a familiar snickering laugh. Eddie.

"I saw what you did," he whispered, in a singsong, taunting voice. "Women go in there. Poof! They're gone! I'll bet McCabe would love to know what his little virgin songbird has been up to."

She clawed at his hand. He released her only to punch her in the head. An explosion of pain brought a wave of darkness. Her eyes rolled but she fought unconsciousness. Twisting away, she dug in her toes, and grabbed for the nearest branch. She managed to pull away and began to slide down the hill. Eddie caught her hair and she was on her back again. He straddled her thighs and held her arms down.

"You wanna scream?" Eddie's teeth gleamed in the moonlight, wet lips shining. "You go right ahead. Bring on the guards, so I can point out your little escape route."

"You're the one who should be afraid of the guards."

She yanked an arm free and swung at him, hard, but he ducked. A blow to her ribs pushed the air from her lungs. While she struggled for breath, he sat on her feet and pushed up her skirt. She threw fists of dirt at him as she felt her pantaloons ripped and pulled open.

Rocks, branches, and cactus spines scraped her bare skin. She fought him, punching and thrashing.

Something hard poked her belly. Rough, hairy legs pressed onto hers. Fingers pushed between her thighs but she squeezed together with all the strength she had. He punched her legs and her stomach but she would not let him open her.

With a snarl, he fell on her again and wrapped his hands

around her throat. She scratched and pulled at them, desperate to relieve the pressure, the crushing pain—this time she couldn't fight off the darkness. When she came to, Eddie loomed above her. Her knees were on his shoulders, her feet on his back. Cold wind blasted her exposed skin. A line of spittle hung from his gaping mouth. When he saw her eyes were open, he smiled. The hardness of him pressed against her.

She gasped at the first stab of searing pain. He rammed into her again and again. She could only whimper with each thrust. His hands were on either side of her as he rose up, arching his back, his eyes closed, breathing hard.

Terror and humiliation gave way to sudden rage.

He fell onto her, and she managed to move her leg closer, working her hand into her shoe. Then the knife was in her palm. A tight grip on the hilt.

She stuck it into his neck.

She twisted the blade, and blood surged around the knife's shaft. Eddie's eyes bulged. He opened his mouth, but no sound came. She pulled the knife loose and blood shot sideways, spattering the bushes. Eddie pressed a hand to his neck. Blood filled his mouth and poured out onto her naked stomach, steam rising from it. She dug her elbows into the rocky ground and pulled herself out from under him. He toppled onto his side, gagged and retched, and blew blood onto the dirt.

Her hand touched the mallet. As if it held some kind of electrical charge that ignited more of her violent frenzy, she raised it above her head and swung. Her own gasping breath hid the sound of Eddie's skull cracking. She dropped the mallet, leaned close, and whispered. "Hope it was worth it, *doing me.*"

She tried to wipe the blood off her stomach and thighs with her petticoat, gave up, pulled her ripped drawers together, and her skirt as best she could. She pushed her knife back into her shoe and remembered how Eddie had smirked as the buzzards circled above Sam. Tomorrow the buzzards would rip the smirking lips off his face. She crawled around, searching for the mallet until approaching footsteps and voices stopped her. She froze, hoping they wouldn't see her.

"Told ya I heard something from over this way."

Rough hands slid under her armpits and hoisted her to her feet.

"Well, well, what do we have here?"

"It's McCabe's songstress. Don't look so *darrrrlin'* right now."

The man holding her up asked, "Ain't that Eddie?"

"Jesus." The other one spat into the dirt. "He never did learn to leave the women alone." He pushed Eddie's crushed head with his boot, revealing the black wound in his neck. He turned to her. "Where's the knife?"

In answer to her silence, they put their hands on her, pressing against her bodice, shoving fingers into her waist, lifting her skirts, running their callused hands up her legs. She kicked, twisted, threw back her head, and screamed. They laughed and shoved her to the ground, pulled off her shoes, and shook the knife out.

They half carried, half dragged her, down the hill. As they approached the house, she tried to break free and screamed again. Their grip on her only tightened.

Mason himself opened the door, already yelling. "What the fuck is—" His eyes widened with surprise when he saw her.

"Take her to the parlor."

They dragged her in. The room full of guests ran for the door when McCabe bellowed, "Get out! Get out!" Only the two guards remained in the room, holding Rose between them, and Caleb, who stood before the hearth with his back to her. He watched the flames, hands resting on the mantel.

"Look at me!" she screamed at him. "You brought me here!

Look at me, you son of a bitch!"

But Caleb did not turn from the fire.

"What happened?" Mason's mouth was an ugly frown.

"It was that Eddie, sir. We found 'em on the hill above the jakes." The guard's voice had a nervous quaver in it.

"And why did you not stop him?" Mason's face reddened as his rage built.

"They was quiet. We wasn't sure what was happening, just heard a—"

"I could hear her screaming here in the house!"

Both guards flinched. "Sir, she didn't start screamin' until after we got there."

Mason's face was suddenly inches from her own. "What did he do to you?" His thick fingers pressed into her cheeks. "Has he ruined ye? *Tell me!*" The smell of whiskey and cigars gusted into her face.

Dazed and sick and pained as she was, she knew full well her value to Mason, and it wasn't just her singing voice. "He punched me." The words rasped in her throat. She glanced at the men who had dragged her to the house. They did not lift their eyes.

Mason gave her a shake. He pushed his face closer to hers. "Punched, ye say. Beat you to a pulp is more like it. And that is *all* he did?"

When she didn't answer, he looked from her to the two men, then started to open his mouth to speak.

"Yes!" she cried. "That's *all* he did. Punched and choked and hit me. Isn't that *enough*?"

He backed away. "Aye, that be enough. You men, bring me this Eddie."

"He's dead, Mr. McCabe."

He nodded, patches of red remaining on his cheeks as his normal color returned. " 'Tis well you killed him. Good boys. I want to see the body."

She almost fell when the guards released her arms, and she grabbed the arm of a chair to steady herself. Mason followed the guards out of the house. Caleb brought a crocheted afghan from the back of one of the parlor chairs and draped it over her shoulders.

She pulled the afghan close. Chills overcame her; her knees buckled. Caleb helped her over to the fireplace and sat her on a footstool. "I'll be right back." He returned in minutes to crouch beside her and handed her a cup of hot tea laced with brandy.

In a low voice, he asked, "What were you doing up on that hill? What have you been up to?"

Flames leaped around the logs, cracking and popping.

"That's where Eddie dragged me. He grabbed me when I came out of the jake."

"You're lying. You were going to run for it."

She kept her head down, staring at the flames.

"Don't do it. Stay with me." The afghan slipped down and he pulled it up over her shoulders. She pulled her arms in tight against her body to keep from flinching at his touch. "I'll keep you safe. I have so far, haven't I?"

"Do I look like I was kept safe?"

"This is what happens when you try to leave. When you don't stay close to me."

Just then Mason returned, smiling as he opened the door. "Those boys did a fine job with that Eddie." He pushed the door shut and saw the teacup and saucer in her lap. "Ah, darlin', I see you're in good hands, as always. This fine man is watchin' out for you." He looked at Caleb. "I hope you put something strong in that tea!"

"Of course."

Mason slapped Caleb's back. "*Mac an cheana.* Me favorite son!" He looked down at Rose. "Well, I'll have the bed made up in the big room upstairs. She'll stay there from now on, where she'll be safe."

"No!" Rose tried to stand, but Caleb's hand on her shoulder held her down.

"Now, now, 'twill be okay. I didn't mean you were to share it with me. I have many rooms up there that I use. The big one will be yours alone, and I believe you'll find it comfortable."

Find comfort in the bed where Patience had been tortured? She drained the teacup. "Thank you for your kindness. But I'd just as soon stay in the tent. Caleb will look after me."

"Not after what happened tonight. No more tent for you."

The teacup fell from her hands and shattered on the hearth. She hated Caleb's smug look. Her hands shook. She raised her voice. "I don't want—"

Mrs. Ling ran in with a rag and started cleaning up the spilled tea and broken china.

"Now, now," Mason said. "Let's not be havin' a conniption. You'll find the accommodations here quite pleasant." He watched her for a moment, smiling, and then he sighed, as if he had endured a troubling night. "I'll be goin' to bed now. Tomorrow's a busy day." He kissed Rose's cheek. "I'll order a hot bath for you. Mrs. Ling will see to your comfort." He turned to the woman standing with the broken china in her hand. "Come see me while the water is being heated. I have some extra treats in mind for the lass." To Rose, he said, "We shall have you all shipshape for the surprise I have in store for you."

"Surprise?"

Mason laughed. "Don't look so concerned. A pleasant surprise, at least I hope you'll agree. But not until tomorrow night."

As soon as Mason left, Caleb held the afghan around her shoulders and helped her up. In the center of the stool was a dark stain. He placed his boot against the stool and quietly pushed it under the nearby chair. "I'm sorry," he whispered. "It was my fault."

She pushed him away, clutched the afghan across her chest, and followed Mrs. Ling upstairs.

Seated at the vanity, Rose stared at the bed where Patience had been tortured. She closed her eyes and tried to imagine she was in her room at Auntie's. Servants went up and down the stairs, carrying buckets of steaming water. Soon the scent of lavender wafted through the room.

Mrs. Ling returned, carrying several jars that she placed by the tub.

"Come, Miss. I help you into tub."

Rose sank into the steaming water and gave herself over to Mrs. Ling's ministrations.

CHAPTER TWENTY-EIGHT

Mary Alice sat by the bed and listened to Mr. Sheldon's steady breathing. She welcomed the warmth of the fireplace as the first rays of sunlight touched the top of Thumb Butte. Another dawn. The last few days had been far too troubling. First a half-dead man and two orphans, and now two bedraggled women and their children had found their way to her doorstep. The walking scarecrows had been ushered to an upstairs bedroom where, after baths and clean nightclothes and food, they huddled together and remained terrified.

And this man in the bed. When he first arrived, she'd been sure he would die. But now Kam Le said he had slept comfortably most of the night. Even in the dimly lit room, Mary Alice could see that some color had returned to his gaunt face. As she watched, he stirred and his eyes opened.

"Good morning, Mr. Sheldon."

His brows raised, and he looked toward her with confusion in his eyes.

"I'm Mary Alice, Mrs. Bradford, Rose's aunt."

He ran a hand over sunken eyes. "You're the auntie?"

"Yes. Don't you remember—?"

"Where are the children?" He pushed himself up on his elbows.

"No, no, don't try to move," Mary Alice said, but he tried to sit up. "Kam Le!" she yelled.

Kam Le rushed into the room. Mr. Sheldon calmed a bit

214

when she promised in her quiet voice that the children were there and they were fine. "Lie down. I will get them." She returned with the two sleepy children, in their nightclothes, rubbing their eyes. At the sight of them, Mr. Sheldon fell back and closed his eyes.

Mary Alice settled into her chair while Kam Le took the children away, but the moment of peace was short-lived.

"What day is it?" Mr. Sheldon asked.

"Tuesday."

"I told her I'd return on Tuesday."

"Mr. Sheldon, you've been here for a week."

Even as she spoke, he threw off the covers and swung his legs over the edge of the bed. Kam Le's compresses fell from beneath Walter's stained nightshirt. He stood, took one step, then grabbed the nightstand, pulling it to the floor as he fell. Tea tray and dishes went flying, and the man hit the floor hard. Mary Alice jumped from her chair, but before she could even call for help Kimo and Walter appeared. They'd heard the racket and came running from the kitchen. Each grabbed an arm and were able to raise Mr. Sheldon to his feet. He tried to push them away but the moment he put weight on the swollen leg, down he went again, this time with a loud cry of pain when he hit the floor.

Walter and Kimo lifted him into the bed. "God damn it, man!" Walter said. He pushed the man down and pulled up the sheet. "Do you want to lose that leg?"

Kam Le hovered in the doorway, a horrified expression on her face. Mary Alice could imagine her thoughts: all her hard work for naught because this crazed man wouldn't stay in bed. When Walter and Kimo moved out of the way, Kam Le rushed in, checking for damage and speaking agitated Chinese. Mary Alice guessed the word she spoke most vehemently and often— *sha*—must be Chinese for stupid.

"I have to get back," Mr. Sheldon said. "I told Rose I'd return the next day."

"You're not going anywhere right now," Walter said. "Let Kam Le tend to you. Then you and I can talk about what to do next."

Mary Alice knew Walter was just as desperate to get to Rose as Mr. Sheldon. She half expected him to pull the ailing man from his sickbed, now that he was fully awake, drag him to that meadow and make him point out the tunnel entrance, show which mountain held his daughter's fate. Instead he placed a hand on Mr. Sheldon's arm. "I'm going to have my breakfast and suggest you do the same. You need to build your strength."

Mr. Sheldon let Kam Le feed him some oatmeal, then he drank the medicine she provided. He slept the rest of the morning while Sarah and Mrs. Coppage sat on the floor beside Mary Alice's chair, content to keep an eye on the sleeping patient and watch Kam Le change bandages and poultices. Mary Alice, also content, sat by the fire and sipped her whiskey-laced tea.

By midday, Mr. Sheldon awakened. Kam Le plumped the pillows and allowed her patient to sit up. "I will make you some soup. Do not move."

A short time later Sarah walked into the room with excruciating slowness, her eyes riveted on the steaming bowl on the tray she carried. A bit of liquid sloshed, and the child's pace slowed even more. Finally, Sarah slid the tray carefully onto the table beside the bed. She shook open a large linen napkin and laid it across Mr. Sheldon's chest.

"Gotta keep the nightshirt clean," she said.

"What's in that bowl?" Mr. Sheldon eyed it with suspicion.

Mary Alice wondered if he realized his hair was sticking up on top like a burro's mane, and she lifted her hand to stifle a giggle.

"Don't matter what's in it," Sarah said. "You have to eat, Mr.

Sheldon. Miss Kam Le says you must, if you're to get better."

"Just put the tray on my lap. I can feed myself."

"No! Miss Kam Le said I was to do this. You just lay there. She said you're to take it easy!"

"Get on with it, then."

She dipped a spoonful, blew on it until it cooled, and brought the spoon to his mouth.

"Not bad. Chicken?"

"I think she said it was rattlesnake."

Mr. Sheldon almost choked as he burst out laughing. The laughter startled Mary Alice, who had been lulled into a contented stupor by the heat of the fire, the warmth of the whiskey-laced tea, and the pretty picture of the little girl playing nurse.

Sarah shared his laughter, her smile turning her eyes into merry crescents. "Miss Kam Le says the Americans call it 'hair of dog.' Don't know what dogs has to do with rattlesnakes!" She peered into the bowl and swirled its contents with the spoon. "I don't see no dog hair."

She spooned up some more and Mr. Sheldon ate.

Mary Alice sipped her tea and thought how sweet a scene it was, the young girl caring for the man who had saved her life and her brother's. They were like soldiers after the war—bonded forever by the horrors they'd experienced together. Joseph had told her few stories about the war but, to the day he died, comrades who had served with him would come by to reminisce, almost fondly, of their hellish time together. Grown men could not forget what they had endured. That girl was no more than ten years old. How sad. But Mary Alice had enough whiskey in her to smooth the rough edges of those thoughts. Enough whiskey to conjure an image of her niece being waited on in the same way, safe in her bedroom upstairs. Perhaps soon.

"How come you keep squintin' like that?" Sarah asked.

The girl's voice made Mary Alice jump. She didn't know she'd been squinting. Then she realized the girl was talking to Mr. Sheldon.

"The light from the windows," he said.

"It's hurtin' your eyes?"

He nodded. "It's all right. When you're through making me eat, I can close them again."

The girl put down the bowl and left. She returned with another napkin, this one damp and smelling of Kam Le's herbal concoctions. "Here." The girl folded it carefully. "Close your eyes. Lean your head back just a little. Against them pillows."

He did as told, and she placed the compress over his eyes.

"Feels good," he said. "Thank you."

"Okay, now just open up. Wide."

Harry opened his mouth, obviously suppressing a smile. Sarah gave notice each time the spoon was approaching, and Mr. Sheldon opened wide. The girl carefully inserted the spoon, dabbing Mr. Sheldon's face when necessary, so intent on her mission she didn't speak again until the bowl was empty. She removed the napkin from Mr. Sheldon's chest, folding it neatly and placing it on the tray.

"Does your eyes still hurt?"

"Just a little. Can you leave the cloth on?"

"I'm sorry you're so sick. It's Jonathan's fault, I know. And mine too."

His arm rested atop the covers and he beckoned her with his fingers. "Come here."

She stood by the edge of the bed and put her hand in his.

"We just had an accident, that's all. It wasn't anybody's fault."

"Yes, it was! It was Jona—"

"No, it was an accident. Listen. If someone had told me this would happen, I still would've taken you both away from there. I would've taken you no matter what."

"Mr. Sheldon, I sure hope there's some piece of you somewhere that don't hurt."

"Well, my stomach feels fine right now, since you filled it up."

A little smile played across Sarah's lips. When Mr. Sheldon fell asleep, she pulled her hand away and took the tray to the kitchen.

Sleeping. He sleeps peacefully while my Rose still suffers. The women upstairs did not speak of what went on while held captive. The women upstairs were terrorized. Even though they'd escaped that place called Hellgate, they didn't behave like normal people. They refused to come downstairs, they started at every sound, wept at every kindness, clung to their children as if they would be spirited away if let go.

What kind of nightmare place had they been in, that the effects continued so? And that was where Rose remained. Left behind by this man, no matter how noble he might have been in saving the children. Mary Alice poured more whiskey into her teacup and glared at the sleeping Mr. Sheldon. How would he ever show Walter the way to Hellgate? Her pleasant dream of Rose being cared for slipped away. Despair and panic gained a foothold in her mind; it would be best if she went to her room to try to fight them off. The bottle and teacup clinked together as she passed the bed, and Mr. Sheldon turned his head.

"I didn't mean to wake you."

"I wasn't asleep. I hear a clock chiming the hour. I hear it all the time."

"It's the clock on the courthouse. You can often hear it in this room. I'm sorry it's disturbing you."

"Each hour passing disturbs me."

She could see now that all his peaceful rest was anything but. Underneath the calm façade, he was seething with impatience. Her judgment and her anger subsided a bit.

"You won't be able to do it, Mr. Sheldon. You're too sick to even ride in a carriage to show Walter where the tunnel is. This plan you and Rose cooked up won't happen."

Walter had tried again that morning to get the escaped women to go with him, to show him where the tunnel was, but the women clutched their children and shook with fear. They'd become so hysterical, Walter had yelled for Kam Le to tend them. He'd left the house and still hadn't returned—no doubt he was out there looking for the tunnel. Or some other way to get into Hellgate. "Mr. LaBelle will find the place somehow. He and his men will attack."

"If they do, they'll be slaughtered, along with all the hostages."

"Please, Mr. Sheldon. Don't try to get up again!"

"Then you must listen to me." He told her of the plan Rose had conceived.

"Mr. Sheldon, you do not understand. The army will not help us!" She told him of their suspicions that Lieutenant Schiffman and the lawmen in the city were colluding with McCabe.

"Then instead of the army, it will be Mr. LaBelle and his men."

The plan was ill-conceived. The plan had too many things that could go wrong. But the worst of it was she could think of no other way to get Rose out of that place, despite the hopelessness and panic she felt. Despite certain defeat. "I pray Rose and Walter will somehow survive."

Mr. Sheldon pulled the cloth from his eyes. "I'll show him where the tunnel is." His pale blue eyes were clear and filled with determination. "And then I will go to Hellgate and get Rose. I will bring your niece to you."

She almost believed him. Almost.

"Thank you, Mr. Sheldon. Now I think we both need to get some rest."

His words followed her across the hallway. "Tomorrow. I'm going tomorrow."

When Walter came home, she repeated what she'd been told.

Walter said, "So that is the plan he was trying to tell me. Mary Alice, it could work!" He hurried to consult with Mr. Sheldon.

Mary Alice spent the evening keeping her doubts awash in whiskey. The morphine was long gone, and she hadn't yet worked up the courage to ask Kimo to get her more. She refused dinner, too drunk to walk to the dining room and too embarrassed to let Kam Le bring a tray. When darkness fell she stumbled to her bed, fell across it, and slept through to dawn.

Chapter Twenty-Nine

Rose stretched and threw off the soft cotton sheet and down-filled quilts. Although the room was dark, it felt like morning. Maybe the noises from the kitchen below had awakened her, or the smell of fresh coffee. She went to the window, lifted an edge of the curtain, and blinked at the bright sunlight. How late had she slept? She closed her eyes until they could adjust to the light.

She let the curtains fall and lit a lamp on the dresser. Mrs. Ling had laid out a plain outfit, skirt and bodice of sturdy cotton, a drab brown color, all draped across the easy chair near the window. She dressed and sat at the vanity. A woman with a bruised and swollen face, chopped hair, and despondent eyes stared at her from the mirror.

Someone knocked. A spiral of fear crawled up her back. "Who is it?"

The door opened a few inches. Caleb poked his head in. "Are you dressed?"

"Yes, come in."

He stepped a few feet into the room, then stopped.

"You look tired," she said. She picked up the brush, but Caleb came up behind her and grabbed her hand mid-stroke.

"You're hurting me. Stop it!" She tried to twist away from him but he held tight.

"Your hair."

"What about it? It's clean for once."

Caleb strode to the window and yanked the drapes wide open. Sunshine streamed into the room. In the flood of light, she looked at herself again and the brush fell from her hand.

All those potions and creams administered by Mrs. Ling last night during her bath . . .

Mrs. Ling had dyed her hair yellow.

It was so long before Caleb said anything else that when he did speak, Rose jumped.

"I just need that map."

He needed the map? The map was more important than this? He knew Mason only wanted yellow-haired women, and now he'd turned her into one. "Don't you know what this means?"

Caleb was at the dresser, pulling the drawers open.

"What are you doing? What if he comes in here?"

He moved on to the wardrobe, pulling doors and drawers open. He straightened up, looked around the room, and walked to the fireplace. On the mantel, in plain sight, lay the rolled-up map. He untied it and spread it out on the bed, studying it. Memorizing it, Rose thought.

"Now what?" she asked.

"Now I know where his hideout is. I don't need him to get there."

"So you can leave. Just go on to Mexico?"

"I told you, I won't leave you." He kept his eyes on the map.

"You left me last night. You left me alone up here. And tonight—you heard him—he has a *surprise* for me."

"He's the one who'll be surprised."

She laughed. "When? Oh, after he rapes me? After he tortures me? You do realize that's the very bed Harry and I found your sister—" Her words caught in her throat when she saw the stricken look on his face.

He rolled the map, tied it, and returned it to its place on the mantel. Then he walked out of the room. She hurried into the hallway after him, "Caleb! Wait!" But he was already down the stairs, his boots echoing in the hallway below.

She turned to return to the bedroom. The first door at the top of the stairs was open, and she looked inside. Just beyond the threshold a dark stain remained where the last yellow-haired woman had died. Now *she* was the yellow-haired woman.

Pistols, shotguns, rifles were piled everywhere; some of the rifles leaned against crates labeled "Warning" and "Explosives." She leaned across a wooden box pushed under the window and looked down on the compound. A row of wagons waited by the corral, some filled with crates, some to be loaded tomorrow. Horses milled in the corral.

No alarm had sounded over the missing women. Nobody, thank God, realized the children were gone, although she'd seen that missing children could be explained easily enough by pointing to the ditch.

She picked up a pistol and checked to make sure it was loaded. She closed the door quietly behind her and crossed the hall to Mason's bedroom.

Voices came from downstairs, Caleb's and Mason's. She hid the pistol in a drawer, under some of Mason's shirts. By the time she went downstairs the voices had grown loud. They didn't notice her standing in the doorway.

"You brought the *maighdean* for *me*. Why else? You know the rules. The women are mine."

"I brought her here because she had a talent I thought you'd appreciate. Not so you could fuck her."

"Aye. And the only reason *you* didn't fuck her? Because she be a virgin and would bring a good price in Mexico. I recall the conversation, even if you do not."

"You let me have her. You *told* me to keep her."

Mason turned his head and closed his eyes, as if seeking patience to deal with someone stupid. He spoke slowly, with an edge to his voice. "Because at the time, all the rooms here were full, if you be gettin' my drift."

"And now they're not. I wonder why."

Mason laughed. "We've had a few misfortunes."

They saw her in the doorway. Mason rushed over and made a show of bowing to her, raising her hand to his lips. "*Alainn. Tá sí go hálainn.* Beautiful. She is beautiful." His arm snaked around her waist and pulled her close. "Come and stand by the fire, darlin'. You're trembling from the cold."

He guided her to the hearth and prattled on about the night's party plans, stroking her hair. "The color suits you. This makes everything perfect. You see, after the entertainment tonight, I have something very special planned for ye."

At that, one side of Caleb's mouth curved up.

"I think I'll practice one more time if that's all right with you, Mason."

Mason beamed. "See? She understands all must be perfect tonight."

Rose rested her fingers on the keys until the final note of her last practice faded. She went to the coatrack by the door and bundled herself up in a heavy shawl, put on her hat and gloves, and picked up her reticule. Horace, lurking in the hallway, made his presence known as soon as she got near the door but when she turned toward the hall, he relaxed and let her pass by him to the dining room. Caleb and Mason were deep in conversation, going over paperwork, checking items off a list. They both looked up when she stopped in the doorway.

"Done with your practice?" Mason looked up, and his pleased smile disappeared. "Do you think you're goin' somewhere?" He scraped back his chair and stood. "Darlin', you're staying here now. There be no need to go out in the cold."

"I have a few things in the tent I'd like to take with me when we leave tomorrow."

Mason's face broke into a wide smile. "Why, of course, of course! Horace! Get one of the guards to accompany—"

"I'll go with her." Caleb got up and took her arm.

"Get on with you both, then. But be back in time to dress for supper. You'll be sittin' at my side tonight."

As they walked past the guards, Caleb's grip tightened until it hurt, until she hit him and pulled her arm away.

"You don't care about protecting me. You're just afraid I'll make a run for it."

When they were inside the tent, he said, "I'm doing everything I can to keep you safe."

"Protect your investment, you mean. You still think you can use me to bargain with Mason."

"Bargain for what? I've seen the map. I have what I want. Tonight I'll finish it and we'll be free."

"*You'll* be free!" She pointed to the pile of chains in the corner. "That's what you want for me. Admit it."

His gaze followed her finger. "You need, for once, to shut up." He backed away and disappeared through the tent flap. Too late, she realized he'd thought she was pointing at Patience's grave.

It didn't matter. Shackles or a grave—given a choice, she'd take the grave.

She dug through the piles of supplies and found the trousers and shirt she'd worn on her first escape attempt. As soon as she finished playing and singing tonight, these clothes would get her across the compound—she wouldn't stand out as she would if she were dressed in the finery McCabe provided. She'd hide the clothes, a candle, matches, and a canteen of water in the drawer where she'd hidden the pistol.

Caleb, waiting outside, yelled. "Hey, where've you been?" She heard him walking away.

She finished wrapping her bundle of supplies in a sheet and was about to leave when the flap opened. "I'm ready—"

Harry stood before her. He wiped sweat from his forehead even though she shivered in the cold breeze he'd allowed in. He came toward her but she backed away, a part of her still not believing it was actually him. Not a ghost, although as pale as one. Anger welled up within her. If he hadn't died, where had he been?

When the tightness in her throat eased, when she could speak, she asked, "Where are the children?"

"With your aunt. I came as soon as I could." He pulled a small bottle from within his coat and took a sip. The same kind of bottle Eddie had always been sucking at, held with the same tremor. Twitching the way Eddie did.

"I thought you were dead. You look like you spent the last week in the Chinatown opium dens."

"Jesus, Rose." He eased himself down onto a wooden crate, one leg stretched out. "Can you get me some water, please?" He rolled up his trouser leg, revealing a boot cut off at the ankle. As he painstakingly unwrapped a bandage from around his swollen leg, a stained cloth packet fell to the ground. Digging into his saddlebag, he pulled out a fresh one. "Please, some water. This needs to be damp."

She winced at the sight of the discolored leg, the seeping, gaping wound a few inches below his knee. "Snakebite," she whispered, and dropped the sheet-wrapped bundle. She rushed to get a canteen and pour water over the poultice for him, then placed it on the gash.

"Kam Le," he said. "She sent packets with me. I'm to replace them when they dry out." He took another deep swallow from the brown bottle. "Laudanum. Kam Le can only do so much."

She knelt beside him, took the bandages from him, and wrapped his leg. While she worked, she told him about the lieutenant and the pieces of conversation she had overheard. "I thought you were dead." She tied the bandage and rolled the pant leg down. "McCabe's been warned. They've been expecting an attack. They doubled the guards up on the rim."

Harry wiped sweat from his face. "And there's no way to warn your father—"

"My father!"

She sank to her knees and Harry pulled her to him.

"Papa is alive. Oh, Papa. What will he think of me . . . ?"

He lifted her face but she couldn't look at him. "What's wrong? You should be happy. Something has happened to you." He gently touched the swollen bruise on her cheek. "God damn it. I never should've left you here."

His eyes darkened as he took in the other scratches and cuts. "Who did this?"

"It doesn't matter. There are worse things to worry about."

"Worse than you being beaten?"

"Mason wants me for himself." She untied her bonnet and pulled it off so Harry could see what she had become. McCabe's woman. "I wish Caleb had killed him. I wish I had killed him. But it will all be over tonight."

"Did Caleb tell you he's going to kill McCabe tonight?"

"I don't know what Caleb will do. I know I won't let McCabe touch me. Either he'll be dead or I will. That's my new plan."

"No, it isn't. I told your father about your idea. I showed him where the tunnel is. It's going to happen as you hoped. Tonight. I just wish there was a way to warn them about the extra guards."

Harry actually thought the plan would work. He believed they had some control over what the outcome would be, but Rose could see things clearly. The lieutenant, forewarned, would stop her father before he got anywhere near Hellgate or the tunnel.

"No, you don't understand," she said. "It won't work.

Lieutenant Schiffman works for McCabe. He won't let any soldiers come."

"No," Harry said. "*You* don't understand—your father knows about Schiffman. He tried to arrest me so I wouldn't be able to tell your father about this place."

"My father can't come alone!"

"He has hired men. Listen to me—"

"I told the women about the tunnel. At least some of them will escape tonight, no matter what else happens. Now I need to get back. We can talk later."

She hurried across the compound with Caleb and Harry following. Her time in Hellgate was coming to an end. She'd escape tonight or she'd be murdered when Mason realized she was no longer the virgin he desired. Either way, tonight she would be free.

Above her scattered clouds cast soft pools of darkness on the surrounding slopes. Even the buzzards seemed graceful, soaring on outstretched wings, feathers splayed like fingers.

Beauty among the horror, she thought. Or did she now find horror to be beautiful?

She entered the house and was hanging up her cape and hat when Mason came into the parlor, smiling at Rose and hurrying to take the bundle from her arms. "Is this all?"

"It's all I'll need."

He called for Horace to put the items in her room upstairs. "You'll have all the finest things when we get to Mexico." Then he noticed Harry standing behind Caleb, and his smile turned to a scowl. "Well, look what the cat drug in. Where the hell've you been, leavin' the poor lass to accompany herself all these days?"

"Please leave him alone," Rose said. "You can see he's been ill, yet he came to play tonight. That's all that matters."

Mason's face softened. He patted her cheek. "If that's what

you desire. I'll not want anything other than perfect tonight, for the big surprise. If it makes it easier for you, then play he shall." He turned to Harry. "But keep your hands off the girl. Now get yourself into the kitchen and have some food and drink. You look like hell."

"Mason?" Rose asked. "May I bring him some clean clothes? We do want him to look presentable tonight."

"A wonderful idea!" Mason said, beaming. "You'll find suitable attire in my wardrobe. You go ahead and select what you think is best. The trousers may be a bit short for him but they'll do."

She hurried up the stairs and rummaged through Mason's clothes. She chose a pair of trousers and braces, a suitable shirt, in another drawer a collar and tie, a vest. She folded all the items, stopped into the room across the hall, and slid a loaded pistol into the middle of the clothes. She found Harry in the kitchen and placed the clothing carefully in his hands. She saw the knowing flicker in his eyes when he felt the weight of it before he put the bundle on the floor beside his chair.

CHAPTER THIRTY

The night of the full moon had arrived. Possibly her last night on earth, Rose thought, as she held back the draperies and looked out at the compound. Heavy clouds had moved in during the afternoon, bringing an early dusk and oppressive dampness. A few tents glowed with lamplight as the men got ready for the big soirée; otherwise all was blackness. There'd be no moon tonight. That meant less chance of the guards spotting the women as they made their way to the tunnel. On the other hand, Rose worried about their ability to find the entrance with no one to show the way.

Fat raindrops splatted against the window.

Mrs. Ling came in and helped her with her chemise, corset, corset cover, and petticoat. Then the older woman ran the brush through Rose's yellow hair, rouged her cheeks and lips, and powdered her face. Rose sat in her undergarments and studied the whore she saw in the mirror, bruises and swollen cheek showing through the garish make-up. Mrs. Ling went downstairs but would soon return to help her with her bustle and into the gown lying across the bed. The gown's low-cut bodice of midnight blue silk—same shade as her eyes—was lined with polished cotton and trimmed with delicate ivory lace and seed pearls. The ivory lace overskirt matched layers of ruffles that trailed down the gathered train.

Mrs. Ling knocked and slipped into the room along with men's voices, whores' laughter, and Mason's thunderous voice.

The merriment floated in from downstairs and filled the room until the door closed. Mrs. Ling stood by the bed, waiting.

Rose breathed deeply to calm her heartbeat while Mrs. Ling fastened all the hooks and eyes down the back of her bodice. The last time Rose wore such fine attire was at a ball in Tucson. She'd been on Arthur's arm. There would be no more balls, no marriage to Arthur, no respectable life she had planned to please her father and make him and Auntie proud of her.

Downstairs in the music room, Harry played Beethoven's Fourth. The music reached a crescendo as she started down the stairs. Mason leaned on the banister and watched her descend. Dressed in a dark suit, a red brocade vest, and cravat, he looked clean. Whiskers trimmed, hair combed back. He held out his hand to help her down the last few steps, then presented her with a jewelry box.

"Open it, darlin'. I think you will like it."

She opened the velvet box. In it lay diamond and sapphire ear bobs and a matching pendant on a gold chain.

"Here, let me help you." With his thick fingers, he inserted one of the ear bobs. His fingers brushed against her neck, and Rose stiffened at his touch. His cold eyes narrowed; one side of his mouth twitched.

"I'm sorry," she said. "I'm nervous about performing. It's made me tense."

He ran his finger down her cheek, then tapped the dangling ear bob, making it tinkle. "You've nothin' to be nervous about. You have a lovely voice." He inserted the other ear bob, then made her twirl around so he could fasten the gold chain.

She wanted to pull off the chain and throw it at him. She didn't want his garish jewelry. Stolen jewelry. She wanted her silver locket. She wanted the memory of her mother. She wanted her father.

Mason pulled her hand into the crook of his arm and swept

her down the hall and into the parlor. Men rushed to their feet, while the whores looked away, sullen expressions turned surly. Mason escorted her to the piano, then returned to mingle with his guests.

Harry made a show of arranging the sheet music while he spoke in a low voice. "Your father will be here tonight. I promise you that. Nothing will keep him away. And I will make sure you are delivered safely to him."

He sounded so sincere. He actually believed everything would be resolved and she'd be safely reunited with her family tonight. What if Lieutenant Schiffman had tricked her father into thinking the soldiers would help him? And at the last moment they'd turn on him and his men, haul them away to the fort and lock them up. Rose's mind was racing as she thought about the million ways their plans could go wrong.

Rain battered the windowpanes. Wind howled and gusted through the compound and blew down into the chimney, making the roaring fire sputter.

Mason came toward Rose and Harry. "Are you ready?"

"Yes," she said. "I think we should start with 'Mockingbird.' "

Harry shuffled the sheet music, then nodded.

Mason faced the audience and clapped to get their attention. "The entertainment is about to begin. Take your seats, please!" He settled himself on the sofa, glowing with pride as Rose sang that song and then several others, popular tunes the men would be familiar with. No hymns.

During the applause for the fourth song, Mason stood. "Let us have just one more song, and then Mr. Sheldon will play for us. Miss LaBelle will be going upstairs to prepare for the next event of the evening."

The front door flew open and a rush of cold, wet air pushed Lieutenant Schiffman into the room. Horace had to lean against the door to slam it shut again.

Mason hurried over, reaching for the officer's hand and pumping it, slapping him on the back, spraying water all over. "Just in time, just in time!" he shouted. The lieutenant took off his oilcloth slicker. Horace hung it on the coatrack, and a puddle quickly formed beneath it.

Rose steadied herself with a hand on the piano, stricken with terror at what would happen when the officer saw Harry. But Schiffman's eyes took in the scene, his gaze landing on Harry for just a second, and moved on. He had not recognized him as the man he'd tried to arrest. Harry looked up at her, his fingers playing idly across the keys, and his eyes softened. *All will be well*, they seemed to say.

He began the opening bars of what would be Rose's last song. Mason played host, arranging the serving of drinks and food to the lieutenant and the rest of the guests. Rose took a deep breath and, at a nod from Harry, began to sing.

> *Beautiful dreamer, wake unto me,*
> *Starlight and dewdrops are waiting for thee;*
> *Sounds of the rude world heard in the day,*
> *Lull'd by the moonlight, have all pass'd away!*
> *Beautiful dreamer . . . awake unto me.*

Yes, the sounds of the rude world would soon pass away. She glanced over at Caleb, at his usual blank expression, while Harry played the last few notes of the bridge. Then the second verse.

> *Beautiful dreamer, beam on my heart,*
> *E'en as the morn on the streamlet and sea;*
> *Then will all clouds of sorrow depart,*
> *Beautiful dreamer, awake unto me!*

She stepped forward, put her hand on Harry's shoulder, and felt the heat of his fever through his shirt. He looked up, glassy eyes flashing in the lamplight. She sang the closing bar with passion.

Beautiful dreamer, awake unto me.

The crowd burst into loud applause. Mason wiped away a tear. He leaped up from the sofa, pulled her into his arms, and spun her around. "Exquisite! 'Twas lovely!" He guided her to the hallway where Mrs. Ling waited. "Go on now. Mrs. Ling will take you upstairs and help you get ready."

"Get ready for what?"

Mason laughed. "Have you no idea? Well, get yourself upstairs and all will become clear."

She followed Mrs. Ling into the bedroom, which was awash with bright light from extra lamps and candles. There, spread across the bed, lay another gown, finer and more detailed than the one she wore. Made of exquisitely embroidered white silk, trimmed with the finest, most delicate lace and seed pearls. Silk roses appliquéd to the bodice matched those on the pleated, three-quarter sleeves and shoulder flounce. Beside it lay a white lace mantilla, long enough to serve as a train, and combs decorated with dried baby roses to secure it to her hair and hold a veil to cover her face.

Mason wanted to *marry* her? That's what he was so excited about? This was his surprise?

After Mrs. Ling helped her get dressed, Rose dismissed her and went to the window. Her reflection, her wedding dress, wavered on the rain-streaked panes. High winds scudded clouds to the west and the full moon burst forth, casting shimmering light on the soaked compound. Puddles reflected the huge white orb. Tents, fences, wagons—all sparkled, a diamond-encrusted fairyland.

In the stockade, though, the blankets had absorbed the rain into their darkness. No glinting light. No sparkle. Just black mounds. If all had gone well, those blankets covered only rocks, logs, piles of scraped-up dirt. Then a blanket shifted. Other blankets moved, plain to see in the bright moonlight. Something had gone wrong. *The women were still there!* They must have been afraid to try for the tunnel in the pitch-black night and the rain.

Rose let the draperies fall into place, shutting out the dismal image. She sat at the vanity. In the mirror she saw a face gone pale and shrouded in a white mantilla—a ghost.

There was a knock on the door. It swung open, and Mason and Caleb entered. Caleb stayed near the door, gently kicked it shut, and kept his eyes on Mason.

Her future husband came to stand behind her. "You look as lovely as I imagined. Pleased with the dress?"

She stared into the mirror through the gauzy lace covering her face. His thick hands hovered over her shoulders.

"You didn't ask me. You did not propose marriage to me."

He didn't seem to be listening, all his energy focused on the low-cut gown. He put a heavy hand on her shoulder and the other reached down and touched her breast. He stopped for just a second, bliss on his face now, as he leaned over her. "Ah, darlin'!" He clutched her breast and squeezed until she gasped. At the door, Caleb's long fingers rested on the sheathed knife at his waist.

Suddenly Mason understood what she had said. "Ask you?" he said loudly, continuing to squeeze, his leering face now peering into the mirror above her shoulder. "You have been *mine* since ye arrived. Why would I *ask* if you accept the *honor* of being my bride?" He let her go and straightened. "But if you insist."

With a heavy sigh and a condescending expression on his face, he knelt on one knee, took her hand, raised it to his lips, and looked into her eyes. "My precious *maighdean.* Please do me the honor of being my wife. Marry me tonight."

"No. I cannot."

He looked shocked, then his eyes narrowed. His hold on her hand became painful.

"There's no priest," she said, trying to pull free.

"Ah, I see." He patted her hand. "Well, 'tis true, there'll be no holy sacrament of matrimony. But you saw that I summoned the lieutenant from Fort Whipple. He will officiate at the ceremony. 'Twill be legal enough."

She pulled her hand away from him and let her head hang, while he continued to talk.

"We can find a proper priest and make our vows before God when we get to Mexico." His voice grew impatient. "If that be so important."

Caleb had stayed near the door, next to Mason's shillelagh, his expression unreadable. "And what is your part in all this?" Rose asked him.

"Why, he is to be my witness," Mason said. " 'Twas my great friendship with him that started me thinking. He's like a son to me, but that's not quite the same as a son of me own, now is it? 'Twas high time I had an heir."

He got up from his knee, pulled her up with him, and turned toward the door. "Come along now. The guests are waiting and I be eager—"

She felt the quick motion, heard the whoosh and the sharp crack as Caleb swung the shillelagh. Mason dropped to his knees, howling. Blood poured through hands held to his face. She jumped back, then jumped again when gunfire erupted outside, coming from the stockade.

Rose ripped the veil from her head as Mason seized her skirts and smeared them with his bloody hands even as Caleb dragged him away. She got to the window in time to see perimeter guards falling from their stations, some rolling down the cliff, some disappearing into the blackness beyond the edge. The mounds in the stockade tossed off their blankets. They rose to their feet, rifles in their hands, and headed for the house.

"They're coming!" She yelled over Mason's howling and the continuing gunfire. "We must go!"

"You go. I've got business here." Caleb held the shillelagh over Mason, who lay rolled into a ball at his feet.

She yanked open the drawer where she'd hidden the gun, then ran. She pulled the door open and almost fell into Harry's arms.

He held the pistol she'd given him. "Downstairs. Hurry."

Men pounded up the stairway, racing for the room storing their weapons. They yelled and jabbed with their elbows, trampling over anybody who fell beneath them. There were more men than had been at the party. They were coming in from the compound, mud dropping from their pounding boots and turning the carpet slick. Harry pushed through, shoving with the pistol to create an opening, hauling her along behind him.

They reached the landing. No more men going up. They were all crowded into that room, scuffling over the pistols and ammunition, arming themselves. Gunfire erupted within the room and was returned from outside.

In the deserted parlor, the lieutenant had pressed himself against a wall by a window, watching the invaders work their way toward the house. Horace's bloodied body propped the front door open. Two more men lay motionless on the porch.

The lieutenant shouted over the steady gunfire coming from outside. "Give her to me. She's our only hostage now." Harry pushed Rose behind him, and the lieutenant raised his pistol. "I said give her to me!"

Harry fired. The lieutenant's pistol fell to the floor. He slid down the wall and sat, blood flowing from a hole in his forehead.

Harry pulled her onto the porch. He guided her to the side of the house and pushed her ahead. "Run!"

The bright moon revealed chaos. Skirmishes near the corral. Outlaws trying to get to their horses to make a break for it. Bullets dug into the dirt below the porch, biting into the wall of the house. It was impossible to tell who was shooting at what. Rose ducked, panic rising, until Harry grabbed her arm and shouted in her ear. "We have to make a run for it. Head for the stockade."

He kicked out the porch banister and they jumped. They landed hard. Harry fell. Rose tried to help him up, but he waved her on. He struggled to his feet, caught up with her, and together they dove for the stockade gate. Harry tried to get up, but his leg gave out and he fell again.

Rose looked over the wooden slats, searching for a glimpse of her father. And Caleb—she had not seen him leave the house.

Deafening noise, blue smoke, and the smell of sulfur filled the air.

Then a flash burst from a second-floor window, followed by a loud crack and a low, percussive boom. Pressure against her ears smothered all sound. In the dreamlike silence, the roof of the house floated upwards. The second floor above the porch blew out. Flames filled the first-floor windows. Her hearing returned—pieces of the roof, the house, slammed to the ground, glittering shards of glass showered onto flaming men who clung to the porch roof or jumped. They crawled on the ground, screaming for help as they burned.

Rose ran toward the hellish image.

"Papa!" Again she fought against a tide of men. She held up her filthy white skirts and raced toward the flames. "Papa!" Bullets exploded in the dirt all around her. She tried to see through the dust and smoke as she grew closer to the smell of charred wood and burning flesh.

Something slammed into her leg, knocking her down. She

tried to get up but the leg, gone numb, would not move. Dragging herself toward the house, numbness gave way to searing pain and thick, warm wetness soaked through her clothes.

Harry fell on top of her, covering her body with his. She could barely hear him as he shouted, "Stay down!"

Then blackness.

CHAPTER THIRTY-ONE

In the turret of Rose's room, Mary Alice clutched her rosary beads, hands resting on the writing desk. In the yard below, the full moon turned the dead lawn gray and edged it with quaking shadows of the lifeless vine tangled in the picket fence.

Black smoke billowed from a cauldron of fire within a mountain to the west, spilled downward, and settled at the bottom of Thumb Butte.

"That's where my mama died," Sarah said.

The girl's comment so startled Mary Alice that she automatically reached for her flask, then remembered she had dropped it on the porch when Mr. Sheldon had come racing up the hill on a lathered horse with Rose in his arms.

Now her beloved niece lay in her own bed, in her own room. Alive and safe, her superficial wound being cared for by Kam Le.

Mr. Sheldon, pale and haggard, looked like he should also be lying down and tended by Kam Le. He had not moved from his position at the foot of the bed since he'd lowered Rose into it.

"You need to sit," Mary Alice said.

Mr. Sheldon nodded, limped to the easy chair, and fell into it.

"Sarah, go ask Kimo for whiskey and a glass for Mr. Sheldon," she said. "Two glasses."

When Sarah returned, Mr. Sheldon poured and handed a glass to the girl. "Give this to the auntie," he said, and sat back with a sigh.

Now that she knew Rose was home, Mary Alice wanted nothing more than to go to her own room, but she wanted to see Walter first. He had not yet returned, although Mr. Sheldon said he'd be along, said he was fine, just overseeing the jailing of the captured outlaws.

Two nights ago, two women with children had arrived at Mary Alice's door, another group last night, and tonight came a steady stream of refugees who now filled the rooms meant for the children she and Joseph never had. All emaciated, filthy, and scared. She'd had to turn many away, sending them to Sacred Heart Church where the nuns would take care of them.

Half a dozen Chinese women, related in some way to Kam Le and Kimo, were banging around in the kitchen, fixing trays of tea and toast and soup to soothe the frightened guests. Too many people. Too much commotion. And her niece, too quiet.

"Dear, can I please get you something to eat? Drink?"

Rose shook her head.

The clock in the courthouse tower tolled the hour. It tolled again before Mary Alice's heart leapt at Walter's voice coming from downstairs. He burst into the room and straight to the bed, grabbed Rose, and held her.

"Papa. I thought you were dead."

"I'm right here, sweetheart."

"They shot you."

"I know. I'm all right. Better every day. And fine now, now that my girl is safe."

"Sarah, dear, please get me a hankie." Mary Alice pointed to the dresser. "Top drawer."

Sarah brought the hankie, then curled up on a quilt in front of the fireplace, Mrs. Coppage tucked against her neck.

"Here, my precious daughter, you should lie down." Walter helped her back onto the pillows and straightened the bedding.

"Are you sure you're not badly hurt?"

"No, Papa. I'll be fine."

"Yes, you will. Everything will be fine now." He wiped tears from his face.

"Please, have a seat," Mr. Sheldon said, and offered the easy chair to Walter who, despite his claim of being all right, seemed grateful to take it and the glass of whiskey. Mr. Sheldon went to the window and pushed it open a few inches. While he rolled a cigarette, the raucous racket from Whiskey Row sounded as if the entire town celebrated the destruction of Hellgate and the capture of the outlaws. Music, gunfire, and cheers erupted nonstop. Mr. Sheldon looked toward the courthouse square and smoked, drinking now and then from Mary Alice's bottle of whiskey. She watched each time he raised it to his lips, her own glass long since empty.

Sarah broke the silence within the room. "Miss Rose? Where is Uncle Caleb?"

"Caleb Connor?" Walter grunted. "Don't be worrying about the likes of him."

"Papa, hush! He's the child's uncle."

"He's in jail waiting to be hanged along with the rest of those hooligans." Walter heaved himself up from the chair, his voice rising in anger. "And it can't be soon enough. That man is an animal—worse than McCabe himself."

Sarah burst into tears and ran to Rose. Walter stormed from the room, slamming the door behind him.

Mr. Sheldon went to the bed and gently pulled the little girl to him. "Now, now. Don't cry. Your uncle will be all right." He asked Mary Alice to take the girl from the room. "I need to talk to Rose."

Mary Alice took Sarah's hand, but when they got into the hallway, she sent the girl away to find her brother while she lingered close enough to the door to hear the conversation.

"Your father was there when they found McCabe. Tied to his bed, half on fire. Charred black in places, blood all over."

Mary Alice pressed her hankie to her mouth. Mr. Sheldon lowered his voice even more, and she strained to hear him.

"They got to the courthouse, him twisting and thrashing around, trying to get away the whole time. They got him downstairs and threw him into a cell. That's when they—"

Mr. Sheldon stopped talking.

"Tell me," Rose said.

"You know, everyone came out of there burned, bloody, ashes stuck to them. Most of 'em were yelling as loud as McCabe."

"Tell me."

"His shillelagh. Shoved up inside him."

Mary Alice pressed the hankie harder against her mouth, against the bile that rose in her throat.

Rose whispered, "Caleb did it."

"That's why your father said that, about Caleb being an animal. He doesn't know what Mason did to his sister. He doesn't know McCabe deserved that and more. *He's* the animal, not Caleb. Your father doesn't know, but *we* do."

"Did what to my mama?" Sarah had come up beside Mary Alice.

"Shush, child. Shush." Mary Alice hoped the child hadn't heard too much.

"Is he dead yet?" Rose asked.

"Not yet. They're not giving him anything for the pain. They're giving whiskey to everyone else, the other prisoners, so they can stand to listen to him. And the smell. He's suffering, Rose. They're letting him suffer."

Sarah hugged Mrs. Coppage and looked up at Mary Alice. "Mama would say Mr. McCabe was gettin' a taste of his own medicine."

★ ★ ★ ★ ★

In the morning, Mary Alice had Kimo fix a tray for Rose, and she carried it upstairs. Walter slept in the chair, legs sprawled. His chin rested on his chest, which rose and fell with gentle snores, and one arm dangled over the chair's arm. Mr. Sheldon was again at the turret window, watching the construction activity in the courthouse square. He wore the same clothes—stained with mud, blood, and soot—he had arrived in last night.

"Music to my ears," Mary Alice said over the sound of banging hammers from the courthouse square. She put the tray on the bedside table. "Soon enough those criminals will be swinging. Nooses around their necks."

Sarah stepped out from in front of Mr. Sheldon. "Are they gonna hang Uncle Caleb?"

Mary Alice hadn't seen the girl, and now tried to think of some way to smooth over her harsh words, but Walter woke up and said, "Hanging's too good for such a monster."

"He ain't no monster. He cried when Mama died." Tears ran down the girl's face and she wiped her nose with Mrs. Coppage's skirt. Mr. Sheldon picked the girl up, and she buried her face in his shoulder. He carried her out of the room, her little hands clinging to his shoulders, Mrs. Coppage dangling against his back.

"Walter, why don't you go downstairs with them? Kimo has breakfast ready. And ask him to fix a bath for Mr. Sheldon."

Alone, finally, with her niece, Mary Alice sat on the edge of the bed and took Rose's hand. "It's all over now, dear. I'm so glad you're safe."

"When they took me away, Papa was lying in the road. I thought he was dead. That was the hardest part."

"Oh, no, you don't want to talk about this." Mary Alice quickly poured a cup of coffee and tried to get Rose to take it. She'd heard enough gruesome stories from the children, the escaped women, and Walter to last her a lifetime. They'd left her tossing and turning all night. Each time she awoke, another ugly scene played through her mind. Or she saw the sunken, frightened eyes of the emaciated women who had come to her door seeking help.

But Rose wanted to talk.

She told the whole story of the robbery, the trip to Hellgate, the stockade, being forced to practice for Mason's party. Mary Alice asked her, several times, to stop.

"And then Lieutenant Schiffman from the fort—I think you know his wife—he came to the house, and I realized he was helping Mason. Auntie, he said his wife had heard something about a plan to rescue the prisoners, and they made plans to stop it. I think that was the first time I felt hopeless, the first time I knew I would die there."

She told of becoming desperate to get the rest of the children out of there before an attack ensured their deaths. "But once I revealed the tunnel, the women wouldn't wait. Three of them broke down the fence and ran, and the guards shot them dead." Rose squeezed Mary Alice's hand.

Mary Alice cried out. "What? What are you saying? Those women were killed right in front of you?"

Rose kept talking, but Mary Alice no longer heard her. *Those women are dead because of me.* Because she had got drunk and gone to that meeting and opened her mouth in an attempt to put the officers' wives in their place. She'd said things she shouldn't have, and those women had paid the price.

Then she heard Rose say, "—was on my way down the mountain and Eddie attacked me."

"Attacked?"

"He hurt me, Auntie. He . . . violated me."

Mary Alice began to cry. "My fault, my fault," she muttered through her sobs.

Her niece was stone-faced. "I don't need your pity, Auntie."

"Oh, God. Rose! Is he one of the men in the jail? We must tell the authorities! Be sure he is the first to hang!"

"He's not in the jail. I killed him."

Mary Alice stopped crying. *Killed him?* With an overwrought laugh, she said, "You couldn't kill anybody. How could you kill a man?"

"With the knife Papa always makes me carry. While Eddie was on top of me."

While he was on top of me. That phrase made the scene real, created a hideous image in her mind. Mary Alice buried her face in her handkerchief.

Rose's story had ended. Mary Alice's quiet sobs and the sound of hammering filled the silence. "I'm sorry, Auntie. All I wanted was to get here, get to you, so you wouldn't worry. Yet here I am, and you worry still." Rose picked at a thread in the quilt, pulled it loose, and cotton batting poked from the hole. "I wish they would stop that banging."

"Please excuse me," Mary Alice said. "I'll be right back."

In her room, Mary Alice got the whiskey bottle but before she had loosened the cork Sarah called to her. "Auntie! Auntie, where are you?" Mary Alice took the bottle with her and climbed the stairs again. She found the little girl standing beside Rose's bed.

"Miss Rose won't speak to me."

"It's all right." Mary Alice tucked the bottle under her arm and put her hands on the girl's shoulders. "She's not feeling well. We can visit Miss Rose later, after she's had time to rest." Her gaze fell upon the crucifix hanging on the wall behind the bed. "Dear," she said to Rose, "I shall send for Father Lyons." Yes, *those* were the words! Words that would bring comfort and peace. "He can hear your confession."

"You have to repent to be forgiven." Rose turned away and

pulled the sheet up over her shoulders.

Mary Alice's head pounded with each strike of the hammers. She took Sarah's hand. "Come, child. She's not herself."

Holding the little girl's hand, she started down the stairs. Now she was glad Mad Mason McCabe had suffered as Mr. Sheldon had described. This was all *his* fault! Her mind whirled. She leaned sideways, banged the whiskey bottle into the wall, and almost fell. Sarah began to cry and tried to pull her hand away, but Mary Alice clung to it.

When they reached the bottom, Mary Alice half-tripped, half-fell, and sat hard on the last step. She lifted Sarah onto her lap. "You're all right. You're not hurt. Don't cry, little girl. You have your whole life ahead of you."

For some reason that made the girl cry harder. "What will happen to us? Me and Jonathan. What will happen to us now?"

Mary Alice stroked the girl's hair and made shushing noises. Indeed, what would happen now?

"Auntie? Can we live with you? Me and Jonathan? Can we live here?"

The girl's upturned face was so innocent, it pained Mary Alice to look at it.

"I'm not fit to care for a child. We'll find a good home for you and your brother."

Mary Alice held the sobbing child as whiskey dripped from the bottle she had dropped. "Here, sit on the step for a minute." She moved the child from her lap, fell to her knees, and crawled to retrieve what little whiskey was left.

Mary Alice awoke in darkness. Bloated, overheated, unsure of where she was, she wondered where Sarah had gone. Had she tried to soothe the crying child or was it a dream? Maybe it was little Rose she'd tried to comfort. That seemed right but also seemed many years ago.

She lay in bed, fully dressed, the room spinning as consciousness slowly returned. The courthouse clock struck six times. Evening? Morning? Crawling from her bed, Mary Alice found the chamber pot and threw up in it. She needed laudanum to soothe her splitting headache but the bottle was empty. She sought whiskey, brandy, anything, but could find none in her room. She searched the parlor, saw Mr. Sheldon's bed in the music room was empty, and looked in there. She ended up in the kitchen. The sink was full of bottles. All empty.

Kam Le came in and stopped by the window, bathed in moonlight. Or was it dawn? She held an unlit candle. "Missus, can I help you?"

Mary Alice shook a bottle at her. "How could you? You know I need it for my rheumatism."

"Missus, *you* emptied the bottles. Last night. You said you had murdered people and you poured it all into the sink. I tried to stop you. You slapped me."

Mary Alice wanted to deny that she would lay a hand on her, but the mark on Kam Le's cheek was obvious.

"You were drunk."

Kam Le had never spoken that word to her before. Mary Alice ran back to the parlor, opened a window, and sucked in frigid air tinged with acrid Hellgate smoke.

At the bottom of the hill the gallows rose from a shadowy mist caught between the courthouse and the small chapel at the east end of the square. Four nooses swung in a slight breeze. There would be no more hammering. The courthouse clock struck once. Half past the hour. Mary Alice pulled the window shut and returned to her bedroom.

She sat at her dressing table. Seeking a match, her hand touched a paper tucked in the back of the drawer. A pamphlet someone had slipped into her hand at a Friday ladies' meeting some months ago, after a discussion of the temperance movement. She read the words of Mr. Francis Murphy.

> With malice toward none, with charity for all, I hereby
> pledge my sacred honor that, God helping me, I will
> abstain from the use of all intoxicating liquors as a bever-
> age, and that I will encourage others to abstain.

A line provided a place to pledge one's sacred honor by sign-
ing one's name.

Mary Alice took pen and ink from the drawer, scratched the
nib across the heavy paper, and wrote her name. "There," she
said. "That should do it." She had signed her sacred honor. She
waved the pamphlet to dry the ink. A Bible quote was printed
on the back.

> Speak unto the children of Israel . . . that they put upon
> the fringe of the borders a ribband of blue . . . that ye may
> look upon it, and remember all the commandments of the
> Lord, and do them.

She took a length of blue ribbon from her sewing basket, cut
off a piece, folded it, and fastened it with a straight pin. The
symbol of temperance.

She pulled out her rosary and twisted the beads in her fingers.
She wondered if those women, the ones Rose had told they
would be safe here with her aunt, had witnessed her drunken
tirade. Or worse, had Mr. Sheldon? Walter?

Her head throbbed. She thought about asking Kam Le to get
her a cold compress, then thought about getting it herself. She'd
caused enough trouble. She could see her words, alcohol-fueled
words that had slithered like a snake all the way from a Friday
meeting to that horrible place. Words that had risen up and
stricken down those poor women. She searched for some way to

exonerate herself, but there was none.

If only she had kept silent. It was drink that had loosened her tongue, made her want to brag and put the officers' wives in their places. It wasn't how a lady behaved. And, of course, Mrs. Schiffman had to run right home to tell her husband.

That's right. The blame belonged to Mrs. Schiffman. Or to her husband, who was one of Mad Mason's minions. A disgrace to his uniform. But the blame insisted on circling around, landing right where it belonged: with her. Rose would not have revealed the tunnel, and those women wouldn't have made their fatal run for freedom, if Mary Alice had just kept her mouth shut. And Rose would not have been on that hill when—! Oh, no; that was more than she could bear, that she be held responsible for her niece being ravished by that criminal.

She laughed. She had offered to call the priest for Rose to confess. *She* was the one who needed forgiveness. She would go herself and see Father Lyons, but she rose too quickly and fell. As she lay on the rug, she spotted a bottle of whiskey under the bed.

Oh, the joy to find it was almost half full!

Of course she could not go to Father now. It was the middle of the night, for God's sake!

She sat leaning against the bed, sipping, hoping each taste would erase the images Rose had placed in her mind. Women running, rifles firing, bodies falling. Dead women. Blood. Children screaming. Rose on the hillside with that Eddie *on top of her.* All the whiskey in the world could not wash those images away.

She pulled herself to her knees, leaned against the bed, and cried, sobbed, prayed. Only one thing would ease her heart. Unlike Rose, she *was* remorseful. She *wanted* to do penance. She rushed to the hallway and, in her hurry to get her cape and hat, knocked over the hall tree. Kam Le came running from the kitchen.

"What are you doing? You cannot go out! It is still dark out!"

Mary Alice put on her hat, pulling her cape over her shoulders. By now Kam Le was yelling for Kimo. He came down the hallway, hair sticking out, dressed only in his nightshirt, and tried to guide Mary Alice back to her room.

She shrieked like a banshee. "I must confess! I must confess!" Kimo tightened his hold. She grabbed her walking stick and swung, hitting the wall, the banister, knocking over the vase on the hall table as Kimo clung to her shoulders.

Kam Le handed a coat to her brother. "Take her to the priest. Go with her and wait."

"Mr. LaBelle should accompany her."

"He is not here. He and Mr. Sheldon went to the jail last night to talk to a prisoner. Just take her!"

They stepped onto the porch and Kimo pulled the door shut, but not before Mary Alice saw the women clustered at the landing on the stairway, the little girl staring, Mrs. Coppage hanging limp from her hand. Kam Le watched from the hallway with worried eyes, holding her fingers to her red-marked cheek.

By the time Mary Alice walked the two and a half blocks to the building that served the Sunday needs of the Sacred Heart parish, her legs gave out. She could not climb the outside stairs leading to Father Lyons's quarters. Kimo left her sitting on the bottom step. The fresh air restored her. She tried to push her hair up under her hat and wiped her running nose on her cape's hem. Father Lyons came down the stairs, pulling a robe over his nightshirt, his face puffy and pillow-creased.

"Dear God in Heaven, Mrs. Bradford." He looked shocked. "What brings you out at this hour? With your cook still in his nightshirt?"

He helped her to her feet and into the hall where he

celebrated Mass, sat her on a bench, and went to the altar. He returned with a bottle of sacramental wine, poured a glass, and handed it to her.

"Drink this, Mrs. Bradford. It will calm your nerves."

She took the glass with shaking hands and raised it to her lips. Thick red liquid spilled over the rim and ran down her fingers. The blood of Christ. She lowered the glass and looked up at Father Lyons.

"Bless me Father, for I have sinned."

CHAPTER THIRTY-TWO

Rose couldn't find out why Auntie had been in her room all morning, with Kam Le running in and out, carrying trays of food and strange smelling brews in a teapot. She refused to say anything other than, "Missus is not feeling well, but she will be fine. Better than ever!"

"Sarah, is Auntie still in her room?"

Sarah left the window and came over to the bed. "Yes, ma'am."

"Have you been crying?" The girl's bloodshot eyes and splotchy face belied her denial. "Why are you so sad? Don't you like it here?"

"I do, Miss Rose. I like it here. But Auntie says Jonathan and I can't stay."

"What? Of course you can stay! You can stay here or with me on my ranch. Until you're both grown up."

Sarah wrapped her arms around Rose's waist, but when Rose lifted her face tears were running.

"Now why are you crying?"

"Because they's gonna hang Uncle Caleb. He's my mama's brother and my uncle and . . . and . . ." She finished through wrenching sobs. "Even as nice as you are, he's the only relative we got left!"

"Help me get some clothes out of the wardrobe. You'll have to help me get dressed. I don't want Kam Le to know I'm going out."

"You ain't 'sposed to be goin' nowhere."

"Sarah, I'm going to help your uncle."

The little girl wiped her wet face and smiled.

Rose managed to limp around the room and get her undergarments and skirt and bodice on, with Sarah tying this and hooking that. She sat at her dressing table and stared at the woman in the mirror, her sunken eyes, the gaunt face with bruises spreading purple and yellow across it. She picked up the brush, but it was hopeless. "I need a hat with a veil," she said, and rummaged through the wardrobe until she found something good enough.

"Sarah, here. Go downstairs and give this note to Kimo, and don't talk to anybody. And come right back." The note told Kimo to go to the livery and rent an enclosed carriage and not to say anything to her father.

Rose stayed at the writing desk and watched the men gathered by the courthouse. They wore heavy coats and hats pulled down against the frigid morning. Four nooses on the scaffold twisted in the breeze. A man struggled to haul a burlap sack up the stairs. He placed it under one of the ropes, then another man in a long frock coat nodded and held up a hand. When his arm suddenly dropped, someone pulled a lever and the floor opened up under the sack. It fell to the ground with a heavy thud she could almost feel in her bones.

Sarah's footsteps again, coming up the stairs.

"I brought you one of Auntie's canes. You might need it. And Kimo's gone for the buggy."

Kimo reined to a stop at the Fremonts' home, only a block away from Auntie's on Marina Street, and the first stop in Rose's plan. She climbed down and Sarah started to follow.

"No. You wait here. I'll be back shortly."

Rose limped up the steps, knocked, and the governor's

daughter, Lily, opened the door.

"Miss Fremont, good morning. I'd like to speak with the governor, please," Rose said.

"I'm sorry. I'm afraid he's out of town."

"I'm Walter LaBelle's daughter. We met a few times for tea at my aunt's house, Mary Alice Bradford—she lives just a block west on Marina Street—"

"I know who you are. Everyone knows who you are. *The Miner* published a special edition. It tells all about your father's raid, and of your role in saving those poor women."

"I need to speak to someone about the prisoners in the jail. One in particular."

Lily's brow knitted. "You needn't concern yourself about any of the prisoners. There will be no escape for them."

"No, you don't understand. I wanted to speak about clemency for Caleb Connor."

"Mr. Connor? Isn't he the one who shot the sheriff in Phoenix?"

"Well, yes, but—"

"I heard he was the worst of them all. The men won't even talk about what he did to that Mad Mason McCabe, but you could hear him screaming all the way to Gurley Street. Not that he doesn't deserve to suffer, of course."

"I'm sorry, but someone has to listen to me. Mr. Connor is the only kin of two small children. They've been through so much. It's not right to hang their uncle. He's the only family they have. Is there some way I can send a telegram, then, to the governor? Or is there someone else I can talk to about Mr. Connor's sentence?"

"I believe Mr. Connor's sentence has been carried out."

"I'm sure if I could just explain it to somebody, they would see that he shouldn't be hanged. Maybe sent to prison if not pardoned."

Lily squeezed Rose's hand. "You don't understand, Miss La-Belle. Mr. Connor isn't going to prison."

"He isn't? They've set him free?"

Lily shook her head.

Rose felt perspiration dampening her collar. "If they haven't set him free, is there some way I can see him then? Take his niece to at least visit with him in the jail?"

"Miss LaBelle, there are no prisoners remaining at the jail except the devil himself, Mad Mason McCabe, and those deputies accused of taking bribes from that corrupt lieutenant. The rest were shipped to Yuma or hanged this morning. Mr. Connor, I heard, is in the latter group. I'm afraid the only place you could visit Mr. Connor would be at his grave."

Rose's leg throbbed with each jolt of the coupé carriage, but the pain was more bearable than the constant delays as the horses slowed to a walk or stopped.

"What is holding us up?"

Sarah knelt on the seat and stuck her head out the window. She yelled up at Kimo, then ducked back inside. "He says there's a lot of traffic today." Sarah wore a hooded cape, lined and trimmed with white rabbit fur. It used to belong to Rose, worn on those rare occasions when she came to Prescott in the winter, and Auntie had saved it all these years.

They stopped as near to the courthouse as Kimo could get in the crowded street. Rose climbed down, then reached inside for the walking stick. Below the gallows, two men held up a body while another pulled the noose off over stringy black hair. Dodger. They laid him down next to three other bodies covered with blankets.

Sarah climbed down, and Rose held the girl's face against her shoulder to keep her from seeing the grisly sight in the square. At least Sarah hadn't seen her uncle hanging from a noose.

The tall brick courthouse sat in the middle of an entire city block. Kimo insisted on accompanying her inside, so all three of them climbed the wide stairway of concrete steps that led to double doors. A deputy who was standing guard stopped them.

"There's no city business today, ma'am. The courts and the offices are all closed, on account of . . . you know." He nodded toward the north side of the building, where the gallows stood. "The hangin'."

"I'm not here on city business. I want to see one of your prisoners."

"Well, there ain't no prisoners either. Except a couple of crooked U.S. deputies and that Mad Mason McCabe. You wouldn't want to be seein' him, believe me."

"Where are the stairs to the jail? At the other end?" She pointed her walking stick down the long aisle of gleaming hardwood floor and plaster walls. There were benches along the sides for people waiting to meet with officials of the court. "Kimo, you and Sarah wait here. I won't be long."

"Wait a minute now, ma'am, you can't—"

At the far end of the hall she found the stairs, guided by McCabe's screams. She pushed past a second guard and headed down the stairs.

It wasn't hard to find Mason's cell between the moaning and the smell. She held a handkerchief over her nose and mouth. Mason didn't notice her at first. He lay in his own filth and feces, curled up with his arms around his swollen stomach, muttering in Gaelic. When he noticed her standing there, he lifted a shaking hand, stiff fingers spread wide.

"Me *maighdean,* come to save me from this hell!" A ghastly smile appeared within whiskers caked with blood and vomit. Behind the handkerchief shielding her from the stink, Rose returned his smile.

Then she stuck her arm through the bars and hit him with

the walking stick. She hit him again and again. He covered his head, shrieking. She struck his back, thrust the cane in and stabbed at his stomach. He doubled over, bellowing a spray of pink spit into the air. She hit him even as city marshals tried to pull her away. She held onto the bars and struck again. Mason rolled off his cot and hit the floor hard. He lay there whimpering.

They dragged her up the stairs and turned her loose in the hallway. Her heels echoed down the shiny hardwood floor. Kimo held the door for her. Before it swung shut behind them, someone yelled from deep within the courthouse. "He's dead. McCabe is dead."

Rose stopped halfway down the steps. A rush of emotion made her dizzy—the nightmare of Hellgate was over. If she had hastened McCabe's trip to hell, she was glad of it, but what about Caleb? Was he in hell now? He hadn't killed anyone. She'd seen he had a heart but, even so, she was surprised at the depths of her sadness.

She must have swayed, because Kimo took her elbow.

Sarah's hand slipped into hers. "That's what Mama would call a job well done."

"Let's go home, Sarah."

"What about Uncle Caleb?"

"I'm sorry. I couldn't help him."

Sarah's eyes filled. "Miss Rose, did they hang my uncle?"

Rose nodded and pulled the girl into an embrace. "I'm sorry. I'm so sorry. Let's just go home now, all right?"

"I don't have no home."

"Yes, you do. You and Jonathan. With Auntie and me." She took a handkerchief out of her reticule to wipe Sarah's tears away. "It's all right to be sad, but don't be afraid."

When they got home, Rose settled Sarah with the women and children in the guest rooms upstairs. She wanted nothing more than to go to her room, shut the door, and lie on her bed. The turret windows filled with blue sky, the kind of blue only seen in the fall: sharp, almost glowing, softened by fluffy white clouds. She stared for a long time, then dozed until Auntie knocked and came in, a piece of paper in hand.

"This was on the hall table."

"Are you feeling better? You look tired. What's that blue ribbon?"

Auntie looked down at the ribbon pinned to her bodice. "Just a promise I made to myself. Kam Le is helping me find other ways to deal with my rheumatism than laudanum and whiskey. And Mrs. Pumfrey is going to come over daily to help me with these women and children. But why are you dressed? You know you're not well enough to leave your room."

Her aunt folded and unfolded the paper.

"Auntie, why are you so nervous? Your hands are shaking." Rose sat up in the bed. "Is that a telegram?"

"It's actually addressed to your father. But it's from Arthur, so I thought you should see it."

"Arthur." Rose lay down and let her gaze return to blue sky, but the fluffy clouds had dispersed to thin shreds of white.

"Don't you want to know what it says?"

Rose shrugged. "Does it matter?"

"Oh, dear. I'm so very sorry, but I think you have to be told. It says"—Auntie cleared her throat—"that under the circumstances, he sees no way he can go through with the marriage."

"Under the circumstances?" Rose gave a little laugh. "*He* can't go through with it?"

All those nights, wondering when Arthur would arrive, clinging to the hope that he would come to her rescue. She turned toward the window, but Auntie still saw her smile.

"Rose! Do you find this humorous?"

She tried not to laugh. "Yes, Auntie. Don't you?" Then she

did laugh. Despite Auntie's worried expression, or maybe because of it, she lay on the bed, holding her stomach, and laughed as hard as she could remember ever doing. The more she tried not to, the more she laughed.

Auntie grabbed her arms, squeezing them. "Stop it! Stop this, Rose!"

"I'm sorry." She wondered what Auntie would think if she knew about McCabe. Mason had wanted to marry her at one time, too. And now she had killed him. Or at least helped along what Caleb had started. She stopped laughing.

"Auntie? What did Papa say about the telegram?" She imagined he was neither surprised nor disappointed.

"Why, he hasn't seen it. Your father isn't here. You didn't know? You must have been asleep. He wouldn't have wanted to wake you."

She sat up. "What are you talking about?"

"He left early this morning. For Mexico. That Caleb Connor finagled his way out of jail by promising to show them where McCabe's hideout is. Your father and Mr. Sheldon went to get him before dawn."

Rose fell back onto the bed. "Someone needs to tell the children. Sarah thinks her uncle was hanged!"

"I'll tell them. Don't worry."

Rose turned her pillow over, resting her cheek on its cool, crisp linen. Suddenly exhausted, her eyelids grew heavy. She felt the quilt being pulled up over her shoulders. "Auntie?"

"Yes, dear."

"Please be an auntie to the children. They are all alone."

"I will do that, dear. I will take care of them. I will take care of you. And, I swear, I'll be the kind of person you think I am. With God's help."

"You seem different, Auntie."

She tried to listen to what her aunt was saying. Just to hear her aunt's voice still seemed like a miracle. But the bed was so soft, and she was so tired. She slept.

Chapter Thirty-Three

At the top of the ridge, Rose sat on a flat rock overlooking the depression that had once been Hellgate. Late fall rains, unhindered by living vegetation, had swept the detritus of buildings and burnt trees to the bottom of the cauldron, then rinsed the charred cliffs clean, washing ash and soot down the slopes to seal the ditches. The first time she came, the odor sickened her. The men her father had hired weren't interested in dead criminals. They hauled away the ones they wanted to hang and left the bodies behind. The fire consumed them along with the abandoned animals. The stench lingered even now, a month later.

Today she had ridden up in light snow showers. A dusting of white covered everything, leaving no testimony to the suffering that had happened here.

She pulled down the bowler she'd taken to wearing. Her hair had grown out a little and the yellow color had faded, but she felt better keeping it hidden. The sky hung low, gray and overcast. She wrapped her wool scarf around her neck. From the corner of her eye, she saw a rider slowly ascending the trail. Snow had muffled the horse's hooves and allowed him to get too close before she noticed.

Some outlaw looking for Hellgate. Some outlaw who hadn't heard what happened.

The rider disappeared at a bend in the trail. At the top of the last switchback, he emerged from behind a juniper that partially hid the path. Rose stood by her horse, rifle aimed.

"Don't shoot." He put his hands in the air.

She lowered the rifle.

Harry slid off the horse and tied the reins next to hers.

"When did you get back?"

"Just now. Your aunt said I might find you up here."

"Papa?"

"He's at the house, getting fussed over by your aunt. Waiting to see you."

"I've been waiting to see him too. You've been gone over a month." She propped her rifle against the flat boulder and sat. "How'd you know exactly where I was? There are a lot of trails coming up the hill."

He limped over and eased down beside her. She pulled a flask from within her coat and offered it to him.

"You know I'm good at tracking," he said.

They sat looking into the hole that had been Hellgate.

"Auntie doesn't like me to come here. She says it's morbid."

She wondered what memories played in Harry's mind. So many ugly images filled hers. But looking at Harry's profile, his hair grown longer, curling past his coat collar, stubble on his cheeks and chin, the image that came to her was of him playing Beethoven at McCabe's piano, his earnest expression when he explained who he was. Bathing Sarah's mother. Looking over his shoulder at her as he took the children into the tunnel.

His breath blew out as vapor and the cold reddened his nose. The lines around his eyes seemed deeper, his cheekbones more prominent in a thinner face.

"How's your leg?"

He shrugged, took another swallow, and handed her the flask.

"Go ahead," he said. "Ask."

"Caleb?"

"Slipped away from us. Still somewhere in Mexico, far as we

know. No doubt headed for McCabe's hideout down there."

"What do you mean he slipped away? I thought you were so good at tracking?"

The corner of his mouth turned up, just a hint of a smile. "Ground was rocky. Not like here." He nodded toward the trail where their horse's hoofprints were obvious in the snow.

"Does Papa know you let him get away?"

Caleb would be all right in Mexico. Part of her was glad. Auntie had pretty much adopted Sarah and Jonathan. What if Caleb had come back? Ridden in with Harry and Papa, returning stolen merchandise and maybe stolen people. They'd all have been heroes. The governor might have pardoned Caleb. What would it have done to Auntie if Caleb wanted the children? She'd become so attached to Sarah.

Maybe she'd have started drinking again. Given up on Kam Le's potions and gone back to the hard stuff. Whiskey! That wouldn't look good for the new leader of the Prescott temperance movement.

"What's that look on your face? My God, it's almost a smile."

"Auntie. She quit drinking. So I *have* to come up here now and then. There's no alcohol in the house anymore."

He was polite enough not to say anything. He would know there were plenty of places she could drink. And she did. Mostly in her room. Kimo was always willing to go and get her a bottle. There was no harm to it. She only drank on the bad days, when the memories were not of Harry playing the piano.

"Rose? Why do you really come up here?"

"It's quiet. I can think."

"Think about what? Let it go, Rose. It's in the past. There's nothing we can do but go forward."

"It's not in the past. It's inside me. I'm not the same. I'm never going to be the same."

"You *are* the same." His voice bordered on anger. "I never

met a woman brave as you. You know what I remember of this place?" He waved an arm toward the crater. "How you stayed behind. How much you gave up to stay behind and save those women."

"You don't know what I gave up. You weren't there when—"

He took her hand, holding it in both of his. His rough skin was warm, his touch gentle. It seemed to penetrate the darkness of her heart, just a small crack.

"I know what happened. Caleb told me."

She pulled her hand away, folding her arms across her chest.

"Do you think I care?" he asked. "That it makes any difference to me? Look at me."

She turned her head away.

"You asked about my leg. Truth is, it's not healed. It's worse. If Kam Le can't do something to help . . . if they amputate my leg, are you going to turn your back on me? If part of me is cut away through no fault of my own? Would that mean I'm ruined? Good for nothing?"

"It's not the same."

"It is the same." The anger in his voice was gone. "We both paid a price for what we did. If you'd known what would happen, would you have done things differently? You were on the hillside because you were helping women escape. Isn't that true?"

She didn't want to feel his pain or the pain his kind words inflicted upon her. She didn't want to feel anything.

He pulled a small box from his pocket. "I picked this up on our way into town." He raised the lid, opened her hand, and placed a delicate chain across her palm.

A silver locket hung from the chain. Shiny, new looking. She opened the clasp. Two photographs.

"I like that picture of your mother. That's how I remember her," Harry said. "Here. Take that hat off."

He took the chain, shifting so he could hook it behind her neck. "Dodger gave it to me when your father and I went to get Caleb. I had one of the deputies take it to Morgan's jewelry store to be fixed."

His warm breath blew against her hair and his fingers brushed her neck as he struggled with the delicate clasp. "There," he said, and the locket fell over the front of her coat, resting on her heart.

A light snow began to fall.

She put her hands over her eyes and wept.

He took her in his arms and she sank into them, shaking, her face pressed into the rough wool of his coat. He held her for a long, long time, until the snow filled the tracks on the trail and the setting sun glowed red upon the flakes that clung to their clothes.

ABOUT THE AUTHOR

P. Grady Cox, a member of Western Writers of America and Women Writing the West, volunteered for several years at a nineteenth-century living history museum near Phoenix, Arizona. This immersion in the everyday life of territorial Arizona spurred her creativity and filled her imagination with stories, leading her to study novel writing through Phoenix College's Creative Writing program. Her goal is to transport readers to another era, and her love of the southwest—the landscape, the history, the culture—infuses her work with the authenticity to do so. Called to move to Arizona from Rhode Island twenty-six years ago, she loves being able to travel to the locations used as settings in her work. *Hellgate* is her second novel.

The employees of Five Star Publishing hope you have enjoyed this book.

Our Five Star novels explore little-known chapters from America's history, stories told from unique perspectives that will entertain a broad range of readers.

Other Five Star books are available at your local library, bookstore, all major book distributors, and directly from Five Star/Gale.

Connect with Five Star Publishing

Visit us on Facebook:
 https://www.facebook.com/FiveStarCengage

Email:
 FiveStar@cengage.com

For information about titles and placing orders:
 (800) 223-1244
 gale.orders@cengage.com

To share your comments, write to us:
 Five Star Publishing
 Attn: Publisher
 10 Water St., Suite 310
 Waterville, ME 04901